Erebus

By Steven C. Bird

Erebus

Erebus

Published by Steven C. Bird at Homefront Books on 8-29-2017
Illustrated by Hristo Kovatliev

Print Edition 12.23.19

ISBN-13: 978-1975895402

ISBN-10: 1975895401

Edited by:
Carol Madding at Hope Springs Editing &
Sabrina Jean at Fast-Track Editing

www.homefrontbooks.com
www.stevencbird.com
facebook.com/homefrontbooks
facebook.com/stvbird
twitter.com/stevencbird
scbird@homefrontbooks.com

Erebus

Table of Contents

Disclaimer

The characters and events in this book are fictitious. Any similarities to real events or persons, past or present, living or dead, are purely coincidental and are not intended by the author. Although this book is based on real places, and some real events and trends, it is a work of fiction for entertainment purposes only. None of the activities in this book are intended to replace legal activities and your own good judgment.

Erebus

Dedication

This book is dedicated, of course, to my loving family, Monica, Seth, Olivia, and Sophia. They are the reason I do everything I do and am everything I am.

I would also like to dedicate this book to the brave men and women who face the rigors of life at the bottom of the world, especially the outstanding team of professionals at MEVO. I hope that the fictitious story I have woven into this real and amazing place peaks the interest of others around the world about your amazing work. You truly deserve to stand in the spotlight. You and those who follow in your footsteps have my eternal admiration.

Erebus

Introduction

In 1841, when the British vessel H.M.S. Terror first charted Antarctica under the command of explorer James Clark Ross, the crew laid eyes on a volcano reaching 12,500 feet above the surface of the frozen ice of Antarctica. Ross and his men saw the huge white plume rising from its crater at the summit, and it has been erupting ever since. Mount Erebus, as it was later named by explorer Ernest Shackleton, was named after the Greek god Erebus, the god of primeval darkness. To anyone who has visited the mountain and its incredibly harsh environment, this name is found to be more than appropriate.

Today, on the steep and icy slopes of Mount Erebus, can be found a rugged team of scientists, researchers, and mountaineers carrying out their work in one of the harshest and most remote parts of the planet, at a facility known as the Mount Erebus Volcano Observatory, or simply MEVO. These professionals, tough enough to brave the extreme climate of Mount Erebus, include experts in the fields of gravity and magnetotellurics, volcanology, geophysics, and even astrobiology. These doctorate-level professionals travel each year from several major universities such as Cambridge, Missouri State, the New Mexico Institute of Mining and Technology, and the University of Washington in order to study Erebus, as well as the unique environment it has created for itself in one of the most remote places on Earth. They are assisted by a professional mountaineer, as well as graduate students from their respective institutions who study under them.

Erebus

The researchers at MEVO, when not on the mountain at the research camp simply called the Lower Erebus Hut, are based out of McMurdo Station. Mac-Town, as McMurdo Station is fondly referred to by its residents, was founded by the U.S. Navy in 1956. What was initially called Naval Air Facility McMurdo is now simply McMurdo Station. McMurdo Station is currently run by the United States Antarctic Program and is governed by the Antarctic Treaty, signed by forty-five world governments. The Antarctic Treaty regulates daily life at McMurdo, as well as the research conducted there.

In many respects, the inhabitants of McMurdo Station are on their own on the vast and remote continent of Antarctica. This is especially true during the winter months, when most of the station's one thousand residents return to warmer climates, leaving behind a skeleton crew of only two hundred to face the rigors and potential horrors of life at the bottom of the world— alone.

Chapter One

Mount Erebus Volcano Observatory (MEVO)

Holding on tightly to the core sample drill as it bored into the side of one of the massive ice towers that reach high into the sky, Dr. Hunter focused on his task at hand with relentless determination. Standing over him like giants from ancient-Greek mythology, the ice towers, formed by condensing air as it vents from one of the many fumaroles on Antarctica's largest and most active volcano, Mount Erebus, reach as high as sixty-feet above the ground.

With the frigid arctic winds atop Mount Erebus pounding his body, his coat buffeted violently as he struggled to maintain his footing. His beard, nearly full of ice and snow, clung to his face like a rigid mask as he wiped his goggles, attempting to see the drill as it bored its way into the ice before him. The season's expedition was about to come to an end, and he could not afford to leave without the core samples he desperately needed in order to complete his research.

"Doc, we've got to get moving," Mason yelled through the howling winds, placing his hand on Dr. Hunter's shoulder as if to urge him away from his work. "If the storm gets any worse, we won't be able to see well enough to make it back to the hut! It's already damn near zero visibility."

Ignoring the plea, knowing his task was nearly complete, Dr. Hunter yelled, "Got it!" as he pulled the core sample gently from the tower of ice. Without saying a word, he patted Mason on the shoulder, and they began their hike through the pounding weather to their snowmobiles, to return to the Lower Erebus

Hut before the mountain claimed them, as it had tried so many times before.

~~~~

Entering the Lower Erebus Hut, Mason slammed the door shut as quickly as he could to keep the fierce frigid winds at bay. Everyone in the room turned to look at the two ice-and-snow-covered men. Having just returned from the summit with Dr. Hunter's core samples in hand, they placed them gently on the floor and began to dust off the fresh snow that covered them, in preparation for removing their heavy outer layers of protective clothing.

"I was starting to worry about you two," said Dr. Linda Graves, a forty-four-year-old astrobiology researcher with the University of Washington.

"So was I," replied Mason, as he began peeling off his balaclava and removing his many layers of clothing. Mason, or Derrick Mason to be exact, was a graduate student of geochemistry at the New Mexico Institute of Mining and Technology (NMT).

As a student of Dr. Nathan Hunter, the Principle Investigator for the expedition and a professor of geochemistry at NMT, Mason had been hand-selected to come along on this year's expedition to Mount Erebus. Dr. Hunter not only chose him for his academic prowess, but also for his abilities as a seasoned mountain climber and avid outdoor adventurer. Mason was an experienced hunter, long distance hiker, mountain climber, and most importantly of all, a survivalist at heart. There were plenty of students academically up to the task, perhaps even more so than Derrick Mason, but Dr. Hunter refused to let his research be slowed by having to babysit a graduate student who wasn't physically up to the extreme conditions that Antarctica, and specifically, Mount Erebus, thrust upon those ill-suited for the challenge.

With Derrick Mason, however, he had a stout, twenty-eight-year-old outdoorsman that he knew could be counted on when things became challenging and treacherous on the volcano.

Peeling off his gloves, Dr. Hunter quipped, "If we were gonna leave without one of our critical core samples, what would be the point of coming? I'm not waiting until next year to come back just to fill in the gaps, and I know you didn't come all the way from Seattle to leave just yet either—all things considered. Caution is wise, but risk yields rewards."

"That it does," joked Mason, rubbing his face in an attempt to return warmth to his skin. "But it's days like this that remind you of the fact that Shackleton named this mountain after the Greek god Erebus, the god of primeval darkness."

"Did you get what we were looking for?" Dr. Graves asked.

"I think so," Dr. Hunter replied. "I still want to get down as far as I can into the fumarole on the north side of Tramway Ridge and get a sample before we leave. But today's cores contain some of the material we were looking for."

Changing the subject, Dr. Hunter looked around the room, and asked, "Any word from Mac-Town?" referring to Antarctica's McMurdo Station.

"The first helicopter will be here in the morning," answered Jared Davis, a volcanologist and a junior member of the research team from NMT. "We'll have them available through the end of the week, but after that, Mac-Town will be buttoned up for the winter. The last Air Force C-17 leaves Saturday. If you've not done what you need to get done by then, you'll either have to leave it behind until spring or be stuck here with the wintering-over crew at Mac-Town."

"I suppose so," Dr. Hunter replied. "Now, getting back to the important business at hand, what was for dinner and is there any left?" he asked, looking around the crowded and cluttered living area and seeing dishes piled high in the kitchen sink. "It looks like we missed out on whatever it was."

Brett Thompson, a Homer, Alaska native and the team's mountaineer and safety specialist, spoke up and said, "Neville made us a pot of his famous Worcestershire stew."

"He made what?" asked Mason with a confused look.

Neville Wallace, a tall, lanky, curly-haired British graduate student who had accompanied Dr. Gerald Bentley, the Co-Principle Investigator and volcanologist from the University of Cambridge said, "I simply concocted a basic vegetable stew from what was left of the fresh produce, before it spoiled. It was already getting a tad bit long on the shelf, so I opted to put it to good use. To mask the rather dismal condition of the ingredients, I kicked it up a bit with what was left of the Worcestershire sauce. It wasn't anything to write home to mum about, but it filled the void."

In a deflated tone, Dr. Hunter replied, "Wasn't? I assume that means it's all gone."

"I told Lester and Ronald not to go for seconds until you had returned and eaten your share, but you know how those two buggers can be," Neville said, poking fun at the two men who had finished off the rest of the soup.

"Oh, well... we'll survive," said Mason as he plopped down onto the only empty spot on the old, worn-out sofa. "I was in the mood for some sort of canned meat anyway. As a matter of fact, I'm so hungry I could go for one of those one-hundred-year-old cans of mutton still on the shelf in Shackleton's Hut."

Tossing him a can of pickled herring, Dr. Hunter said, "Here ya go. It's not century-old mutton, but it'll do. We're scraping the bottom of that sort of thing, too," he said as he searched for food in each of the nearly empty cabinets.

"If something happens and the helicopters don't show up soon to give us our ride back to Mac-Town, we may have to decide who we're gonna eat first," chuckled Mason, as he peeled open the can.

"I vote for Lester and Ronald then, since they ate the last of the soup," said Dr. Jenny Duval, the official camp scientific assistant. "It only seems fair."

"Hey, now!" replied Lester Stevens, an engineer brought along as the team's lava-lake-imaging technical guru.

Lester Stevens and Ronald Weber were the resident non-scientific technical experts, and though they had never met before traveling to Antarctica, the pair often seemed as if they were long-lost brothers. The others frequently joked that they spent way too much time in the hut and needed to get out on the mountain more. They often teased about the two having a fictitious mental condition they called *MEVO Fever* from being isolated on the mountain for too long. If anyone in the camp had it, it was truly those two jokers.

As the rest of the group settled into their nightly routine of watching old black-and-white science fiction movies, Dr. Walter Perkins, a researcher from Missouri State University who specialized in gravity and magnetotellurics, stood and waded through the tired bodies strewn about the floor. The researchers lay about the hut with their heads propped up on boots, jackets, or whatever they could find to help them see the television. To an outsider, it would appear to have been the scene of some apocalyptic movie where the dead lay scattered on the floor wherever they had fallen.

Approaching Hunter and Mason, he asked, "Dr. Hunter, would you like me to put your samples away in the cold room while you two finish your five-star cuisine?"

"Thanks, Walt, but we can get it," Dr. Hunter replied. "There's no reason for you to get the chills after warming up from your day out and about. The two of us are barely thawed, so we won't even notice."

Looking to Mason, watching as he devoured his canned meal of compressed fish, he said, "Actually, Derrick, I can get it. I'm hitting the sack after that. Get your stuff together and be ready to accompany me to Mac-Town in the morning when the helicopter comes. We'll get our samples on the next transport and then head back up to the summit when we return tomorrow afternoon. I saw something interesting that I want to check out."

"Yes, sir," Mason replied sharply. Taking another bite of pickled herring, he turned and asked, "What did you see?"

"We'll talk about it in the morning; it may be nothing."

"Roger that," Mason replied, turning his attention back to his half-eaten can of fish.

~~~~

Early the next morning after the weather had cleared, Dr. Hunter looked off into the distance, scanning the horizon for the arrival of the helicopter that was scheduled to transport his core samples back to McMurdo Station. Once at McMurdo, they would arrange to have the samples loaded onboard a U.S. Air Force C-17 for transportation back to the states where he could continue the analysis of his samples in a proper laboratory environment.

"There they are!" shouted Mason over the howling winds of the clear, arctic morning.

Looking at his watch, Dr. Hunter replied, "It's about damn time! We're cutting it close. We barely have time to get them on today's flight. We haven't got time for delays."

Upon landing, Dr. Hunter and Mason loaded the crate of core samples, as well as some other gear that was packed and ready for shipment, on board the Eurocopter AS350. Once everything was securely lashed to the floor, the pilot was given a thumbs-up and they were quickly on their way.

During the flight, Mason couldn't help but look across the frozen continent, thinking of how, strangely, he would miss it during their time back in New Mexico. Antarctica, a place that to a casual observer may seem to be merely empty, cold, and harsh, somehow endears itself in the hearts of those who spend time there. There is a beauty and peace about the frozen continent that feels like home to a wandering soul, and a wandering soul he was.

As the helicopter approached McMurdo Station, a research base that more closely resembled an industrial mining town than an environmentally-friendly research facility, Mason's mind switched gears as he chuckled to himself, thinking, *then again, I could use those warm New Mexico nights right about now.*

After landing, Dr. Hunter and Mason quickly unloaded their core samples and placed them on a forklift for transportation to McMurdo's Ship Off Load Command Center.

Walking into the facility behind the forklift, Dr. Hunter and Derrick Mason were immediately greeted by George Humboldt, a logistics specialist at McMurdo. Pulling his scarf away from his mouth, George said, "Dr. Hunter, I'm glad you made it."

"Have we missed it?" Dr. Hunter impatiently inquired.

"No, but unfortunately, the flight is delayed until tomorrow due to mechanical issues." Pointing at the crate on the forklift, he asked, "Is that the samples we spoke of?"

"Yes. Yes, it is," Dr. Hunter replied with tension in his voice. "I can't stress enough how these samples need to remain frozen at all times. They contain...well, they contain material that is critical to my research. I just can't do without them."

"Don't worry, Doctor," George replied. "It's no problem at all. I don't think I need to point out that transporting ice samples is a fairly routine task for us here at McMurdo."

"I know. I know," Dr. Hunter replied. "Forgive me, but I believe I'm onto something special and if my samples are lost for any reason, it will be a setback that will require me to wait until next year just to catch back up."

"Every sample from every research team is important, Doctor. But you have my word that I will ensure that exceptional care is given to yours. By this time tomorrow, your samples will be well on their way back to the U.S., and will be in good hands."

Patting Dr. Hunter on the arm, Mason interrupted by saying, "C'mon, Doc. George has a handle on things here. Let's get some lunch before we head back out to MEVO. I've been looking forward to a hot meal after what we've been down to for the past few days."

Nodding in agreement, Dr. Hunter said, "Yes, of course. Thanks, George," as the two men turned and began their walk toward the station's cafeteria.

~~~~

Completing the paperwork for Dr. Hunter's shipment, George watched as Mason and Dr. Hunter left the facility.

Turning to see Vince Gruber approaching with the forklift, he chuckled, placing his clipboard on top of Dr. Hunter's samples.

Stepping off the forklift, Vince said, "They always wait until the last minute. Every year, it's the same damn thing."

Patting Vince on the shoulder, George smiled, saying, "Yep. They all think their work is more important than everyone else's, too. You'd think these ice samples were tubes of gold the way that guy acts. He's one of the worst. He's always uptight about his stuff. He could carry it on the plane his damn self, if it were up to me."

Pausing to look around at the vast amount of cargo they had yet to load, George continued, "Oh, well. You'll be home in Florida soon, and I'll be back in Philly eating a real cheesesteak, not the sorry excuses for a sandwich they have here. Let's just get on with it and mark our last few days of the season off the calendar."

~~~~

Arriving at the station's cafeteria, still referred to as the galley due to McMurdo's roots as a naval facility, both Mason and Dr. Hunter grabbed a plastic tray, a large and a small plate, and silverware as they began working their way through the hot food line. Plopping a heaping scoop of barbecued pulled-pork onto his plate, Mason said, "Man, I've been looking forward to this."

"I know what you mean," replied Dr. Hunter. "MEVO is like a second home to me, but when provisions begin running low, it's not like we can run out and get more. Being based on the side of a major volcano has its inherent limits."

As the two men sat down and began to eat, they were approached by Dr. Raju Tashi, a particle physics researcher from the University of Wisconsin. "Dr. Hunter, may I join you?" he asked.

"Of course, Raj," Dr. Hunter replied. "And this is one of my best and brightest graduate students from NMT, Derrick Mason," he said, gesturing to Mason. "Derrick, this is Dr. Tashi. He's one of the particle chasers out at the IceCube facility. They're researching neutrinos. Pretty exciting stuff for a particle chaser."

"Pleased to meet you," Dr. Tashi said to Mason with a smile as the two shook hands.

"Likewise, Doctor."

"How are things going at IceCube?" Dr. Hunter asked.

With a look of excitement on his face, Dr. Tashi replied, "Excellent. Our experiments with the high-altitude balloon went very well. We're excited to get back to Wisconsin to study our results in more detail. We have wrapped up our operations for the season and are all awaiting transportation back to the states. And yourself? How are things at MEVO?"

"Excellent as well," he replied. "Although I wish I could say we've wrapped things up as you have. No matter how much I accomplish, I always feel a step behind the mountain. There is so much to learn. So much to explore. And of course, as soon as you're on to something good, Erebus throws you a curve ball and a critical piece of equipment gets smashed by a crater bomb or the like."

"Well, at least you haven't been smashed by a crater bomb yourself," Dr. Tashi said with a chuckle.

"He came close a few times," Mason said, looking to Dr. Hunter with taunting smile. "Last week, a crater bomb the size of a Volkswagen almost nailed him.

"Is that so?" asked Dr. Tashi with a raised eyebrow.

Placing his glass of tea on the table while poking around at his tray for the next bite of food, Dr. Hunter responded, "Let's just say Erebus doesn't give up its secrets without you having to earn them."

"I don't envy you for that," Dr. Tashi replied. "At IceCube, all we have to contend with is the cold."

"Well, gentlemen," Mason said as he pushed himself back from the table with a satisfied look on his face. "I'm gonna grab dessert. Can I get anyone something while I'm up?"

"Frostyboy is down again," Dr. Tashi said in a tone of frustration, referring to the cafeteria's famous soft-serve ice cream machine.

"No! Ah, damn it," Mason said, exasperated by Dr. Tashi's news.

Patting Mason on the back, Dr. Hunter laughed and said, "Don't fret about it. By next week, you'll be getting yourself a scoop at Cold Stone Creamery from that cute blonde who has her eye on you back at NMT."

With that, Dr. Hunter stood and said, "It was great seeing you again, Raj. Are you coming back next summer?"

"That has yet to be decided," Dr. Tashi replied. "If not, keep in touch. I'm sure we'll cross paths again. We may not be in the same field, but science is a small world."

Shaking his hand, Dr. Hunter smiled and said, "You take care. And yes, yes, it is."

Chapter Two

Mount Erebus Volcano Observatory

As the helicopter touched down near the Lower Erebus Hut, snow and ice crystals swirled around them as the twenty-five-mile-per-hour wind gusts pounded the craft. Shoving open the door and holding it against the violent winds, Mason signaled for Dr. Hunter to exit the still-running helicopter. Once Dr. Hunter was clear and on his way to the Lower Erebus Hut, Mason shut the door firmly and signaled to the pilot that they were clear. Before the two men reached the door of the facility, the helicopter pilot had lifted off and was on his way back to McMurdo Station and the comforts it provided.

Closing the door securely behind them, Dr. Hunter looked around the room and asked, "Where is Linda?"

Looking up from his work of packing up some of the team's sensitive data-recording equipment, Ronald answered, "Linda? Oh, Dr. Graves. She and Brett went back up on the mountain this morning just after the two of you took the helicopter out to McMurdo."

"I hope they hurry. It's getting late. There isn't much daylight left as it is," Dr. Hunter said with a noticeable uneasiness in his voice.

"They'll be fine," Mason replied. "Brett is a top-notch mountaineer. I wish I had just half of his climbing skills."

"You find your way around the mountain pretty well," Dr. Hunter said as he walked over to the coffee maker.

"I'm an outdoor junkie, but I'm your average outdoor junkie," Mason replied with a thankful smile. "But Brett—he's hardcore. That's why I know they'll be fine. Besides, Dr. Graves is a fitness freak. She can scurry up a vertical ascent and be looking down at us from the top, while the rest of us are stopping to catch our breath a quarter of the way up."

With a chuckle, Ronald added, "And Doc, you know better than to let her catch you uttering words of concern about her. She'll rip you a new one."

Smiling as he took a sip of hot, black coffee, Dr. Hunter said, "You're right about that, Ronald. She's not one to tolerate a male counterpart's acknowledgment that she's a lady."

~~~~

Opening her eyes and seeing nothing but darkness around her, Dr. Graves realized she was lying flat on her back. With her head pounding from the impact, she paused for a moment before she attempted to move when she heard Brett yelling down to her from above.

"Dr. Graves!" he shouted. "Dr. Graves, are you okay?"

With his words echoing off the walls throughout the ice cave, it was disorienting and difficult for her to tell from which direction his shouts were coming. Sitting up, she felt herself become dizzy and light-headed as she replied in a weak, shaky voice, "Yeah. Yeah, I'm fine—I think."

"I can barely hear you!" he shouted. "Are you okay?"

Mustering the strength to shout back, she yelled, "Yes! Yes, I'm okay!" She instantly regretted her efforts as the intensity of her throbbing headache increased with each word she uttered, as if the words were bouncing around inside her head.

"I'm coming down!" he shouted.

Struggling to get to her knees, Dr. Graves reached for her headlamp, only to find that it had been irreparably damaged in the fall. Pulling her hand-held flashlight from her pocket, she flicked it on, only to discover in amazement that the walls of the cave around her contained traces of grayish microorganisms, unlike anything she had ever seen.

Hearing a rope bounce off the wall behind her, she turned and pointed her hand-held flashlight skyward and into the small, tubular vertical fumarole shaft from which she had fallen into this previously undiscovered chamber deep beneath the ice. Seeing Brett's climbing rope, she shouted, "I've got your rope. Come on down. I'll belay you from here."

Within a moment, Brett Thompson, the MEVO research team's professional mountaineer, appeared above her with his feet dangling as he descended into the dark chamber. Brett, still an Alaskan at heart, had been in and around large mountains his entire life. Standing six-foot-two with a slim build and sandy brown hair, Brett had always been popular with the ladies. However, his heart belonged to the extreme environments created by the mountains.

After working as a guide on Denali since his mid-twenties and having climbed the likes of Everest, Kilimanjaro, and the Matterhorn, Erebus seemed like the next logical place for his mountaineering career. It had yet to disappoint him in that regard.

Dropping into the chamber in front of Dr. Graves, he said, "You scared me half to death. That fumarole has to be at least one-hundred and fifty feet nearly straight down."

"Thank goodness for helmets," she said, tapping her gloved knuckles on her head. "That, and I tried to ball up the best I could to create drag on the sides of the ice tube to slow my descent. That way, it wasn't really a fall so much as it was a slide—at least until I reached the opening in the ceiling here. That part was a free-fall."

"Either way, I'm amazed you're up and walking," he said, scanning the chamber with his headlight.

"Hand me one of your sample containers," she said, reaching out to him as she began to look closely at the life-forms that appeared to be thriving on the chamber walls. "We've stumbled across something special here. It's hard to tell exactly, given the conditions, but I don't think we've documented microbes such as these before."

Handing her the container with the lid removed, Dr. Graves took it and immediately began collecting specimens with her Zero Tolerance brand folding pocket-knife, a gift from her brother that she carried with her at all times. "These walls are almost wet to the touch. What temperature is it in here?"

"I'm showing thirty-three," Brett replied, looking at his thermometer with his headlamp. "It's almost warm enough to remove a few layers of gear."

"Don't," she quickly replied. "These chambers have all sorts of gasses flowing through them, and we don't have any O2 with us. We may find ourselves having to egress in a hurry, and you won't have those few precious seconds to spare."

Screwing the lid back onto the container, Dr. Graves said, "Turn around. Let me put this in your pack, if you don't mind."

"Of course," he said, allowing her to stow her precious sample safely in his pack.

"Do you hear that?" she asked.

"What?"

"Nothing," she replied with amazement. "It's so quiet down here. Everything is so still. In most of the caves and tunnels created by the fumaroles, you can see the light shining through the walls and ceiling from the sun above. You can hear the wind pounding the mountain. But here, there's nothing. It's silent."

Looking around, he said, "Amazing, isn't it? I'm not sure we've ventured this deep before."

"Of all the trips we've made into the ice caves, I've never noticed that particular vent."

"The one you fell into?" he asked.

"Yeah. It's like it simply appeared."

"The heat from the mountain mixed with the cold ice above can do some crazy things," he said. "Helo Cave, and others like it that are close to the surface, appear steady to us because they have the cold to keep them solid. This far into the volcano, though, who knows what hot gasses come and go, cutting a swath through the ice only to have it fill in and refreeze later before we've had a chance to discover it."

Walking over to Brett's climbing rope that dangled into the chamber, Dr. Graves asked, "Do you have your ascenders?"

"Yes, ma'am," he replied.

"Get them set up while I take a few more samples. We'd better get going. Who knows when the next blast of hot gasses will come rushing through."

~~~~

Looking impatiently at the clock that hung on the wall in the Lower Erebus Hut, Dr. Hunter began to speak when the door opened, allowing a rush of frigid arctic wind to enter, blowing papers off the table in front of him. "Linda, so glad you two are back. How did it go?" he asked, attempting to mask his concern.

"It's a long story," she confessed, "but it's one you'll want to hear."

Chapter Three

Mount Erebus Volcano Observatory

Early the next day, Dr. Hunter stood outside on what was a beautiful morning and watched his long-time friend, Dr. Linda Graves and the junior member of their team, Volcanologist Jared Davis, climb aboard the helicopter to fly back to McMurdo Station. He couldn't help but wonder when he would see her again to discuss her laboratory analysis and the findings of her sample once she'd made it back to her lab at the University of Washington. He was deeply curious about her recent discovery deep within the bowels of Mount Erebus, but as a professor of geochemistry and not an astrobiology researcher such as herself, he left the work of analyzing the life-forms discovered within Erebus to her.

Dr. Hunter and Dr. Graves had, over the past few years at MEVO, begun to realize that their work was closely intertwined. Being an Astrobiology Professor at the University of Washington, she had come to Erebus to study life in one of the most isolated places and harshest conditions on Earth. She hoped that her research on Erebus would lead to a better understanding of how life could not only exist but thrive in the far reaches of space where such conditions may exist.

Mt. Erebus, being located on Antarctica, with temperatures far below zero and miles from anything, presented itself as the perfect study environment. The microbes, which appeared to thrive in the warm caves and fumaroles reaching deep into the mountain, did not have organic matter on which to feed. There was no plant or animal life on the surface of the volcano to create organic material that could be washed down to them, as would be the case for most other subsurface microbial life. On Erebus, the microbes seemed to exist by eating the rock itself, subsisting on minerals. Instead of being photosynthetic, they were chemolithoautotrophic. They took their energy from chemical reactions between themselves and the rock.

But where did they come from? Erebus was far too isolated and far too cold for them to have simply traveled here on the wind, by animal, or by water flow. No, the life-forms on Erebus seemed to have come from far beneath the surface of the Earth. They seemed to have risen from deep within the planet, finding themselves near the surface of one of the harshest places on Earth, yet they thrived.

What else was down there? Could there be vast colonies of sub-surface dwelling life-forms far beneath our feet? Could they be living in the total absence of light, thriving on the heat deep within the Earth, and by converting minerals and other resources into energy in ways we have yet to discover? This and many other questions begged to be answered by the researchers and scientists of MEVO.

~~~~

"Snap out of it, man," Dr. Gerald Bentley said sharply. "It's not as if she's going off to war. You'll see her again soon enough."

"What?" Dr. Hunter said, momentarily confused as he was still somewhere between his thoughts and reality. "I've got a lot going on is all, and our clock is ticking. While the rest of you are busy packing up and taking pictures to commemorate your trip, Mason and I have more trips to make up to the mountain."

"What is it you Americans sometimes say?" Dr. Bentley said as he scratched his chin, pretending to be occupied by deep thought. "Prior proper planning prevents piss-poor performance—or something like that?"

With his face taking on a perturbed look, Dr. Hunter replied, "You may be here to check a box in your scientific career or to simply be interesting enough to get one of your articles published, but I am here for different reasons. Discovery doesn't start and stop with a University's research schedule, or even with McMurdo's logistical schedule; it is all around us, all the time."

"Come, now; don't get your knickers in a twist. I was merely teasing you," Dr. Bentley said, in an attempt to quell the hostility growing in Dr. Hunter's voice. "Neville needs only to get the remainder of our equipment packed up, and we'll be ready to jet back to Cambridge. If you good chaps from NMT need any assistance, we would be delighted to lend a hand and assist in any manner possible."

Smiling, Dr. Hunter replied, "Thanks, Gerald. I appreciate that."

Hearing several snowmobiles approaching, Dr. Hunter and Dr. Bentley turned to see Dr. Jared Davis, volcanologist and junior member of the research team from NMT, along with Derrick Mason and Brett Thompson returning to the Lower Erebus Hut from a trip to Fang Ridge to check on some of the team's sensory equipment.

"I thought you'd lost it for sure," Mason said to Dr. Davis in a jovial manner, as he climbed off his machine and removed his facemask.

"I can't believe I did that," Dr. Davis replied in a humble tone.

"Did what?" Dr. Hunter enquired as he noticed the downward angle of the snowmobile's handlebars and the crack in its fiberglass hood.

Confessing his folly, Dr. Davis sheepishly explained, "We were side-hilling it just below the rock outcrop before you get to Fang Ridge. I had a few too many thoughts swirling around in my head about going home, and failed to heed Brett's constant warnings to keep both feet on the uphill side of the snow machine when in such a situation. I hit an icy patch and began to slide downhill with the machine still horizontal to the mountain. When the skis on the front caught a rock, the back of the machine swung around and the next thing I knew, I was sliding down the mountain backward. I barely got off and out of the way before the machine took a few hard tumbles, coming to rest on its top. It was a close one. My heart is still racing."

Shaking his head, Dr. Hunter said, "You're almost out of here. Don't screw it up now. Keep your head focused on the mountain until you're off the mountain."

"I know. I know," Dr. Davis replied.

Looking to Mason and Brett Thompson, Dr. Hunter said, "I know you guys just got back, but do you think you could make it a quick turn and head back up with Lester and Ronald? They have some gear to retrieve from the crater, as well as some small wind-turbine charging systems to install to keep our wintering-over equipment powered while we're away."

Sharing a glance, Brett and Mason both nodded as Brett said, "Sure thing, Doc."

"I really hate to ask, guys, but the sand is getting low in our hourglass, and we've got a lot of stuff to do before we head off the mountain for the last time."

"That's why you pay us the big bucks," Brett replied.

"Pay YOU the big bucks," Mason quipped. "I'm just here because my grades would have reflected it if I had refused his offer to come along." Looking to Dr. Hunter to gauge the reaction to his joke, Mason added, "Nah, but seriously, Doc, we'd be glad to head back up. I'm gonna miss this place. The mountains in New Mexico don't actively try to kill you every step of the way. That'll be boring. I've got to keep my heart rate up with near-death experiences while I can."

~~~~

For the rest of the day and well into the evening, everyone at MEVO worked feverishly to mothball the Lower Erebus Hut, their seasonal home away from home and research station, for the coming cruelty of the rapidly approaching austral winter.

As the group gathered around the folding table that doubled as their dining room furniture, Dr. Bentley presented the group with a bottle of Moët & Chandon champagne. Standing before everyone, he said, "I would like to take this opportunity to thank each and every one of you for making this year's expedition to Mount Erebus both memorable and full of great scientific accomplishments. I fear this will be my last trip to Erebus as the University is rumored to have new plans for me, but I'm sure Neville here will be back next year with whatever hack they send in my stead. I wish you all the best of luck in your future endeavors, and may we all cross paths again in whatever journeys our lives take in the future."

After a round of applause, Neville began handing out plastic champagne glasses while Dr. Bentley filled them all with the bubbling goodness.

Once everyone had been served, Dr. Bentley held his glass high and said, "To science, and our mutual pursuit of knowledge."

Lifting their glasses above their heads, the group shouted, "Hear, hear!"

The rest of the evening was spent joking and discussing their discoveries and setbacks during their time on Erebus.

As the mood began to turn from celebration to fatigue, Mason stood, and with a yawn, said, "Well, folks. We've got to get up early to have our gear staged outside and ready for the helicopters when they arrive. With that in mind, I'm gonna hit the sack."

"Me, too," seconded Dr. Jenny Duval. "That champagne has suddenly gone to my head in this thin air. I'm going to bed while I have at least a modest amount of good judgment left."

"Oh, C'mon, Jenny," pleaded Ronald Weber. "It's our last night on the mountain. Besides, what happens at MEVO stays at MEVO."

"Very funny," she replied. "And just so you know, you're even creepier when you drink. I didn't think that was even possible."

As laughter swept the room, Ronald's face turned red with embarrassment as he attempted to retract his statement by saying, "I was only kidding, Jenny."

"I wasn't," she scoffed as she left the room, heading for her cot.

Chapter Four

Mount Erebus Volcano Observatory

Early the next morning, the remaining members of the MEVO team were informed by radio that due to inclement weather moving in, their pack-out and transportation back to McMurdo station by helicopter would be delayed to the following day. This didn't seem to bother anyone too greatly, with the exception of the fact that their food supplies had gotten very low.

"It looks like we may have to eat Lester and Ronald after all," Mason said jokingly as he perused the cabinets in search of food.

Laughing at Mason's comment, Dr. Bentley replied, "Good Lord, can you imagine the preservatives and toxins you would be ingesting if you did such a thing? Why, I would rather eat shoe leather instead of one of those rancid old chaps."

Quickly chiming in, Neville added, "And I'm all out of Worcestershire sauce. I'm afraid you'd have to taste them as they are, which is dreadful to imagine."

Reaching into one of the cabinets, Mason said, "It'll be okay. We've got salt and pepper."

"I know you guys are joking around, but all this talk of cannibalism still makes my skin crawl," remarked Dr. Jenny Duval.

"Just imagine if they were joking about eating you," replied Ronald as he stood and stretched. "The saving grace for me is that I would have the last laugh. This meat is tainted, but you won't know from what until you receive your diagnosis."

Walking into the room with his hands in the air, Dr. Perkins said, "Okay, okay, that's enough. This group sounds more like a pack of college kids than a group of distinguished researchers."

"Hey, now," Mason disputed. "I'm still a college kid."

"You're far from a kid, Derrick. Besides, you know what I mean."

"Dr. Perkins is right," said Dr. Hunter, speaking up for the first time. "We've only got to make it through one more day cooped up in here together without going mad. Who's got kitchen duty today?"

"I do," replied Brett.

"Good. See what you can whip up to get us through the day. We've got to ration out what we have left in the event the helicopters can't fly tomorrow either."

As the day dragged on, the residents of MEVO passed the time by reading, watching old movies, and catching up on some much-needed rest.

~~~~

Early the next morning, Dr. Hunter approached Ronald Weber, who was manning the radio, and asked, "Any word from Mac-Town?"

"Nothing," Ronald replied with frustration in his voice. "I've literally got nothing. Those bastards won't reply. I've been calling them for an hour now."

"Hmmm," Dr. Hunter murmured as he scratched his chin through his short, brown beard. "That's odd. The weather isn't bad enough to interfere with our comms. It's cleared up quite a bit since yesterday."

"Well, I sure as hell hope they didn't forget about us. We're out of food and I'm ready to get the hell out of here."

"What's going on?" Dr. Jenny Duval asked.

"Ronald is having a hard time reaching Mac-Town," Dr. Hunter replied.

"What do you mean?" she queried.

"They just aren't answering the radio," Ronald answered.

"This is no time to be messing around, Ronald," she said in a serious tone. "What did they say? When will they be here?"

"I'm not joking, Dr. Duval," he insisted. "I've been trying to reach them for an hour now."

"Well, keep trying," she said.

"Of course, I will, but getting mad at me won't make them answer."

"I'm not mad, I'm just concerned," she said, placing her hands on her hips and walking over to the frost-covered window. "What could be going on to cause them not to answer?"

Trying to ease her concerns, Dr. Hunter replied, "It's probably just a technical glitch. Radio or not, they will send helicopters to get us. Don't worry about that. The folks at Mac-Town are always on their game."

~~~~

Over the course of the day, tensions began to rise throughout MEVO, as neither radio communications nor signs of their scheduled transportation by helicopter materialized. Their usual jovial moods had turned to near silence as thoughts of their situation raced through their minds.

Taking charge, Dr. Hunter gathered the group in the main living area and said, "Many of us have been coming out to MEVO for years. For myself, this is my tenth season. I don't have to tell you I've never seen anything like this. There have been occasional technical difficulties regarding communications equipment, but McMurdo has several layers of redundancies built into everything they do. It simply shouldn't have taken this long to respond to us, or to make contact via alternate means."

"Surely, they'd have sent the helicopters regardless of our comms status," Brett said.

"Exactly," replied Dr. Hunter. "Which is why we've got to start putting our own contingency plan together. We can't wait them out forever as our food supplies are already running dangerously low."

Speaking up, Mason said, "We've got enough food for two more days max, and that's eating small portions and staying hungry. We don't have much time at all to sit around hoping for something to happen."

"What do you suggest?" asked Dr. Perkins.

"I think we need to be ready to make the trek to Mac-Town by snowmobile first thing in the morning."

"What?" asked Dr. Duval. "That's a long way to go over a lot of rough terrain. We'll freeze to death. Besides, there are only six snowmobiles and eight of us."

"Some of us will have to double-up, and those who are lucky to be able to ride solo will have to carry extra fuel and emergency supplies. We'll have to leave all our research gear behind. We just won't be able to carry it."

"Good Lord, Dr. Hunter!" Dr. Bentley said with excitement in his voice. "Not only does leaving our work behind sound like scientific heresy, but if I might be so bold to suggest, it also sounds like suicide!"

Seeing looks of fear and confusion sweep through the faces of the group, Dr. Hunter explained, "I'm open to suggestions, Gerald. But with our current food stores being what they are, I just don't see how we can sit here and do nothing. If our communications are restored or if the helicopters arrive between now and in the morning, then all is well. But what if they don't?"

Standing up to address the group, mountaineer Brett Thompson said, "Dr. Hunter is right. We can't just sit here without adequate food supplies and hope someone comes to the rescue."

Camp Assistant Dr. Jenny Duval asked, "But what if they do come, but we're already out there freezing to death, or lying at the bottom of a one-hundred-meter-deep crevasse? They'll have no idea where to find us."

"Good point, Dr. Duval," Brett replied. "But here's the facts of the matter. We're running out of food, and it's the end of the season. McMurdo Station is going through what is essentially an annual planned evacuation as we speak, while the weather is still good enough to allow it. The deteriorating weather won't merely make it difficult for aircraft. It will make it more difficult for all modes of transportation, including snowmobiles with exposed riders.

"It's an arduous and dangerous trek to McMurdo from here by snowmobile, I'll give you that, but would you rather do it three or four days from now in a weakened state when you're feeling the full effects of hunger and starvation? If we're gonna be able to handle whatever struggles are ahead of us, we need to get moving while we still have our strength and a few reserve calories.

"Besides, I know in our modern day and age virtually everything physical seems daunting. We've become accustomed to traversing the ice in heated helicopters, but remember, Shackleton's party reached the summit of Mount Erebus in 1908. They were traveling by dogsled and foot and made it in five days. We've got better clothing, better transportation, and a better understanding of the terrain ahead of us. Not to mention

39

we'll be going down the mountain instead of up. If we head out first thing in the morning as Dr. Hunter suggested, we should be able to make it to McMurdo by nightfall."

Showing his firm support for the plan, Mason spoke up. "I agree. There's no reason to think we can't make it back on our own, and there's definitely no reason to just sit and wait for the situation to potentially deteriorate before we set out."

"So, Nathan," Dr. Perkins said, addressing Dr. Hunter casually. "Do you really intend on leaving behind some of your work after stressing over it as you have?"

"My work is important, Walt," Dr. Hunter replied. "But if I don't survive, how will I finish it? Your priorities can't be so rigidly fixed into place that they cause you to lead yourself down a foolish path."

"Well, I believe it's settled then," Dr. Bentley said, confidently addressing the room. "If our seasoned mountaineers here say we should set out by snowmobile, then I'll gladly put my reservations aside and join them. I don' t want anyone questioning my expertise, so I won't question theirs."

Chapter Five

Mount Erebus Volcano Observatory

After a long and sleepless night, the researchers began crawling out of their bunks and preparing themselves for the challenging day ahead. As Mason handed a cup of coffee to Brett, he said, "You know this is on your head, right? Wise decision or not, if anything happens to anyone, their University will have your ass."

"Yeah, I know," Brett replied, taking the coffee and savoring the aroma as it warmed his face. "But they'll also have my ass if we sit here and do nothing, allowing them to simply starve to death. It's lose-lose. Either way, we've got to get moving and worry about the potential civil actions later."

"It's sad that these days you can't make a decision without worrying about the potential legal liability involved."

"Yeah, I often feel like guides need malpractice insurance like medical doctors. We take the affluent into dangerous situations every day upon their own request, and if anything were to happen, well, like you said, someone would have my ass," Brett said with a chuckle.

"Mr. Thompson," Dr. Bentley said from across the room. "Are you ready to lead our intrepid group of laboratory dwellers into the myriad dangers ahead?"

"Yes, sir," Brett replied smartly. "Where's Neville?" he asked.

"He is busy gathering as many of our notes as he can. There's no reason to leave our ideas behind, even if we have to dispense with our gear."

Once everyone had eaten their last meal in the relative comfort of the Lower Erebus Hut, they all suited up, donning their many layers of protective garments for the harrowing journey that awaited them.

"Listen up, everyone," Dr. Hunter announced. "The minute we step foot out of the hut, Brett is in charge. I don't care what your position is at your respective universities. Once we get out on the mountain and the vast expanse of snow and ice ahead of us, he's our leader. There will be no arguments there. He's our expert guide and mountaineer, and your level of tenure does not supersede that."

Looking around and seeing that everyone was in agreement, Dr. Hunter said, "Good," with a smile and a nod. Turning to face Brett, he said, "Mr. Thompson, you have it from here. We're all equals out there on the ice. You give the orders as you see fit for the good of the group and don't worry about hurting anyone's feelings or pride. You'll have my full support in that as the Principle Investigator of the expedition, though I will yield that authority to you until we reach McMurdo Station."

"Thanks, Nathan," Brett replied with a grin. He then quickly said, "Sorry, Doc. I had to test drive my position."

"Call me 'Hey, You' if you want until we get to McMurdo," Dr. Hunter replied with a chuckle. "Just get us there. There is no room for titles or social status from here on out."

Looking around the room, Brett said, "Okay, folks. Two of the snowmobiles will have to be ridden double-up. Dr. Duval, you and Neville share a ski, if you don't mind. Lester, you and Ronald share one, too. You four are the lightest of the group, and the machines will handle your combined weight in the snow better than the others."

"It's Jenny," Dr. Duval replied. "Call me Jenny. Like Nathan said, let's dispense with the formalities and just get us the hell out of here."

Replying only with a smile, Brett continued, "Now, we won't be taking our familiar route up the mountain that we've taken so many times before. That route is all many of you have ridden. The trail is well established and the dangers are known. What we will be facing today is the opposite of that. It's unmarked terrain with many unknowns. I'll take the lead position so that I can evaluate any hazards before I lead you into them. Mason, I'd like you to take up the rear. With the two of us being the most experienced, if I get swallowed up by a snow-covered crevasse or something, I want to ensure that you're still around to get everyone else back to McMurdo. We can't both go down together."

"Understood," Mason replied.

"You and I will meet up to confer about things when necessary, but when the group is moving, I want us at opposite ends. As far as the rest of you go, pay close attention to the ski in front of you. Stay in my tracks to avoid any undetected hazards."

~ ~ ~ ~

After a brief question and answer period, the group joined up with their snowmobiles outside. With rescue gear, emergency shelters, and first aid kits strapped to some, extra fuel cans were lashed securely to others. With their engines running and warmed up, Brett signaled, and the group headed down the mountain to begin their journey to McMurdo.

Working their way down the steep, snow-and-rock-covered grades of Erebus, the group carefully picked their way around the rock outcrops and sections too steep for snowmobile travel.

Side-hilling above a nearly vertical icy slope, Lester and Ronald began to slide sideways toward the ledge.

Mason's heart nearly skipped a beat as he saw the two men sliding uncontrollably. Seeing them come to an abrupt stop just feet from certain death, Mason parked his ski and worked his way past several of the others to reach them.

"Holy fuckin' shit!" Ronald screamed as Lester silently clenched the handlebars, afraid to move. "Get us off this thing! Get us the hell off this thing!"

"Calm down, Ronald!" Mason replied as he radioed ahead to Brett. "Brett! We've got a problem!" he shouted over the radio.

"On my way," Brett said in return, as he halted the movement of the group.

Quickly grabbing a climbing rope that Brett had lashed to Dr. Hunter's ski, Mason said, "Take this end and run it through your ski somewhere, then tie it off to Dr. Bentley's ski as well. We need a good anchor point."

Nodding in reply, Dr. Hunter did as Mason asked, as Brett joined up with them and said, "Damn it, we just got started."

"No offense, but you put Lester and Ronald on the same sled," Mason replied. "That's asking for trouble."

"Yeah, well, let's get to this," Brett said as he threaded the climbing rope through the figure eight clipped to a carabiner on his harness. Taking a second rope, he handed it to Mason and said, "Tie this one off to something secure. I'm gonna have Tweedles Dee and Dumb work their way up to you with ascenders, one at a time. I don't trust them enough to let them climb untethered."

Turning to look down at the two and their perilous position, he then said to Mason, "Tie off a third rope and toss it down. I'll tie off the ski. If I can get it turned up the hill I'll ride it back up, or try, at least. We can't be losing equipment this early into the trip."

Working his way down the steep, icy slope, Brett could see that the rock ledge just beneath them dropped what appeared to be fifty or sixty feet below. *It doesn't matter if it's a thousand feet,* he thought to himself as he allowed the rope to slip through his figure eight, lowering him toward their position. *Even if they survived the fall, the slope below would take them for quite a ride before they came to a stop.*

Closing to within ten feet of them, Brett looked around to see that several rocks sticking up from beneath the ice were the only things that had kept them from going over the drop sideways.

"What the hell, boys?" he asked in dismay.

"Just get us out of here, damn it!" Ronald shouted.

"Calm down," Brett said. "We'll have you out of here in no time."

As he worked his way closer to them, a gust of wind swept Brett off his feet, causing him to fall several feet before catching himself by applying pressure to the rope as it slipped through the figure eight. With his heart racing, he said, "See? Nothing to worry about," as he struggled to his feet, once again leaning back against the rope.

With the fall putting him to the side and just below the snowmobile, he looked up to the two men and tossed them the rope he had brought for them with ascenders attached. "You know the drill!" he shouted. "You learned it at snow school. Ronald, since Lester has a good grip on the machine, you go first. Tie yourself off and use the ascenders to get back up to the group. When you get to the top, have Mason toss the rope back down. Make sure he positions the ascenders to where Lester can reach them without too much physical maneuvering."

45

Nodding nervously, Ronald took hold of the rope and began working his way up. Every few feet, his boots would slip, causing him to whimper in fear as he clutched the ascenders tightly.

Working his way over to Lester Stevens, Brett said calmly, "Nice view, isn't it?"

"That's not funny," Lester said, intensifying his grip on the handlebars.

Talking as he tied the third rope off to the machine, Brett said, "Relax. You'll need some strength in those hands to get to the top. Don't fatigue yourself by hanging on with a death grip. No pun intended, of course."

Relaxing slightly, Lester said, "How the hell are we supposed to make it all the way to McMurdo if we can't even get off the mountain?"

"Trust me, Lester. We'll be fine."

With a shaky voice, Lester replied, "I sure as hell don't feel fine."

Tossing the rope back down to the machine, Mason yelled, "Heads up!" as the weight of the ascenders carried the rope quickly toward them, bouncing off the ice upon impact.

"You're up, Lester," Brett said as he reached for the rope and ascenders, sliding them to within Lester's reach.

Taking hold, Lester began working his way up as Brett pushed away from the steep incline with his feet, swinging around to the front of the snowmobile as he arced around, suspended from the rope. Reaching for the starter button located on the left-side handlebar, Brett pressed start and heard the two-cycle engine sputter to life with a cloud of smoke billowing out of its exhaust. *Thank God it's not flooded out on this angle.*

Yelling up to Mason, Brett said, "Once Lester and Ronald are clear, get the group moving slightly forward and in unison to keep the slack out of the rope tied to the machine! I'm hoping we can get it pointed uphill so I can get it going up while you guys pull!"

Yelling back down to Brett, Mason said, "Roger that!" as he helped Lester get back to his feet once safely on the trail.

Waiting patiently down below, just inches from the sheer drop, Brett looked at the rocks holding the sled up by its track one more time, swallowed the lump in his throat, and said, "Okay, give her a slight pull. The rope should help get the nose pointed uphill. I'll ease her up with the throttle to help while ascending beside it."

"What? You're not gonna just ride it up?" Mason joked, shouting back down at him.

"Hell, no! I ain't gettin' on this thing until it's back on the trail," Brett replied.

Watching the slack of the rope begin to tighten as the five other snowmobiles began pulling in unison from above, Brett's heart skipped a beat as he saw the tracks slip over the rocks, bringing the heavy machine swinging toward him and yanking hard on the rope above.

Sliding over the edge, the snowmobile's free-hanging weight was too much for the sleds above to hold in position. Screaming when she felt the snowmobile that she and Neville occupied begin to lunge backward toward the edge of the trail, being pulled by the rope from below, Jenny Duval held on for dear life as Mason quickly pulled his Medford Praetorian pocket knife, flipped open the blade with his heavily-gloved thumb, and immediately chopped through the climbing rope with the thick, heavy blade, allowing the snowmobile to freefall over the edge.

As the sled began to fall, Brett became entangled in its handlebar and went over the side, his rope smoking as it was pulled through his figure eight with increasing speed.

Erebus

Watching as Brett disappeared over the edge, Mason's mind raced as he immediately second-guessed his actions. Seeing Brett's rope work itself back and forth from a struggle below, Mason shouted, "Brett! Brett, are you okay?"

Reaching over the edge and taking hold of the rocks that once held the snowmobile in place, Brett grunted and said, "Yeah. Yeah, just pull me up."

Chapter Six

En Route to McMurdo Station

After the incident, the group pressed on, working their way down the side of the treacherous volcano. Having only five remaining snowmobiles after Lester and Ronald's mishap, Dr. Hunter now found himself with Lester Stevens as a passenger, while Dr. Bentley carried Ronald Weber.

Taking fewer chances now, the group had each extra rider dismount and walk any terrain that was viewed as potentially tricky. It slowed their pace, but ensured they would each reach the bottom of the mountain safely.

After reaching the base of Erebus, and several hours into the ride across the frozen terrain toward McMurdo Station, Brett raised his hand and brought the group to a halt.

Stopping his snowmobile and walking toward Brett, Mason asked, "What's up?"

Pointing up ahead, Brett said, "See that shift in the snow? It looks as if that section settled suddenly while the rest remained in place. I'm guessing there is a crevasse or something there allowing the snow to shift like that. We need to probe around a bit before pushing any further in that direction."

"I'll go with you," Mason replied.

Speaking up from behind, Dr. Hunter dismounted and said, "No. You stay behind with the group for the reasons Brett mentioned earlier. I'll go with him."

"I can do it myself," Brett replied.

"Nonsense. It'll take twice the time," Dr. Hunter replied. "If we both probe as we move, staggered apart, we can cover twice as much ground and clear a wider safe zone while we're at it."

Correcting himself, he quickly said, "That is, of course, if you agree, Mr. Thompson."

"Okay, Doc," Brett Thompson replied. "You're right, and we need to cover ground more quickly if we're gonna make McMurdo before nightfall. The days are short this time of year as it is."

Following what appeared to be the safest route across the shifting snow, Brett and Dr. Hunter used the long, slender wooden rods with metal tips that they had brought along with the rescue gear to probe beneath the surface for solid ground or ice. If there was a crevasse or a void beneath the snow, they wanted to find it before a snowmobile disappeared with its riders into what would more than likely be a cold, icy death.

After probing for approximately twenty yards, Dr. Hunter said, "Here we go," as his wooden probe went beneath the surface of the snow to his grip. "This is deep. I can't feel a bottom."

With a nod, Brett turned and began to walk and probe perpendicular to Dr. Hunter's position and their direction of travel, jabbing at the ground in front him. After a few moments, his probing rod went several feet down beneath the surface.

Turning to Dr. Hunter, he shouted, "Here's the other edge."

Walking toward Brett Thompson, Dr. Hunter pointed and asked, "So, you think crevasse runs this direction?"

"Yeah, I'd say we've been on it for a while, and luckily remained on its spine. We need to keep heading in that direction," Brett said as he pointed along what he believed to be the ridge between two crevasses.

Walking back to the rest of the group, Brett approached Neville and said, "Neville, give Jenny a break and take my snowmobile for a while. I'm gonna walk ahead of the group, probing as we go."

"Whatever for?" Dr. Bentley enquired.

"It appears we are on top of a ridge of ice, or a snow bridge, with a crevasse on each side hidden by deep snow. Just stay in single file, at least ten feet apart, and follow in my footsteps. This will slow us down a bit, but so will plummeting to the bottom of a crevasse."

"You've got a rather odd sense of humor," Dr. Bentley replied.

"Sorry, but I wasn't joking," Brett responded. "Now, let's get moving. We're gonna be hard-pressed to make it to McMurdo before dark. You all know how cold it gets around here after dark."

~ ~ ~ ~

After pushing hard for the rest of the day, narrowly avoiding several closer calls, the group neared McMurdo Station as the remaining daylight disappeared over the horizon. Tired, hungry, and nearly frozen to the core, the group pushed on with the lights of McMurdo in sight.

As they neared the edge of the research station, they saw flames coming from several locations around the base, prompting Brett to bring the group to a halt. Looking to his left as Dr. Hunter rode up alongside him, he said, "What the hell?"

"Where is everyone?" Dr. Hunter asked. "Why isn't anyone fighting those fires? Come on!" he said as he began to speed toward McMurdo with Lester hanging on for dear life.

Pulling to a stop, Dr. Hunter was horrified to see bodies strewn about on the blood-soaked ice, snow, and dirt of McMurdo. Quickly dismounting, he ran to the side of one of the bodies to see that the person had been beaten so savagely that most of his face was gone, with a smashed and distorted eye dangling from the massive hole that was once an eye socket.

Dry-heaving for a moment in disgust, he stood as the rest of the group reached him, each of them dismounting their snowmobiles, in shock at what they were seeing before them.

Noticing one of the bodies move, Ronald pointed, and said, "Look! He's alive!" as he ran to the person's side.

Kneeling beside the horrifyingly disfigured body of the man who barely clung to life, Ronald saw that the blood on the ground was beginning to freeze. Turning to the others, he shouted, "This just happened!" Feeling the man's arm move, he turned back to see him mouth the word, *Run,* as his life left him and his final breath escaped his lungs, emitting a cloud of frozen mist.

"Run? Run from what? What the hell is going on?" he asked to no avail, as the man lay there still and lifeless.

Turning back to the others, he shouted, "What the fuck is going on?"

Seeing Dr. Hunter turn to face him and then quickly noticing the look of horror in his eyes, Ronald turned just in time to see a crazed man standing before him. In the man's hands was a large, jagged piece of metal, torn loose from a piece of machinery. Ronald immediately recognized the man as someone he had seen around McMurdo many times. Was it in the cafeteria? Was it in the greenhouse? Or was it from Gallagher's Pub or the Southern Exposure Bar, both of which Ronald frequented on his visits to McMurdo when taking a break from the seclusion on Mt. Erebus.

"Hey," Ronald said, holding up his hands in a calming gesture. "I don't know what happened here, but I didn't have anything to do with it. We just got here from MEVO."

Not replying, the man inched closer to him as his heavy breathing intensified. His eyes were wild and unfocused, and he was sweating profusely with the droplets quickly freezing, covering the man with an icy sheen that seemed to freeze and re-melt in a continuous cycle. *Sweating? In this frigid cold?* Ronald thought. The man was facing Ronald directly, but his eyes seemed as if they were looking straight through him, instead of at him. There was a froth around the man's mouth that was freezing to his face in the terrible cold of the Antarctic night.

Turning to look over his shoulder, Ronald heard Dr. Hunter say, "Put it down. Put down your weapon," in a forceful tone directed at the crazed man.

Turning back to the man, Ronald started to back away as the threat continually inched closer, his rate of breathing increasing with each passing moment. As the man drew near, Ronald could see something on the man's neck. There was a film, or substance, algae-like in appearance, though it was gray instead of green, running up the man's neck, appearing to follow his jugular vein.

"Drop it!" Mason shouted as both he and Brett appeared from the darkness to his right, both having retrieved ice axes from the rescue and climbing gear lashed to the snowmobiles.

In an instant, the man let out a primal scream as he charged at Ronald, shoving the broken metal pole through his abdomen.

Falling backward onto the ground, Ronald gripped the metal pole as it protruded from his body. He could feel the warmth of his own blood against his cold skin as the man began clawing and biting at his face and neck, his world slipping into darkness.

Hacking at the man with the axes, Brett and Mason swung wildly, hitting him several times in the back, spilling the man's blood, but seeming to provide little to no deterrence against his aggression. With a well-aimed, powerful swing, Mason landed his axe squarely in the back of the man's head, the blade crashing into his skull and ending the fight.

"What the fuck?!" Lester screamed. "Is he a fucking zombie or something?! What the hell is this?!"

With the crazed attacker's body slumped over Ronald, twitching violently, Brett and Mason each took hold of one of the man's boots, pulling him clear while the others gathered around Ronald's now lifeless body.

"He's gone," Dr. Hunter pronounced after feeling for Ronald's pulse.

In a near hysterical fit, Lester, the member of the group who had grown closest to Ronald, shouted, "We've got to get him to the medical hut!"

Looking around at the scene of the carnage, with bodies and frozen blood spread throughout the area, Dr. Gerald Bentley said, "Mr. Stevens," as he placed his hand on Ronald's shoulder. "I fear the medical hut is not an option for him due to both his current state, as well as that of McMurdo. Something dreadful is afoot, and I don't see anyone responding to the needs of these poor folks. That's very telling, indeed."

"The Operations Center!" insisted Dr. Perkins. "We've got to get to the Operations Center and find out what the hell is going on!"

Taking a deep breath, Dr. Hunter scanned the area and said, "I'm afraid Gerald's assessment of the probable state of the medical hut would also apply to Ops. First things first, we need to get somewhere safe and warm for the night. We'll freeze to death if something—or someone—doesn't kill us first."

Lowering his bloody ice axe to his side, Brett said, "Dr. Hunter is right. We need to find a safe place to hide out and get warmed up. We just need to ride out the night and figure this out in the daylight."

After an awkward moment of silence with many of the group seeming to be in shock, Neville spoke up, saying, "Well, come on, then. Let's get to it. I'm freezing, and I don't like just standing out here in plain sight waiting for the next potential killer to find us."

Kneeling to look at Ronald's attacker, both Dr. Hunter and Dr. Duval noticed the organic-looking substance that seemed to follow along the man's jugular vein. Reaching out to touch it, Dr. Duval's hand was quickly knocked aside as Dr. Hunter said, "Jenny, no! Don't touch it."

"What do you make of it?" she asked.

"Well, I'm a geochemist, not a biologist, but it appears to be some sort of bacterium or a mass of microorganisms of some sort."

"Are you sure it's not just dirt or grease?" she asked. "Or even ash of some sort? There are a lot of fires in the area at the moment."

"I'm not sure, but let's get moving," he said while looking around. "One crazed man didn't do all of this alone."

Chapter Seven

McMurdo Station

Quietly working their way around McMurdo's outer perimeter to the west, Dr. Bentley whispered to Dr. Hunter, who appeared to have reassumed his authority over the group, "Where are we going?"

"The D2 pump house," Dr. Hunter replied.

"What? A pump house? Why?"

"Because until we know what the hell is going on, I don't want to intentionally go where I would expect people to be. Like I said, that man back there didn't do all of that alone. The pump house is heated to keep the pump and its associated valves operating in the extreme cold. We'll be able to stay warm in there for the night, and hopefully, avoid others in the process," Dr. Hunter explained.

"That's sound thinking," Dr. Bentley whispered in reply.

Arriving at the D2 pump house, Brett and Mason stepped ahead of the group and said, "Let us check it out first."

Nodding in agreement, Dr. Hunter gestured for them to proceed.

Grasping the lever on the heavy, steel door, Mason nodded to Brett as he slowly pulled it open. Standing at the ready with his ice axe, Brett listened for sounds from within, and upon hearing nothing, he continued inside.

Feeling along the side of the wall, Brett flipped on the lights to reveal a room full of pipes, valves, and a large electrically powered pump housing. After a quick scan of the building, the two motioned for the others to join them.

Once everyone was inside, Dr. Perkins closed the door as Brett and Mason quickly found several heavy pieces of extra pipe from the supply rack and wedged them firmly against the door to prevent entry from the outside.

Shivering, Dr. Duval said, "It sure feels better in here than it does out there. I don't think I could have taken the cold for much longer."

Looking around, Neville asked, "What is the purpose of all of this?"

Pulling his balaclava over his head and rubbing his cheeks, Dr. Hunter replied, "D2 stands for diesel tank number 2. This is the pumping station to get the fuel to each of the fueling stations for the diesel-powered equipment."

"Like Ivan the Terra Bus?" Neville asked, referring to the facility's famous, large-wheeled passenger bus.

"Exactly. That and the dozers, loaders, and all the other equipment running around the base," Dr. Hunter replied.

"You sure know your way around Mac-Town," remarked Dr. Perkins.

"I've been coming here for over ten seasons. This place has been my second home."

"Okay, someone has to say it," Lester said, redirecting the conversation. "What the hell is going on? Why were there bodies everywhere with no one rendering aid? Who was that man and why did he kill Ronald? What the hell is going on?" he said, his voice becoming more frantic with each question.

Taking a seat on a large purple fuel pipe that spanned the width of the room, Dr. Hunter said, "The only question we have an answer to at the moment is why Mac-Town didn't answer our radio calls and why they didn't send a helicopter. They apparently had more pressing matters to deal with. Beyond that, I'm as shocked, horrified, and confused as you."

"Do you think it was a terror attack or something?" asked Dr. Duval.

"I don't know, Jenny," Dr. Hunter replied. Shaking his head, he added, "Well, I just don't see how it could be. I mean, did you get a look at that guy? He seemed to have lost his mind. Something wasn't right with him, but he couldn't have acted alone. He definitely wasn't taking a conscious action in the name of a jihad or something."

"Then what the hell is it?"

Speaking up, Derrick Mason said, "He almost seemed rabid. Have you ever seen an animal with rabies? They're aggressive and irrational, just like he was."

"I was thinking the same thing," replied Brett.

Standing up and walking to the door, ensuring it was adequately secure, Dr. Hunter said, "Okay, until we have a way to gather more information, we just need to accept the fact that we haven't got a clue as to what's going on. We also need to acknowledge the fact that there are potentially more threats out there. We've had a long, hard day. We all need to get some rest and investigate further in the morning when we have daylight to work with."

"What about the telephone?" Jenny Duval said as she pointed to the station's land-line phone mounted to the wall next to the light panel. "Can't we call around looking for help?"

"I imagine we could, but again, we don't know what's going on, who's involved, or even the extent of the situation," Dr. Hunter explained. "I'd rather not alert anyone to our presence until we can get a better look around and adequately assess the situation."

Looking around at the group, Dr. Hunter then said, "There are seven of us, now. Let's take a rotational watch throughout the night. We don't want to wake up to an unwelcomed guest. I'll take the first watch. I'll then wake someone to relieve me in a few hours, and we can continue rotating throughout the night until morning."

"Who's after you?" Mason asked. "I mean, who are you waking to relieve you?"

"I guess you're volunteering, Derrick," Dr. Hunter proffered. "You can then wake Dr. Perkins to relieve you, who will be relieved by Dr. Bentley, Neville, Brett, and then Jenny. That should get us through until morning."

"What about Lester?" Jenny asked.

"Let him sleep—if he can. He needs it."

~~~~

Early the next morning, Derrick Mason awoke to see Dr. Jenny Duval with her ear to the door. "Hear anything?" he asked softly, trying not to wake the others.

Replying with a whisper, she said, "I heard a metallic thud a few minutes ago. It sounded like it was off in the distance—to the east side of the station, perhaps. I haven't heard any voices or vehicle traffic at all. McMurdo is usually bustling by now."

As the rest of the group began to stir, Dr. Hunter said, "If McMurdo was still functional, we'd have heard a response to the violent scene we saw. The silence is very telling."

Waking the others, Dr. Hunter gathered everyone together and said, "Okay, we need to come up with some sort of plan of action. We can't sit in this pump house waiting for help that may not come."

"I agree," said Brett. "We've gone long enough without food and water, and we need to secure a source of both before we move forward with any other plans."

"The station galley?" Dr. Bentley asked.

"That's a logical choice, and if there were other survivors, surely, they would have gone there as well," added Mason. "Everyone will need food and water."

"Where there is the potential for people, there is a potential for threats," replied Dr. Hunter.

"Agreed, which is why we all need something to defend ourselves with," said Brett as he stood and looked around the room. "Mason and I have our ice axes, but the rest of you need something as well. There are plenty of pipes, tools, and other objects here that can be used as blunt weapons. Everyone, find something that you can comfortably handle."

As the group looked around the room at the resources they had available, Dr. Hunter picked up a pry bar of about four feet in length, swung it through the air a few times, and said, "This will do."

Rummaging through a tool locker, Jenny Duval picked up a forty-ounce ball-peen hammer. Neville Wallace picked up a piece of one-inch steel tubing with a shut off valve on one end, thinking it would make a nice club.

As the rest of the group rummaged aimlessly, Mason said, "Hey, if we saw an angled cut into the end of this one-inch pipe and cut it into four-foot sections, it will make some very handy stabbing weapons. Like spears or lances."

With a look of interest on his face, Dr. Hunter said, "If we run those saws, we'll make too much noise. We don't want to lead who or whatever may be out there to us."

"You mean, lead the zombies to us?" Lester blurted out in frustration.

"Look," Dr. Hunter said, trying to calm Lester's agitated state. "We may not know what's going on out there, but let's not go off the deep end about zombies. Ronald's attacker was clearly not the walking dead. He was as alive as any of the rest of us.

That, Brett and Mason proved without a doubt. He did seem ill—
or something—but we've got to keep our perspectives straight.
There's no such thing as a zombie. We all know that. Let's stick
with what we know and not get ourselves wrapped around the
axle of our minds."

Holding a Milwaukee hand-saw above his head, Brett said,
"Here we go. We can use this hand-saw. It'll take longer, but we
should be able to muffle the sound and not make anywhere near
as much noise as a power saw. Maybe if we wrap the pipe we're
sawing in insulation or something, we can deaden some of the
reverberating sounds of the metal."

"Fine idea," said Dr. Bentley as he selected a section of
tubing for his weapon. "Let's get to it then."

~~~~

After approximately an hour's work, the group's slant-cut,
sharpened pipes were complete, providing everyone other than
Brett and Mason with what was essentially a makeshift spear or
lance.

"I wish I had a damn gun," Mason quipped. "It's ridiculous
to be facing a situation like this with sharpened pipes."

"At least you've got an ice axe," Jenny replied.

"If the politics of the Antarctic Treaty didn't keep this place
so..."

"So, what?" Neville asked. "Demilitarized? What is it with
Americans always needing an armed presence to feel secure?"

"You call it demilitarized. I call it vulnerable. A lot of
different people flow through McMurdo during the research
season. What's to keep one of those people from snapping?
What's to keep a wannabe terrorist from making a name for
himself, wreaking havoc on the place? That could be what's

going on right now, for all we know. And here we are, sharpening pipes when there should have been a security force of some kind."

"There is...or there might be, something along those lines," Dr. Hunter replied.

"What do you mean?" asked Mason.

"The NSF Station Manager is rumored to have a weapon, or weapons, for just such a thing."

"With what we saw, wouldn't you think we'd have heard gunshots last night? And if someone is armed, why aren't they out and about right now, checking on the extent of the situation?" Mason asked.

"I can't answer that," replied Dr. Hunter. "The station manager's office is located in the Ops building, on the top floor. If there are weapons at McMurdo, that's where they'll be."

"What the hell are we waiting for then?" Mason asked.

With a look of agreement on his face, Dr. Hunter said, "The galley is halfway between here and Ops. Ops is at the far end of the berthing complex from the galley. Let's plan on stopping at the galley to get some food and water. Then, based on what we find there, we can make the decision to proceed to the Ops center or not."

Chapter Eight

McMurdo Station

As the team from MEVO worked their way through McMurdo Station toward the galley, they saw signs of recent violence all along the way. A decapitated corpse wearing U.S. Antarctic Program gear lay in front of the National Science Foundation building. Though the head was nowhere to be found, crystallized frozen blood stained the icy ground around the body.

As they paused for a moment, each wondering who the person may have been, undoubtedly an acquaintance or friend of some of them, Brett said, "Come on. Let's keep moving."

"There it is," Mason said, pointing ahead to the large, blue, two-story metal structure.

The galley was housed in the lower floor of the building, with laundry facilities, a billeting office, a library, and a convenience store that contained everything from snacks to liquor, located on the upper floor.

Seeing boot prints going in what appeared to be virtually every direction, Brett knelt and paid special attention to one set and said, "Droplets of blood follow along with these tracks."

Kneeling beside him, Mason noted, "Yep. You've got a good eye. They're tiny and almost lost in the snow from all the commotion."

"Whoever the poor soul was seems to have sought refuge in the galley as well," added Dr. Bentley. "I sure hope the fellow is friendly."

Hearing a door slam behind them, the group turned around to see a disheveled woman, wearing only her bib-overalls, but no jacket and no boots, standing just outside building 211, which was a berthing or dormitory for seasonal workers.

As the woman quietly stood there, staring at them with the same lost, dazed look as the man who had attacked Ronald, Dr. Perkins said, "We've seen that look, and I don't have a good feeling about this."

Agreeing with Dr. Perkins' observation, Dr. Bentley added, "I do believe that young lady would be feeling the effects of her bare feet if she was in a correct state of mind. They're obviously frostbitten."

Lowering her head and intensifying her stare, the woman's breathing began to steadily increase as she moved slowly toward them, almost dragging her frostbitten feet.

"Ma'am?" Neville shouted. "Are you in need of assistance?"

Upon hearing their voices, the woman's cadence increased as her slow, plodding walk turned into a run.

"Shit!" Dr. Duval shouted. "Do something, but don't kill her!"

Readying his axe, Mason said, "Head for the galley."

"What if the person who left the trail of blood is still in there?" Neville asked.

"Then we'll deal with it," replied Brett, as he ran up the steps of the galley to the double doors at the entrance. "Now, come on!" he shouted as Mason squared off with the woman, holding his ice axe in both hands in front of him.

Joining Mason, Dr. Hunter lowered his makeshift pipe spear and pointed it at the woman. Gesturing to Mason's axe, he said, "I'll hold her off so you can do the job."

Nodding in reply, Mason held the axe high as the woman, now at a full sprint, ran straight into Dr. Hunter's sharpened pipe, impaling herself through the stomach.

With the pipe protruding from her back, Mason and Dr. Hunter were both shocked to see the fight and rage that still resided deep inside the woman's eyes. Dr. Hunter struggled against her forward motion as he held her out of reach the best he could.

"What the hell is this?" he asked, staring into her eyes. "Look at her! She's behaving like an animal!" Looking to Mason, he shouted, "You'd better hurry the hell up and get it done!"

With one powerful blow of his axe, Mason sheared off the top of the woman's skull. As her eyes rolled back into her head, she dropped to her knees, grasping Dr. Hunter's spear before rolling over to her side, dead.

The sweat that had been profusely emanating from her pores began to freeze instantly to her skin as the extreme cold of Antarctica overcame her residual body heat. Within seconds, the heavy layer of sweat created an icy sheen on every exposed surface of her skin.

Pulling his spear free, Dr. Hunter said, "Quickly. Get inside with the others."

Joining the others inside, Mason and Dr. Hunter took the opportunity to catch their breath as Dr. Perkins and Neville quickly jammed chair backs into the push-type handles of the doors, preventing the mechanisms from being operated from outside the facility.

"You killed her!" Dr. Jenny Duval shouted. "Why the hell did you have to kill her?"

"Are you blind?" Mason shouted in reply. "She was no different than the man who attacked Ronald."

"You should have just run away," she argued. "We don't know what is going on. We might have been able to help her."

"Fuck that!" shouted Lester. "Ronald tried talking to his killer, and it didn't work. There was no soul inside that monster, if you ask me. Kill them! Kill them all! We need to kill every damn one of them if we have to!"

"Jenny," Dr. Hunter interjected as he carefully wiped his spear clean with a tablecloth, trying his best to avoid touching the blood. "He's right. As crude as he made it sound, he's right. We have no clue what's going on here. All we know is that death—violent death—pervades McMurdo at the moment. Remember the headless body in USAP gear? That person may have tried reason instead of violence to deal with the threat before him. I'm not letting something like that happen to any of us if I can help it."

Looking around the galley, Mason asked Brett, "So, what's our situation?"

"There's a lot of blood on the floor in the kitchen and prep area, along with a few bodies in kitchen staff uniforms. Besides that, the place is a wreck. It looks as if everyone left here in a hurry."

"Let's do a quick sweep of the place to make sure we're alone," Mason said as he began to work his way between the tables. "The last thing I want to do is be surprised by another rabid psychopath when I finally sit down to eat."

"Agreed," replied Brett sharply. "Jenny, you come with me. Neville, you go with Mason. Dr. Bentley, you and Dr. Perkins team up, and Doc Hunter, you take Lester. Let's spread out and sweep the immediate area and meet back here. Yell if you have a problem, otherwise, try to keep quiet. It was our talking outside that probably led our visitor out of the berthing to find us."

As everyone began to split up as directed, Lester protested, "Hell, no. I'm not going to look for something to kill me. My ass is staying right here."

"C'mon, Lester. It'll be fine," Dr. Hunter assured. "We'll keep an eye out for each other. The guys are right; we need to make sure we're secure here before we find ourselves cornered in the back looking for food."

Shaking his head, Lester insisted, "No. I'm staying right here. You're not in charge anymore, Doctor. We're not at MEVO. That little research game you were playing is over."

"Have it your way, Lester," Dr. Hunter replied. "Gerald, I'll go with you and Walt," he said, addressing Dr. Bentley and Dr. Perkins.

Pulling out a chair and sitting down at one of the galley's cafeteria-style tables, Lester huffed under his breath, "I'm sick of this shit. Sick of it."

Gesturing for Dr. Duval to follow, Brett said, "Jenny, let's check out the kitchen."

Following along, they watched as the rest of the group dispersed as Brett had recommended.

Looking underneath the swinging half-doors leading into the kitchen and prep areas, Brett whispered, "I don't see anything, but what's that smell?"

"Something's burning," she said.

Slowly pushing one of the doors to the side, Brett slipped inside, looking in horror at the cook who lay dead on the floor with a meat cleaver buried deep in his chest. Nudging the body with his foot, ensuring no life, Brett crept past the man, being careful not to step in the slippery pools of blood that had begun to thicken and dry in the warm air of the kitchen. Continuing past a row of deep sinks, they came upon the grill and fryer area of the kitchen where they found one unidentifiable worker who had been pushed into a large, commercial deep fat fryer.

"Oh, dear Lord," she said, covering her face with her sweater.

"I guess we know what was burning," Brett said as he reached to the controls, turning the fryer off.

"My God," he said. "The poor bastard's upper half is burnt to a crisp."

Seeing Jenny begin to dry-heave, he motioned for her to continue toward the large, walk-in refrigerator. "Are you gonna be okay?" he asked.

Wiping her mouth, she said, "Yeah. I'll be alright. I just... I just can't..."

"I know," he interrupted. "Me, too. It's just too much."

~~~~

Exploring the horseshoe-shaped stairwell leading up to the second floor, Mason and Neville crept slowly up one step at a time in an attempt to see around the staircase to what might await them above.

Reaching the upper landing, Mason noticed that a portion of the hand-railing alongside the stairs had been beaten off, and was shoved into the door-actuation lever at the top of the stairs, jamming the door shut.

"What the—?" Neville said, joining Mason on the upper landing.

"It looks like someone didn't want anything from the upper level to get down the stairs."

Hearing a crashing sound, as if a display rack of some sort had been knocked over at a distance on the other side of the door, Mason said, "Let's leave well enough alone. Let's get back down to the others."

"Agreed," replied Neville as the two men quietly worked their way back down the stairs to the first floor.

~~~~

Sitting nervously at the cafeteria table alone, an uncontrollable torrent of thoughts raced through Lester's mind. Thoughts of his family back home, the warmth of the sun on his bare skin, and the freedom to simply get in his car and drive as far as he wanted to go reminded him of what he now began to believe he would never see again. *What the hell is going on here? I don't understand. I don't understand. Make it stop. Oh, please, God, make it stop. Wake me up from this nightmare.*

With his panic-laced thoughts being interrupted by the sound of a chair scooting across the floor behind him, Lester jerked around to see Frank Horton, a friend of his and a writer from Virginia who had traveled to McMurdo Station to work as a fry cook in search of an idea for his next great novel.

"Frank," he said nervously. "Thank God, it's you. What the hell is going on?"

As Frank slowly walked toward him, Lester could see a blank, emotionless look on his face as beads of sweat oozed from his skin. "Frank. What's wrong, Frank? Are you okay? It's me, Lester."

Standing up from his chair, Lester recognized the look on Frank's face as the same look he'd seen on the face of the man who had brutally killed Ronald the day before.

"God, no, Frank," he said, backing away. "It's me, Frank. It's me, Lester. Don't do this, Frank. Please, don't do this."

~~~~

Searching the coffee shop, Dr. Hunter saw a twitching body lying in the corner of the room next to the cooler filled with yogurts and parfaits. Several chairs were piled up on top of the body, which he could now see was a woman. Many of the chairs had been broken in what he could only assume was a horrible act of violence and rage.

As he approached the twitching body beneath the pile of chairs, he placed his weaponized piece of steel tubing on the counter and whispered to Doctors Bentley and Perkins, "Be ready. I'm going to see if she can be helped."

With Bentley and Perkins holding their spears at the ready, Dr. Hunter began slowly and quietly removing the broken bits of coffee shop stools and chairs, revealing a blonde woman in her early thirties.

Her eyes darted around wildly, and her breathing was rapid and shallow, but from the position of her head, Dr. Hunter could tell there was nothing he could do for her. Her neck was severely broken and it appeared that both of her arms were as well. *Probably from shielding herself from the violent blows,* he thought.

Kneeling beside her, he said, "I'm sorry. I'm so sorry." as he brushed her hair out of her face.

Seeing a tear appear from the corner of her eye, he said, "I wish there was something we could do. I'm afraid to move you. Your neck looks too badly injured. If we can find help, we'll come back for you. I promise."

As the tear ran down her cheek, her breathing slowed and her life slipped from her mangled, damaged body.

Closing his eyes for a moment, Dr. Hunter's heart ached inside, only finding solace in the fact that she was no longer in pain and that she was free from this terrible ordeal.

Turning to Doctors Bentley and Perkins, Dr. Hunter began to speak when they heard screaming coming from the cafeteria. "Lester!" he exclaimed as the three of them turned and began to run toward the desperate pleas for help.

~~~~

Back in the kitchen, Brett and Dr. Duval had reached the walk-in refrigerator where most of the perishable fresh food was kept. Reaching for the handle, he said, "I sure could go for some fresh fruit right about now."

As he began to rotate the lever to open the large, stainless-steel door, Dr. Duval said, "Try to be quiet about it. Don't let the door make any noise."

"Relax, Jenny," he replied reassuringly. "I'll be nice and easy. Besides, you know you want an apple or orange just as bad as I do."

Placing his hand back on the lever, he rotated it slowly clockwise as the latching mechanism released with a click. Looking at her with a grin on his face, he whispered, "Sorry," with a smile.

Hearing something fall from a shelf inside the refrigerator, she shouted, "Close it! Close it now!" as they both attempted to shove the door closed. Feeling the weight of a fully-grown man slam into the door from the opposite side, both Jenny and Brett were knocked backward and onto the floor.

As a crazed man, dressed in his issued bib-overalls and snow boots, stood over them, they could see sweat running down his face, dripping off his nose as his breathing seemed heavy and rapid.

Watching as he turned to them, looking at them with the same blank stare as the others, Brett exclaimed, "Holy shit! Go! Go! Go!" as he hurried back to his feet, swinging his axe at the man.

With the impact from his ice axe nearly severing the man's left arm, Brett was startled to see that the wound seemed to have no effect on the man at all. As the man let out a primal scream and with his teeth fully exposed, charged Brett. Reacting quickly, Brett swung again, nearly decapitating the man as a stream of blood splattered across the white kitchen wall behind them.

Seeing the man fall to the floor, the threat having been neutralized, Brett turned and followed Jenny, who was now running back toward the cafeteria's seating area in search of help.

~~~~

Rounding the corner and entering the cafeteria, Dr. Hunter saw a figure standing over the location where they had left Lester. The figure, wearing what appeared to be a surgical mask, rubber gloves, and goggles, in addition to the typical cold-weather gear issued by the United States Antarctic Program, was raising a large fire axe, seeming to Dr. Hunter to be preparing to drop it to the floor. Unable to see Lester due to the position of the tables and chairs, Dr. Hunter drew back his spear, preparing to throw it from across the room in an attempt to save Lester.

As Mason and Neville reached the bottom landing of the staircase, they burst into the cafeteria just twenty feet from Lester's bleeding, bludgeoned body.

Recognizing what was going, Mason turned to see Dr. Hunter prepare to thrust his spear into the air. Raising his arms above his head, waving frantically, Mason yelled, "Doctor Hunter! No! No! Don't do it," as he ran toward the person with the axe, seeming to be unafraid.

Confused by what he was seeing, Dr. Hunter paused, only to see the axe-wielding figure remove the surgical mask and goggles, and then the hood of the red, USAP issued parka. To his surprise, Dr. Hunter saw his dear friend, Dr. Linda Graves, turn to him as she lowered the axe. In an instant, he recognized the caring look in her eyes. He knew that she was okay. She wasn't afflicted like the others.

Dropping his spear, he ran to her side to see Lester, lying on the floor still and lifeless, with his jugular vein torn from his throat. Joined alongside Lester in the massive pool of blood beneath him, was Lester's friend, Frank Horton.

Horton's chest had received numerous blows from Linda's axe. With his chest splayed open, his heart was visible, still, and lifeless.

Dropping the axe to the floor, she looked at Dr. Hunter, and cried, "Nathan. Oh, my God, Nathan. I'm so glad you're finally here."

Chapter Nine

McMurdo Station

After an emotional reunion between Dr. Hunter and Dr. Graves, Mason interrupted, saying, "We need to get moving. All that ruckus was surely heard by... uh... others—if they're around."

"Where is Jared?" Dr. Hunter asked.

Before Dr. Graves could answer, Jenny Duval asked "What the hell is going on here? I feel like this is just a nightmare. I feel like I'm in a fucking zombie apocalypse movie like we watched all the time when cooped up back at MEVO. This can't be happening. It can't be!"

"I'll explain more when we get somewhere safe," answered Dr. Linda Graves. "Mason is right, we've got to get moving."

"What are your recommendations?" Dr. Bentley asked. "Being that you've been here amidst the chaos the longest, there is little doubt you have a better idea of what is safe and what is not."

"First, we've got to get to the medical building and get you all suited up," she replied. "This is contagious."

"This?" Dr. Perkins asked with a raised eyebrow.

With a stern facial expression, Dr. Graves reiterated, "I said I would explain more when we get somewhere safe. First, we've got to get to the medical building, as I said. It's not far. It's right behind the galley."

Hurrying over to the double-doors at the main entrance of the galley, she scanned outside for threats, and said, "Come on," as she stepped outside.

Quickly following close behind, Brett, Mason, Dr. Hunter, Dr. Duval, Dr. Bentley, and Dr. Perkins slipped back into the frigid, blowing winds of McMurdo.

Walking as stealthily as they could, following closely along the side of the building to avoid being seen too easily, the group gathered at the back of building 155, just across from the medical facility, commonly known as McMurdo General Hospital.

Though more of a metal, shop-type of structure than a traditional hospital, building 142 was equipped with just about anything that station medical professionals would need to treat the myriad injuries and health conditions that were likely to occur to McMurdo's seasonal residents.

Slipping up to the side door, marked *Mass Casualty Equipment*, Dr. Graves motioned and said, "Quick. In here."

Once everyone was inside, and the door was closed securely behind them, she flipped on the lights and began sifting through the stacks of supplies in the room, which looked as if it had already had a thorough ransacking.

"Okay," Dr. Hunter, said. "What do you know? You can't keep us in the dark forever."

Giving him a stern look, Dr. Graves replied, "Look, Nathan, I'm not keeping you in the dark. The truth is I'm barely keeping myself together. You've not seen half of what I've seen, damn it! So, don't give me any—"

"Hey, hey, hey," he said, holding his hands in the air as if trying to calm her. "Linda. I'm sorry. I didn't mean to—"

Shoving hazmat gloves and a disposable medical face shield against his chest, she said, "Just go and deal with Lester. Don't leave him there like that. Do something respectful with his body," she said, breaking down into tears.

Taking what she'd given him, Dr. Hunter nodded to Mason, gesturing for him to join him in retrieving Lester's remains.

Stopping them before they left the room, Dr. Graves said, "Nathan. Don't touch it. It gets inside you."

"What?" he asked. "Don't touch what?"

Slumping down into the floor, Dr. Graves began to cry uncontrollably. As Jenny Duval rushed to her side, Dr. Hunter knew that Linda had gone through more in the past few days than he could imagine. She had held it all inside—until now. She had managed to suppress the horrors and sorrow, but no more. For the moment, she would let it overtake her. He knew that's what she needed for the time being. She needed to deal with things. With that in mind, he and Mason left the room to do as she'd asked.

~~~~

Closing the heavy, steel door of the unheated storage building adjacent to the galley, Dr. Hunter removed his face shield and looked to Mason, who was standing guard behind him with his ice axe at the ready. "Their bodies will be preserved in here just fine. It's the best we can do for now. It's not like we can dig in this icy ground."

Replying with only a nod, Mason began walking back toward the galley with Dr. Hunter in trail.

As they worked their way around the galley and back to the medical facility, both Mason and Hunter watched and listened for threats. With the wind howling through the station, they could barely hear their own footsteps, much less the approach of any potential threats. Wiping his snow goggles, now covered with blowing snow and debris, Dr. Hunter caught a glimpse of movement to his left. Stopping in his tracks, he watched for a moment, holding his makeshift spear at the ready.

"Did you see that?" he asked Mason, shouting over the noise of the violent winds.

Huddling close, Mason asked, "What? See what?"

Pointing, Dr. Hunter said, "Over there. Between that modular office and the FEMC trade shop."

"I didn't see anything," Mason replied. Tugging at Dr. Hunter's arm, he urged, "Let's get going."

~~~~

Hearing a bang on the door, Dr. Perkins asked, "Dr. Hunter? Mason? Is that you guys?"

Hearing a muffled voice through the door, "Yeah. It's us. Open up," he threw the latch to the side and let them in, quickly closing the door behind them.

"It's done," Dr. Hunter said while removing his gloves and snow goggles.

"Don't get undressed too quickly," Dr. Bentley said, handing him a sack of items picked out by Dr. Graves. "We're off to the Crary Lab." Pausing for a moment, he said, "You've got an office there, right, Nathan?"

"Yes. Yes, I do, but I don't use it much. It's mostly storage for me. I've always preferred to be in the field and on the mountain," Dr. Hunter replied.

As the group left the mass casualty storeroom, Dr. Graves said, "Follow me. The best way into Crary is through Phase Three, the Aquarium Pod. The main doors at Phase One were barricaded shut when the breakout began."

"The breakout?" Dr. Perkins asked.

"I'll explain when we get there," she replied curtly.

Following Dr. Graves as she worked her way carefully toward the Crary Science and Engineering Center, known commonly as Crary Lab, the group was pummeled by the violent winds. Wiping his goggles, Mason looked off to the left to see Gallagher's Pub. Nudging Dr. Hunter, he leaned toward him and said through the noise of the howling winds, "I sure could use a beer right now."

"We all could, Derrick," Dr. Hunter replied. "Or a shot...or three."

Approaching Crary Lab, Dr. Graves signaled for the others to work their way around to the lower steps leading up to the door next to Loading Dock E. Once gathered at the bottom of the steps, she pulled Dr. Hunter close and said, "Dr. Bob Muller was waiting for me in room 303 when I left. It's next to the loading dock door on the inside. He's supposed to be keeping an eye out while I went to look for food at the galley in the main building."

"The GPS guy? He sent you out into this shit while he stayed behind?" Dr. Hunter said, appalled at the thought of Dr. Muller staying safe while sending Linda out to face the madness that had become McMurdo Station.

"I insisted," she replied sharply. Opening the door slightly, Dr. Graves saw no immediate signs of danger and slipped inside. With the group following and closing the door, sheltering them from the foul weather of the day, Dr. Graves removed her goggles and hood, whispering, "Bob. Where are you?"

Hearing movement but no direct reply from room 303, Dr. Hunter and the others placed the sacks and bins of supplies that they had brought from the mass casualty storeroom on the floor and readied their makeshift weapons.

Gripping his spear tightly, Dr. Hunter gestured to Mason to ease open the door to room 303. As Mason rotated the lever-style doorknob, he pushed it gently open and backed out of the way. With virtually no time to react, a male figure ran straight into Dr. Hunter, slamming him violently into the wall behind him, causing both men to fall to the floor.

As his attacker struck the floor, the metallic sound of Dr. Hunter's spear could be heard as it protruded from the man's back. The direct rush of the man's attack had caused him to impale himself on Dr. Hunter's sharpened pipe as the handle struck the wall behind him.

Scurrying to his feet, trying to distance himself from his attacker, Dr. Hunter heard Linda Graves scream aloud, "Bob!" as she ran to the man's side.

Pulling her away as the man known as Bob Muller reached for her ankle, Mason shouted, "No!" as they watched Dr. Muller squirm and struggle on the floor as if his injuries didn't faze him at all.

Dr. Muller had the same violence and rage in his eyes as the others. He was drenched in sweat and his breathing was heavy and fast. Holding him down with the spear shoved against him, Dr. Bentley said, "Look at the tracks on his neck. They're the same as the bloke that attacked Ronald."

Pointing into room 303, Dr. Graves said, "Look!" as a body lay next to the saltwater holding tank, apparently killed by multiple blows to the head by a blood-covered piece of gear lying next to him. The floor was covered with water, as well as dead giant isopods, pteropods, sea spiders, and other strange Antarctic sea life as one of the aquarium tanks had been destroyed during the apparent struggle, spilling its contents throughout the room.

Turning back to Dr. Muller as he lay on the floor, reaching for Dr. Perkins who still held him in place with his spear, Dr. Graves said, "He's going to die from his wounds, anyway. Put him, or what part of him that may remain, out of his misery."

Staring at her with a look of disbelief, Dr. Perkins stammered, "R... re... really? You can't be serious. This is Bob Muller. You know him."

Taking Dr. Duval's spear from her hands, Dr. Graves walked over to her friend, Bob Muller, writhing and struggling on the floor. Watching as he reached for her with pure, unbridled rage on his face, she said in a cold, calculated voice, "I'm not sure that's true anymore. I'm not sure Bob is still in there. Even if he were, he wouldn't survive an injury like this with no medical care."

The group was horrified as she then plunged the rusty pipe, with its sharp, angle-cut at the end, into Dr. Muller's eye socket, penetrating his brain and putting an end to his struggles.

Handing the makeshift spear back to Jenny Duval, Dr. Graves said, "Don't touch the blood. Clean it off the first chance you get." Turning back to the others, she said, "Now, come on. We need to get to the Phase One pod so I can show you what I know."

Looking at the blood on the end of her spear, Jenny Duval was in shock at what she had just witnessed. Dr. Linda Graves was one of the kindest and gentlest people she had ever met, yet she had somehow, over the past few days, gotten to the point where she could plunge a weapon into the eye socket of a friend. What was this madness? When would they wake up from this nightmare?

Watching as the others began to leave, Dr. Duval snapped out of her shock-induced trance and followed her bewildered colleagues as they began to leave.

Leading the group up the connector to the Phase Two of the Crary Lab, which houses the Earth Sciences Pod as well as the Atmospheric Sciences Pod, Dr. Graves stopped, pointing to the

Earth Sciences Pod. Looking to Dr. Hunter, she asked, "Nathan, is there anything in the MEVO office you would like to retrieve?"

Thinking for a moment, he shook his head and said, "No. There's nothing there of use to us in our current situation. Let's just keep moving."

Continuing up the slanted ramp toward the Phase One section of the Crary Lab, Dr. Graves paused, listening intently.

"What is it?" Brett asked.

Turning to him, she replied, "Nothing. I don't hear anything at all. Everyone was in a hurry to leave. A large group left together saying they were heading to Ivan the Terra Bus to get to the airstrip. There were several planes leaving. There was a very unorganized emergency evacuation taking place. I... I was just wondering if any of them had returned."

"But why didn't you escape with them?" Dr. Hunter asked.

Pausing for a moment, seeming to struggle with something in her own mind, Dr. Graves maintained her composure and replied, "I couldn't leave Jared. At the onset of everything, I had no idea what the end result of this condition would be. That's why I got him safely locked away while I focused on just trying to understand what was happening around me. I couldn't leave him. Besides," she said, turning to look at Dr. Hunter, "I knew you were still out there on Erebus. I knew you would find a way back."

Continuing up the connector, affectionately known as the 'skateboard ramp,' Dr. Graves led the group into the Phase One section of Crary Lab.

Looking ahead, the group could see the barricade that Dr. Graves had spoken of at the main doors at the end of the connector. To their left was the Biology Pod, which was, since she was an astrobiology researcher, Dr. Grave's home at McMurdo when not at MEVO with the rest of the group. To their right was the Core Pod, the administrative and support wing of Crary Lab.

With Phase One being the largest section of Crary Lab, the Biology Pod was separated into two hallways with numerous research labs and offices lining both sides of each hallway. Taking the first door on her left and entering the southernmost hallway, Dr. Graves said, "It's this way. What I need to show you is in the microscope room on the right, room 122."

As they reached room 122, a violent, loud impact was heard against the door across the hall, startling everyone but Dr. Graves. Turning to face the threat with their weapons held at the ready, Dr. Hunter asked, "What the hell was that?"

Reaching for the doorknob, Mason said, "Let's deal with this."

"No!" Dr. Graves commanded. "Leave him be."

"Him?" Dr. Perkins queried.

Pausing for a moment, reluctant to answer, Dr. Graves said, "Yes. Him. It's Jared. He's... he's the same as the others."

They were stunned by what they had heard. Their friend and colleague, Dr. Jared Davis, volcanologist and junior member of the research team from Dr. Hunter's own NMT, was on the other side of the door, raving mad and full of the same rage and violence as the others.

"He can't get out," Dr. Graves said. "I locked him in. Just leave him be. I don't have the heart..."

Growing impatient with his own lack of understanding of the situation, Dr. Hunter said, "So, what's in room 122 that you have to show us?"

Chapter Ten

A. P. Crary Science and Engineering Center (Crary Lab)

Once in the microscope room, Dr. Graves turned on the lights, locked the door behind them, and said, "Here. It's over here."

Leading Dr. Hunter to one of the room's many microscopes, she said, "This is the substance you have all noticed following along the major blood vessels of those affected."

Looking into the microscope, Dr. Hunter adjusted the magnification several times and said, "Eukaryotes?"

Removing the sample slide from the microscope's stage with a gloved hand, she replaced it with another and said, "This is a sample of what Brett and I found just before I left the mountain."

"It's the same," he said, startled by what she was clearly laying out for him.

"Yes, it's the same," Dr. Graves replied. "Those eukaryotes are chemolithoautotrophic. Like the many other microorganisms we've seen on Erebus and in other extreme environments around the world, they thrive not by feeding on organic materials, but by deriving their energy from the chemical reactions between themselves and rock. They basically use materials such as iron, carbon, nitrogen, and more, for food."

Sitting up from the microscope and looking to Dr. Graves, Dr. Hunter asked, "But what is happening here?"

"Our bodies are full of iron, carbon, nitrogen, and all of the things they have evolved to process for energy. Our bodies are like a candy shop for them. They can extract the nutrients they seek from our blood far easier than from the cold, hard rock of

Erebus

Erebus. Of all the eukaryotes I've encountered in my studies as an astrobiologist, I've never seen anything quite like this. I don't know why they are interacting with us when all the others remained happily restricted to a diet of rock and minerals, but they are.

"Once inside our blood, they reproduce at a rapid pace and begin to take over. How it is exactly that they interfere with our brain function is still a mystery to me, but that is clearly what is happening here. Is it an unfortunate side reaction of the host/parasite relationship? Or is it something we simply can't grasp, such as an intentional reaction to get the host moving around to encounter other potential hosts so they can increase their population through physical contact? Blood and bodily fluids would make the most convenient vehicle for transfer."

"I don't understand," interrupted Dr. Bentley. "If they latch on to human hosts so easily, why didn't you and Brett become their first vehicles? And how did they get loose here at McMurdo?"

"I've thought about that quite a bit," she replied. "Brett and I never made direct contact with them. We were wearing our protective clothing and never directly touched them with our gloves. I used my knife to scrape a sample from the cave walls. Though they are accustomed to processing things such as iron, they usually make such a reaction with soft rock, not the hardened materials found in modern metallurgy such as the stainless-steel blade of my knife. They simply didn't survive to transfer from my knife to me. That, and if there were surviving hitchhikers on my blade, they probably froze once we exited the caves. The rest were kept relatively warm inside the sample container deep within Brett's pack. That's another reason I believe the human body makes an excellent host. Have you noticed all of those who are infected have been sweating profusely? They seem to be replicating the heat of the caves and fumaroles that run throughout Erebus by heating up their hosts."

"Heating up their hosts?" Doctor Perkins repeated. "You just said you weren't sure if it was a chance reaction and now you're acting as if these simple little microscopic creatures are consciously controlling us."

"First off, they are anything but simple. And yes, I am still guessing at this point. These organisms may be single-celled, but they can group together to make a more complex organism in a relatively short amount of time. Secondly, we don't know how long these things have been dormant, hiding deep within the bowels of Erebus. You know as well as I do that over one-hundred-million years ago, this continent was teeming with life. It had the climate of a rainforest. These creatures probably thrived then. They could have easily lived in the blood of myriad species, merely retreating underground, deep within the bowels of the Earth as the climate changed, trapping them deep below the ice. Fossil record proof of this may merely be hidden thousands of meters below the ice, just out of our reach.

"As an astrobiologist, I have traveled the world in search of the most extreme conditions where life might exist so that we may understand where life may also exist elsewhere in our universe. I've learned not to be surprised by anything. Life will find a way not only to survive, but also to thrive, and it won't restrict itself to the rules of our narrow scope of understanding when doing so."

Turning back to the rest of the group, she continued, "As to how it has spread so rapidly through McMurdo, there was an accident in the Ship Off Load Command Center. My samples and gear were packed away securely as always. Unfortunately, one of the forklift operators had a medical emergency of some sort and crashed into my pallet, knocking it off the stack and down onto a coworker below. I believe this is where the first transfer took place. The open wounds of the injured worker were the perfect ingress points for the freed organisms."

"Whatever happened to the worker?" Dr. Bentley asked. "The one who was exposed."

"In addition to the severe injuries he sustained during the accident, he immediately developed a high fever. He was too injured to transport without stabilizing him, so an emergency surgery was performed at the station hospital. He was then transferred to the next departing aircraft.

"The secondary exposures seemed to come from medical, and spread rapidly through McMurdo over the course of the next day. Even without a basis in facts, I immediately knew what was happening," she said, hanging her head low. "I could feel it deep within my soul. It was my fault. All my fault. I brought this evil from deep within the bowels of the Earth and thrust it upon us all."

Placing his hand on her back, Dr. Hunter said, "Linda, that's nonsense. We've all brought samples from Erebus through McMurdo to get them to our university labs back home. It could have been any of us."

Looking at him with a tear in her eye, she replied, "It could have been. But it wasn't."

Chapter Eleven

Crary Lab

Listening to the thuds against the wall from across the hallway, a continued reminder of the violent struggle deep within the body of their friend and colleague Dr. Jared Davis, the group sat there in silence, contemplating their fate.

"We've got to work up a plan," Brett said. "We can't stay here in the Crary Lab forever. We have the food we took from the galley and that'll get us by for a few days. Now, we need to figure out how we're going to defend ourselves and what we're going to do next. It's only a matter of time before the station power grid goes down without workers to keep it up and running. That means no more heat and no more lights with the flip of a switch. That could happen in days or minutes. We need to act now."

"Brett's right," Dr. Hunter said, standing to face the group. "This is a lot to take in, I know. Our long-term plans may have yet to be formed, but if we don't take care of our short-term needs, it won't matter. Once we've established a secure location, an adequate supply of food, and a way to provide warmth for ourselves, we can start to figure out what comes next."

"And security," Mason said. "All of that will be for nothing without security."

"Suggestions?" Dr. Hunter queried, knowing full well where Mason was going with this.

"We need to get to Mac-Town Ops and find out for ourselves if firearms are, in fact, present at McMurdo. Even if we don't find them there, there may be some sort of written protocol in the station manager's office that will lead us to them."

Seeing Mason look at him as if awaiting a protest or response, Neville said, "Oh, I agree. We need them. I apologize for my earlier remarks about you Yanks and your need to feel secure. That was merely my own social conditioning speaking up, I'm afraid."

"Do we all need to go?" Dr. Bentley asked. "Don't misunderstand. I am not trying to get out of it if you feel you need me. My concern is that our entire merry band being out and about will attract more attention from...well, the infected, of course."

"That's a good point," Mason replied. "A small recon team may have a much better chance of slipping in and out undetected."

"Recon team?" Dr. Perkins said with raised eyebrow. "That's not something one usually hears in a scientific setting. Were you prior military?"

"No, but I've never had the mindset that the world I grew up in would remain safe and stable for the long-term," Mason replied. "That's just not the reality of things when you study history. War, tyranny, instability, and suffering are the standard of the human struggle, not the exception. I've always felt at peace when surrounded by the natural world, which would explain my penchant for long-distance, multi-day hikes. Getting as far away from everyone else and as close to nature as possible has always been my goal when not at work or school.

"That inherent mistrust of society led me, over time, to expand my knowledge of self-defense, both in the most basic forms of hand-to-hand combat and advanced weapons training."

"Really?" Dr. Jenny Duval asked. "You seem so quiet and polite."

Responding with a confused look, Mason said, "What's not polite about being able to defend oneself and others?"

"I didn't mean it that way," she said in an attempt to undo any unintentional insult.

"What sort of training did you attend?" Dr. Bentley asked with peaked interest.

"I've had martial arts training from several dojos of various disciplines. I never stuck with anything specific for very long, though, as all my life I found myself moving around with my parents as my dad traveled for work. As far as weapons training goes, as a hunter I have used firearms all my life, but I've expanded my knowledge to the self-defense side of things with training at several schools, one of which was called Resolute Dynamics in Mt. Zion, Illinois. There, I received tactical rifle and tactical pistol training, as well as active-shooter response training."

"Why is this the first I've heard of this?" Dr. Hunter asked.

With a chuckle, Mason replied, "It's not like firearms training and a belief in the fragility of our modern society is a popular subject on college campuses these days. No. The way things are, I figured I'd just keep those aspects of my life to myself."

"Hell, I'd have asked you to go shooting with me if I'd known that," Dr. Hunter replied.

"And why is this the first I've heard of this?" Mason quipped.

"Same reasons, I guess," Dr. Hunter said with a grin. "Well, let's see a show of hands of who agrees that a small group should set out for Ops to see what we can find or find out?"

With a unanimous response, Dr. Hunter said, "Good. I'm in, and I think it's obvious that Mason is as well. Who else?"

"I'm in," replied Brett.

"I'd feel better if you stayed here, Brett. If anything happens to us, the rest of our team will need your survival expertise."

"That seems to be a recurring theme," Brett replied.

"There's a reason for that," Dr. Hunter said with a raised eyebrow. "Your position here as MEVO's official mountaineer is because those of us who feel we have brilliant scientific minds may not be the best to explain how to survive an avalanche. Your skills have always been in critical need with us."

"I'll go," Neville said anxiously. "I've never been one who could sit and worry. I'll go nuts here just waiting."

"I think three will do just fine," Mason replied. "Everyone suit up, and considering Dr. Graves' concerns about the spread of this thing, I think we should wear our medical masks and gloves underneath our cold-weather gear. Our snow goggles should do just fine for eye protection if we come in contact with contagions."

"That's a mild way to say, 'fight off raving mad, prehistoric organism-controlled zombies,'" Neville remarked.

"They're not zombies," Dr. Graves said sharply, correcting Neville's use of the Z-word. "I feel ridiculous even saying this, since we all know zombies aren't, and never were, real. But even if they were, zombies were portrayed to be the dead, reanimated for the sinister, primal purpose of consuming the living. The infected in this situation are living, breathing human beings. A few days ago, you may have been sitting in the station galley having lunch alongside any one of them. Let's not allow the world of science fiction to blur the lines of reality. For all we know, there may be a way to help them that has yet to be discovered."

Hearing a thud from across the hall, she added, "That's why I have Jared secured safely across the hall. I'm not giving up on him."

"And Bob Muller?" Jenny asked.

"He was going to die no matter what," Linda quickly replied. "There was no reason to risk him spreading the microbes to anyone else just so he could live for a few hours or moments more."

Changing the subject, Dr. Hunter said, "Mason, Neville, let's get going."

"Hurry back," Dr. Graves said.

Dr. Hunter could see the stress and burden of the situation in her eyes. He could tell that, not only had she suffered through several days of horror, she also carried the burden of knowing, or at least believing deep within her own heart, that she was to blame for the spread of the menace that held McMurdo and the remainder of its inhabitants captive. She knew she was unknowingly responsible for the icy embrace of certain death for those who remained.

"It'll be okay," he said with a reassuring smile. "We'll get back as quick as we can."

"We'll be upstairs on the second floor above the Core Pod," she replied. "The lounge up there will be a comfortable place to wait—in the event it takes longer than we all hope for you to return. There's also two sets of stairs, giving us an alternate point of egress if something... well, let's just say there is a second way out if we need it."

~~~~

Slipping quietly out of the microscope room, Dr. Hunter, Derrick Mason, and Neville Wallace worked their way through Phase One of Crary Lab, down the inclined passageway leading to Phase Two. As Mason led the way, his ice axe in hand, Dr. Hunter brought up the rear, keeping a vigilant eye on their potentially threat-filled environment behind them.

Erebus

Exiting Phase Two and entering Phase Three, the aquarium pod, the men were surprised to see Bob Muller's body and the transformation it was taking. Covering his face in a futile attempt to prevent the putrid smell from entering his lungs, Mason pulled his snow goggles down and said, "What the hell?" as the men noticed that Bob Muller's body seemed to be collapsing in on itself.

"Look," Neville said. "That gray film—it's no longer following his veins and arteries. It appears to be gathered around his eyes, nose, mouth, and even his ears."

"I guess when the blood flow stopped, they started expanding their search for nutrients," Dr. Hunter added. "Just imagine what's going on inside him right now."

"I'd rather not," Neville answered. "That's why I study volcanology and not biology. Such things tend to make me weak in the knees."

"Come on," Mason said, urging them forward.

Stepping out and into the painful cold, Mason found himself relieved to breathe the painfully frigid air. *I'd rather have my lungs frost over inside than breathe that wretched stench,* he thought.

Working their way to the south side of the Crary Lab, Mason led the group west, following underneath the structure as it was held above the frozen surface via its pier-style foundation.

Seeing Mason come to an immediate stop in front of them, Neville and Dr. Hunter quickly saw the reason for his halt of their advance. A frozen corpse lay underneath the building. It was the young lady who Mason had met at McMurdo to have lunch with on several of his jaunts from MEVO to the station and back. She was a pretty young brunette in her late twenties who was at McMurdo to work in the greenhouse for the summer, as she had taken a respite from her hectic life back in Chicago.

Placing his hand on Mason's shoulder, Neville said, "I'm sorry, mate. That's the young lady you had a fancy for, isn't it?"

"She was a nice girl," he replied. "She had a bright future ahead of her. She wanted to be a social worker all her life, but was somewhat disenchanted by the bureaucracy of the system. She came down here to find herself. She just wanted to get away from it all and reboot."

"That's yet another common theme down here at the bottom of the world," Neville replied. "All of us who aren't sufficiently grounded to the rest of the world up there seem to fall off and end up down here together."

Changing the rather somber mood of the moment, Dr. Hunter said, "Do you notice the difference between her and Bob Muller? She was clearly infected, but she never advanced past the fever stage," he said, referring to the icy sheen that covered her exposed skin.

Giving them a moment to look her over, he added, "Bob Muller's body rapidly advanced to a different stage after his death. When his body could no longer be used to generate heat, and when his circulation ceased, they appeared to move deeper within, consuming him from the inside. All of the bodies we've seen outside of the warmth provided by the facilities of McMurdo have remained the way they were when they died."

"So, you're saying the microorganisms can't survive in the cold? The same as us?" Neville asked.

"It appears so. Think about it. They haven't been found anywhere on the continent except deep within the warm, gassy caves of Mt. Erebus. They do not exist beyond the boundaries established by the volcano's warmth. Inside the lab, Bob Muller's body had been kept relatively warm by the heat provided by the facility, so the organisms were able to advance to some further stage within him. Out here, they appear to die along with their host. That's something we may be able to use when the situation presents itself."

"What situation?" Mason asked.

"Knowing where they can and cannot live will undoubtedly come in handy."

"The problem is, we can't live where they can't live," Mason replied. "That, we have in common."

"Okay, let's go," Dr. Hunter said. "The chill is starting to work its way into my bones."

~~~~

Arriving just outside of building 165, McMurdo Station's Operations, Air Traffic, and Weather Center, a two-story building with two large spherical radar enclosures and numerous antenna arrays, commonly referred to as Mac Ops, the men sat quietly, patiently observing before continuing toward the building.

Noticing the vast amount of above-ground duct work running into the building from its remote heating source, Dr. Hunter said, "Let's work our way to the side of the building via the duct work. That will help keep us from being seen. We can then climb the service ladder to the roof and try to gain entry via the roof access point."

"Pardon me, Dr. Hunter, but how do you know there is a roof access point?" Neville asked. "What if we risk our necks to get up there, exposed to all the elements without any sort of wind break, only to find that there is, in fact, no way in?"

"Why would there be catwalks around those radomes and antenna arrays if there wasn't a way to access them?"

"Ah, of course," Neville replied, embarrassed, but now understanding the obvious. "Carry on, then."

Working their way along the above-ground duct work as Dr. Hunter had suggested, the men found themselves along the side of the building. Looking up at the ladder that reached the entire height of the building, Neville remarked, "It sure looks higher from here."

Looking at him with his head cocked to the side, Mason said, "Dude, you work on the side of an active volcano, twelve-thousand-five-hundred-feet up. We had to move down the mountain to the Lower Erebus Hut because of the Volkswagen-sized bombs the mountain was spitting out at us, and you see a two-story ladder as high?"

"I was thinking about your safety, not mine," Neville replied with a grin. "I'm good with it. I was just making sure you Yanks were up for it."

Holding his spear in his hand and then looking back up the ladder, Dr. Hunter said, "Mason, do you still have that paracord you always carry with you?"

"Of course, Doc."

"Your axe will be easy to carry. You can just tuck it under your belt. Our spears, on the other hand, present a different problem. Being made of hollow tubing, if we run paracord through the length of them, then back around the outside for the length of the shaft to the beginning point, we can tie it off and make a sling. Cut both Neville and me off a section about eight feet in length—if you have enough, of course."

"Sure thing, doc," Mason said, flipping out his Medford knife.

"You're never without that thing, are you?" Neville asked.

"Nope," Mason matter-of-factly replied. "A climbing buddy of mine in Arizona works at Medford Knife and Tool. It's a small company and these things aren't cheap. But if you think about it, when you live life in the most rugged and remote places on Earth, you can't count on being able to get replacements or sending something in for warranty coverage. Buy it once and be done, I say."

"Now you see why I keep him around," Dr. Hunter said as he took his section of paracord and began threading it through his pipe spear to form a sling. Tugging on it and verifying that it was secure, he said, "This'll do."

Slinging his weapon over his shoulder, Dr. Hunter looked up the ladder and said, "Don't make me wait on you too long. It looks windy up there," as he began his two-story vertical climb.

Following closely behind, Mason kept up with Dr. Hunter's pace as Neville slung his spear and began following suit.

Having only climbed several rungs, Neville stopped to shift his sling to a more comfortable position when he heard rapidly approaching footsteps to his right. Looking quickly, he saw one of them, one of the afflicted, frothing at the mouth from heavy, aggressive breathing and wearing the sheen of frozen sweat.

"Shit!" he yelled as he scurried up the ladder, only to feel the weight of the man, a former maintenance worker at McMurdo, pulling down on his boot, attempting to rip him from the ladder.

With no words, merely a primal scream, the crazed man pulled Neville free from the ladder, causing him to come crashing down onto the icy surface below. Winded from the impact, Neville rolled over, struggling to remove his spear as the man, now only feet from him, salivated as if he intended to feast on Neville himself. His eyes were bulging and swollen, bloodshot and red with ruptured capillaries. The tell-tale signs of the microorganisms traced his veins and the sides of his head.

"Get away from me!" Neville shouted as he freed his spear, pointing it at the man.

As the man let out one final, blood-curdling, primal scream, he began charging at Neville with his teeth exposed and his face full of rage.

Lunging the spear toward the man, Neville was knocked backward, not by his afflicted attacker, but by Mason as he leaped from the ladder nearly ten feet above.

Landing on top of the man, Mason drove his knife directly into the top of the man's skull, ending the man's rage. Falling on top of him, Mason quickly rolled away and began shedding his thick winter gloves, which were now covered in the man's infected blood.

"Shit! Shit! Shit!" Mason shouted, tossing his gloves to the side as he checked himself thoroughly for other signs of contamination.

Running to his side, Neville shouted, "You're good, mate! You're good! It was on your gloves, but nothing else. Your hands are going to freeze soon. You had better scurry on up the ladder while you still have some feeling left in them."

Merely nodding in reply, Mason worked his way back up the ladder, quickly catching up with Dr. Hunter who had paused his ascent during the sudden and vicious attack.

Once all three men had arrived on the roof, Mason shoved his hands into his pockets and said, "I've got to get warmed up, ASAP!"

Seeing the access door at the midpoint of the building's roof, Dr. Hunter urged him forward, saying, "This way!" as he ran to the door.

Opening the access door, Dr. Hunter paused and looked inside. Seeing no signs of an immediate threat, he quickly led the others inside.

"Shit. My hands," Mason said, rubbing them together and blowing on them.

"Put them inside your coat," Dr. Hunter said. "But keep rubbing them. Keep the blood moving."

"Whew! Man, you never realize just how long you can't live without something simple like a glove until you go a few minutes without it," Mason said, frantically trying to warm himself.

"This place has a thousand and one ways to get you," Dr. Hunter said as he attempted to gain his bearings inside the Mac Ops building. Pointing down the hall to his right, he said, "I think it's this way."

Rushing ahead of the other two men, with Mason still focused on his near-frostbitten hands, Dr. Hunter rounded the corner only to feel something catch him around the neck, yanking him violently into one of the offices on the opposite side of the hall. Hearing the door being kicked violently shut behind him, Dr. Hunter tried to turn to see his attacker as his head bounced off the floor, nearly knocking him unconscious.

Seeing a large tanto-bladed knife come directly at his face, Dr. Hunter struggled to free his spear, but the weight of his attacker's body prevented him from using his arms as the spear was lying across him, pinning him to the floor.

Putting the knife up to Dr. Hunter's face, the man pushed Dr. Hunter's goggles out of the way and opened his hood with the cold steel of the blade, nearly grazing his face.

Looking him over, the man, with an olive drab scarf around his face said in a heavy Russian accent, "Do you have it?"

Barely able to speak due to the constriction of what he could now tell was a rope around his neck, Dr. Hunter muttered the words, "Have w... wa... what?"

"The sickness," the man said sternly. "Do you have it?"

"No. No, I don't. None of our group does," he said, hearing Mason and Neville pounding on the door and calling his name.

"Tell them if they enter this room without my permission, I will kill you, and then them," the man said, reflecting light from the blade of his knife into Dr. Hunter's eye.

"It's okay!" Dr. Hunter shouted to Mason and Neville in the hallway. "Just give us a minute, please."

"I'm going to relax my grip around your throat," the man said, tugging on the rope he had used to pull Dr. Hunter into the room, reaffirming the control he had over him at that moment. "Do not move. Do you understand?"

"Yes," Dr. Hunter replied.

"You will answer questions for me, yes?"

"Yes. I'll do my best," Dr. Hunter said, reassuring the man that he would cooperate.

"Good." Releasing the pressure from the rope, the man moved Dr. Hunter's spear to the side and said, "Now, tell me everything."

Chapter Twelve

Crary Lab

Carefully cracking open the door of room 122, Brett checked the hallway for any sign of threats. "Looks clear," he whispered, stepping out into the hallway alone. After waiting a moment, he motioned for the others to follow.

Joining up with Brett, Dr. Graves whispered, "The lounge is on the second floor of the Core Pod." Pointing down the hallway to the left, she said, "Just go through those double-doors, then across the main passageway and through the next set of double-doors. The stairs will then be immediately to your left."

Nodding that he understood, Brett motioned the group forward and began quietly slipping down the hall toward the first set of double-doors. Raising his hand to signal the group to stop, he held his ice axe at the ready, carefully pushing one of the swinging doors open. Hearing a loud and aggressive smashing sound against one of the doors behind him, Brett flinched and spun around, ready to defend the group.

Holding her hand over her heart, recovering from the scare, Dr. Graves said, "It was Jared. He must hear us."

"Holy shit. That scared me half to death," Jenny said, looking around to see that based on the facial expressions from the rest of the group, she wasn't alone.

Turning his attention back to the double-doors leading into the main passageway, Brett once again pushed the door open slowly, looked around, and then stepped across and toward the opposing set of double-doors.

Hearing another violent slam against the door of the room where Dr. Graves had left Jared, the group flinched as Dr. Graves said, "He's getting more violent as time passes."

Seeing her turn and begin to walk back toward Jared, Brett whispered firmly, "Dr. Graves. No. Leave him be."

"I... I just wanted to check on him," she stammered.

"I know. But we've got to keep moving," he said. Motioning for the group to continue, he once again lead them forward and through the second set of doors.

Once the group was inside the Core Pod, directly across from the biology pod, they worked their way up the stairs adjacent to the boiler room and to the Core Pod's second floor. Entering the multi-purpose and lounge area, Brett flipped on the lights to see the familiar body of one of the lab instrument technicians lying awkwardly across a broken coffee table in the break area.

Holding his hand up to urge caution, Brett walked slowly over to the body as Dr. Duval covered her mouth as her eyes began to well up with tears. "That's Cindy. Cindy Wesch. Is she...?"

Walking closer to her, Brett looked her over, seeing what appeared to be a dislocated jaw and severe blunt force trauma to the left side of her face that had nearly dislodged one of her eyes. Nudging her with his ice axe, he shook his head and said, "She's dead."

"So... she's not infected? She's not going to..."

"No," Brett quickly replied. "She's dead."

"I don't understand," Walt Perkins said. "Why is it that some people become infected, and some are simply killed? Why aren't these things consuming the dead the same as they are the living?"

"I was just thinking the same thing," Dr. Bentley replied. "It's as if the microbes have the ability to be selective of their hosts."

"There's a lot we don't understand," Dr. Graves explained. "These life-forms have learned to adapt and thrive in one of the most extreme environments on Earth, nearly totally devoid of any other forms of life. I would imagine they've gained the ability to quickly determine the best available energy sources. If you take microscopic or very small parasites, for example, they have been shown to be able to evolve very rapidly due to their short generational cycles. If they are continually reproducing at a rapid rate, they may be quickly adapting to their new environment in ways that give them the ability to be selective and to determine the best host to make their home.

"It's doubtful any ticks try to suck the blood out of a rock or a tree. They know that the deer is a much better host as it passes by. They know they want that fresh, pulsating flow of blood, and they are very adept at finding it and latching on.

"In just a few short days, these microbes could have gone through many more generational cycles than we are used to seeing in such a short span of time. This could allow their continuously reproducing offspring to pass along the information needed to target us and seek us out, and specifically, to seek out the warmth and energy-rich blood flow that our bodies provide. Their ability to extract energy from the materials found deep within Erebus has already shown us just how resourceful they can be."

"I would still caution against casual contact with the dead, however," Dr. Bentley added. "Some of the organisms may have made the transfer from the attacker to the victim, only to end up lying dormant until a new and viable heat-generating host comes along."

"That could be the case," Dr. Graves answered. "Especially if the death came quickly, before the eukaryotes began to establish a colony on their host with flowing blood as a rapid transportation system. If there was a large and growing population established before the death of the host, they might not be as able to fall into a dormant stage without the need to continue to consume energy, making their presence more noticeable."

"Okay," Brett said. "We'll have plenty of time to discuss such things once we've secured the area to the best of our ability. Dr. Bentley, if you and Dr. Perkins could help me move the furniture up against the doors, I would appreciate it."

"Do you honestly think a sofa pushed up against a door will stop someone exhibiting such aggressive and violent behavior as what we've seen?" Dr. Bentley asked.

"Stop them? No. But it will slow their entry into the room along with alerting us to their presence, allowing us to react," Brett replied. "It's better than nothing."

"Yes. Yes, indeed," Dr. Bentley replied. "It's a shame they didn't install locks on the doors, but then again, the need for such a thing would not have been evident before now. Let's get on with it, then, Walt," he said as the two men began doing as Brett had requested.

Turning to Dr. Graves, Brett asked, "Ma'am, if you and Dr. Duval could search the lounge area for any food or anything else that may be of use to us, I would greatly appreciate it. Preferably packaged, unopened food. I don't have your expertise on the subject of microorganisms, but I would feel better eating only food that has less of a chance of coming in contact with whatever that stuff is."

"That's sound thinking," she replied.

"I've got to go to the bathroom," Dr. Duval said, looking to Brett. "I need to go before they block the doors. Is the nearest restroom the ones we passed downstairs?"

Looking to Dr. Graves for an answer, not being as familiar with the facilities at Crary Lab as her, Brett shrugged his shoulders.

"Yes, Jenny. It is," Dr. Graves replied.

Thinking her answer over, Brett quickly said, "That's out of the question. We all need to stick together. I wouldn't feel good at all about you going back downstairs."

"Well, I'm not peeing in front of you guys, and I really have to go," she said. "I can take care of myself."

"Jenny," Dr. Graves said, giving her a look of concern. "Can't you go on the mezzanine across the hall? That's private enough, and you'll still be on the second floor with us. I agree with Brett about sticking together."

Pausing for a moment, Dr. Duval said, "Yes, that will work. I guess we're long past the need for our customary ways of doing things. Propriety needs to take a back seat here. I guess it will be like camping, but indoors," she said with a half-hearted chuckle.

"Hurry," Brett said. "I mean, please hurry, okay?"

"You can bet I won't want to be out there for much longer than I have to," she replied.

With Dr. Bentley holding the door open for her, Jenny Duval stepped out of the room, and crossed over to the second-floor mezzanine above the biology pod. She then slipped behind the water tanks and the reverse osmosis system equipment, in search of adequate privacy for her needs.

Looking around nervously, she pushed the straps of her overalls off her shoulders and began sliding them down to her lower legs. Hearing movement behind her, Jenny could feel the hairs on the back of her neck stand as chills ran down her spine.

She knew someone was there. She could feel it with the utmost certainty.

Slowly turning her head, she saw Dr. Jared Davis standing there, drenched in sweat and his eyes so bloodshot, they appeared as if they might burst out of his head from the pressure. The veins in his neck and the sides of his head were traced by the grayish-green film of the eukaryotes. Exposing his teeth as his rate of breathing increased, a thick froth of saliva oozed from his mouth as he seemed to be preparing to make a move.

"Jared... it's... it's me," she said. "It's me, Jenny. You know me, don't you?"

Slowly beginning to stand while pulling her bib-overalls back to her shoulders, she began to back away as Jared dragged his right foot forward, initiating a slow, deliberate advance toward her.

"It's me, Jared. We can help you. Dr. Graves can help you. She's working on something to help you right now," she pleaded.

Taking another labored step toward her, his eyes fixated on hers with an empty, soulless stare. Her words seeming to have no meaning to him at all.

"Jared. I know you're still in there. I can see it in you. I know you can hear me. We're going to help you, Jared. That's why Dr. Graves had you somewhere safe—so that she could return with help."

With his breathing now heavy and thick with bubbles of mucus in his lungs, Jenny backed away, whispering softly, "Please... please don't do this."

~~~~

"That's been long enough," Brett said. "Privacy or not, I'm gonna check on her."

Walking past Dr. Perkins and pushing the door open, Brett heard Jenny unleash a blood-curdling scream. Shoving his way through the door, he ran at full speed toward the mezzanine where to his horror, he saw Jared standing over her body, fifty feet in front of him, alongside the water storage tanks.

"Get off her!" he screamed as Jared's head slowly turned toward him.

Exposing his blood-covered teeth in a primal, bloodthirsty manner, Jared began to walk toward Brett, quickly accelerating to a run as he unleashed a visceral, rage-filled cry.

With only seconds to act, Brett drew back his arm and threw his ice axe. Watching it tumble through the air toward his intended target, he was horrified to see it hit handle first, bouncing off Jared's shoulder. Brett immediately turned to run, with Jared now only a few feet behind him and gaining fast.

Seeing Dr. Perkins behind him with his spear drawn back above his head, Brett dropped to the floor as Dr. Perkins thrust the spear overtop him, directly into Jared's forehead, halting his advance. Jared's grotesquely infected body went limp, crashing to the floor with the loud metallic thud of the mezzanine walkway echoing through the complex.

As both Brett and Dr. Perkins turned their attention toward Jenny, Brett cried, "Oh, God. Jenny..."

Chapter Thirteen

McMurdo Station Ops

Sitting upright, his head throbbing with pain from his fall to the floor, Dr. Hunter asked, "What do you mean by 'tell you everything?' What information are you looking for?"

"Do not play stupid with me," the man said through gritted teeth. "You're a scientist here, are you not?"

"My name is Dr. Nathan Hunter. I'm a professor of geochemistry at New Mexico Tech. I'm the Principle Investigator for the MEVO research team."

"So, you are from big volcano?" the man asked with a curious tone.

"Yes, that's right."

"What has caused all of this? What disease has great world of science inflicted upon rest of us? This is no normal sickness. This is something more. Something scientists, perhaps like you, would need to travel to a very remote place to work on, to keep secret. Was this intended to be weapon that escaped your grasp?"

"No. It's not a weapon—at least, not one that man has created," Dr. Hunter insisted. "From what we have gathered, it was a previously unknown microorganism that resided deep within the ground on Mount Erebus. It survived in a very dormant state, feeding off the minerals in the rock, deep within the hot caves that riddle the mountain. There is no way it or the other microbial life found on the volcano could have been transported there. No, it came from deep underground."

"And you brought it here?" the man asked.

"A member of our team who studies extreme life-forms took a sample to study in her lab back home. That sample was involved in an accident before shipping and... well, it seems to have leapt to humans and has begun to spread, and spread rapidly. It wasn't anything anyone could have foreseen. It looked just like so many other microorganisms, but as we've had the misfortune to learn, it's nothing like the others at all."

"Are they," the man started to ask, pausing as if trying to choose his words. "Are they dead? The people infected by it. Are they dead?"

"No. They're alive, but serving as a host for what seems to be a very aggressive parasite in microbial form. The host exhibits symptoms similar to rabies, where they become extremely aggressive and hostile. This is probably a function of the parasites' need for its hosts to make contact with other potential hosts. Once contact is made, they can continue to travel and spread from one host to another before the original host dies from the sickness and physical stress induced by the parasites."

Looking down at the floor and shaking his head in disbelief, the man asked, "How do we stop it?"

"We don't know exactly. At least, not an easy way that would spare the life of the host. They'll die without a source of heat and energy, the same as us. But separating them from the host while leaving the host alive? Well, that's currently a problem with no solution."

"Then hosts can die with them," the man said, clenching his jaw.

"What?" Dr. Hunter asked.

"Look around you! Look how quickly your plague has spread through McMurdo. It has almost wiped us out. Just imagine, if whatever this thing is makes it back to rest of world where things are much warmer, and possibly more hospitable for it.

Entire planet may be in danger. In danger from something God had locked away, deep in fiery hell beneath Earth. Only now, it has been unleashed upon us. We need to send it back to hell where it belongs. We can't let it escape this cold and icy place. It needs to die here."

Knowing in his heart that the man's words were words of wisdom and clarity of thought, Dr. Hunter put his hands on his head and said, "There are others—other survivors who can help us. Most importantly, the biologist of our group. She's an expert in the field of extremophiles."

"Where are they?" the man asked.

"Before I tell you where they are, you need to show me a sign of good faith that you won't hurt them, or my friends in the hallway."

Standing up and putting his knife in its' Kydex sheath, the man pulled his olive-drab green scarf down to his neck, revealing a short, graying beard with an obvious scar across the left side of his face. Reaching for the door knob while keeping his eyes fixed on Dr. Hunter, he unlocked it and said, "Is okay. Come inside."

Entering the room, Mason rushed to Dr. Hunter's side with Neville close behind him. "Doc, are you okay?"

"Yeah. I'm fine. I just tripped and fell. I hit my head pretty hard, but I'm fine," Dr. Hunter replied. Gesturing to his former captor, Dr. Hunter said, "This is, um..."

"Vasily. My name is Vasily," the man replied, reaching out for Mason's hand.

Shaking hands with everyone, Vasily said, "I work in fabrication shop. I am metalsmith by trade, but good with all materials."

"Nice to properly meet you, Vasily," Dr. Hunter replied.

"Why are you here?" Vasily asked. "Why at Operations?"

Giving Mason a look of uncertainty, Dr. Hunter said, "We came to see if the rumors of weapons being in the possession of the station manager were true."

"Ahhh," Vasily said with a smile. "We think alike. I, too, am here for that reason."

"Well, it's good we're on the same page, then," Mason said with a cautious smile.

"Now, come. We must find what we are looking for and get to your friends," Vasily said as he twisted his knife onto a five-foot length of steel tube, held in place by what appeared to be a homemade bayonet mount welded to both the knife and the tube. "I have safe place for us while we work on solution."

"Safe place?" Neville asked. "Why, I think I've forgotten what the notion of a safe place is by now."

Holding his hands out in front of him, Vasily said, "I can do amazing things with my hands." Pointing to his head, he added, "Just as you do with your minds. I have safe place. Trust me. Now, let us get what we came for and go."

Working their way down the hallway toward the station manager's office, Vasily pressed his finger to his lips, gesturing for the men to be quiet. Walking up to the door, he placed his ear to it and began listening for sounds within the room.

Turning to Dr. Hunter, he murmured, "He is in there."

"Who?" Dr. Hunter whispered.

"The station manager," Vasily replied. "He does not sound healthy. I fear he is like others."

"How do you know it's the station manager?" Dr. Hunter asked.

"I follow him here to Ops building two days ago," Vasily replied. "From distance. He did not see me. I did not see his body anywhere in the building, so he must have made it back inside office. I have been keeping eye on Ops, waiting to see signs of being sick like others or if he sent for help. If anyone has access to resources, it is station manager."

"What do you have in mind?" Dr. Hunter asked.

"I will make contact. But if he is like others, if evil consumes him, I think it is best to avoid fighting. By avoiding fight, we avoid the sickness and not draw others near. Only fight if you must." Pointing down the hallway, he said, "We have two main passageways with rooms in center. If one of us leads him down this hallway and around corner, another can quickly open door to one of center rooms, allowing decoy to escape, closing door behind him. Those two can then double back up other side of hallway and be let inside station manager's office by other two. Once inside and secure, we can search for what we have come for."

Looking to Mason and Neville, Dr. Hunter shrugged and said, "Sounds like a plan to me."

Placing his ear against the door once again, Vasily gently knocked and asked, "Is there anyone in there?"

Hearing no response, he placed his hand on the doorknob and attempted to turn it to no avail. "Is locked," he said.

Knocking once again, he was startled by a violent impact on the other side of the door. Taking a step back, readying his knife-bearing staff, he looked to Dr. Hunter and said, "I do not know how we are to remove him without—"

Interrupted by another violent crash, this time breaking the door from its hinges, Vasily jumped back to see a crazed man, sweating profusely, his veins bulging on the sides of his head, and with the tell-tale signs of the grayish film of microbes tracing the arteries in his neck and around the openings of his nose and mouth. The whites of his eyes were filled with red as his capillaries appeared to have begun to rupture from the pressure.

Screaming at the infected man to hold his stare, Vasily ran down the hallway, initiating a chase. He could hear the man running along behind him. Rounding the corner, he nearly slipped and fell on the tile floor, allowing the man to gain a few steps on him. Working his way around the bend at the end of the hallway and back up the other side, he saw a door open. Quickly ducking inside, Mason slammed it shut behind him, locking the door. Hearing the man slam into the door, they ran through the room to the other side, then back into the adjacent hallway. Once in the hallway, they ran back toward the station manager's office where Dr. Hunter and Neville were nervously waiting.

"We can't close the damn door!" Dr. Hunter said in frustration. "He broke it off the hinges."

"Inside. Quickly," Vasily said, shoving Dr. Hunter and Neville into the room while Mason followed close behind.

Shoving a desk in front of the doorway, Vasily readied himself as he said, "This will give me time."

"Time for what?" asked Dr. Hunter.

Just then, the door to the room where they had trapped the man smashed open. The crazed man stumbled into the hallway, turning to look at them with his evil, blood-filled eyes. Taking a step toward them, and then another, the man increased his pace from a slow, methodical walk to a rage-filled run, his feet pounding hard on the floor as he let out a primal scream with his teeth fully exposed.

Raising the steel tube with his bayonet affixed, holding the front with his left hand and the rear of the weapon with his right, Vasily flipped a small wheel on the tube that had previously gone unnoticed by the other men. As Vasily gripped the weapon tightly, a loud crack and a flash of flames and smoke erupted from the knife end of his weapon.

The man's head whipped back violently, with the back of his head exploding into a mist of blood and brain matter.

"Holy shit!" Mason exclaimed. "What the hell is that?"

Staring at the man a moment longer to ensure that he was truly dead, Vasily turned to Mason and responded calmly, "Is gun I made. One shot, though. That was it. They could prevent me from bringing weapons, but they could not stop me from making them."

Looking down at the small wheel he'd flicked with his thumb, Vasily grinned and said, "Zippo lighter wheel and flint. I was afraid it would blow up in my hand where is installed. I had not yet tested it and was not sure if hole drilled for wheel created weak spot." Looking back down to his weapon, he rolled his right hand over to expose a small powder burn from the hot, escaping gasses around the lighter wheel. Turning to the others, Vasily smiled and laughed, saying, "Thank Lord Almighty, it worked."

"I'm sure glad we stumbled across you," Mason said with a smile.

"Okay, guys, let's get to it," Dr. Hunter said as he began searching the room. "Neville, you keep watch at the door. We don't want anyone or anything that may have heard that blast sneaking up on us."

As Neville walked to the doorway, he looked to his left to see a pump-action, Mossberg twelve-gauge shotgun leaning against the trashcan in the corner. "That was easy," he said, pointing to the weapon.

Noting the food that had clearly been stockpiled in the room after the outbreak had begun, Mason said, "That bastard."

"What?" asked Dr. Hunter.

"That bastard locked himself in his office with food and weapons while people around him died." Looking to the radio on the station manager's desk, he said, "He just sat here calling for help, trying to save his own ass. If he had weapons, he should have been out there protecting others."

"Don't be so quick to judge," replied Dr. Hunter. "You don't know that he didn't try. After all, he was exposed somehow. It could have been while he was doing just as you said."

Shrugging, Mason walked over to the shotgun and picked it up. Pressing the small slide release button on the bottom of the action, Mason racked out all the shells and began inspecting the weapon. "Looks like it was topped off. It seems to be in good working order, too," he said as he began feeding the double-ought buckshot shells back into the magazine tube.

Turning to Neville, he said, "Here. If you're gonna be standing watch while the rest of us search for more, you'll need this."

Raising his hands as if to reject the offer, Neville said, "I'm not comfortable with guns. We don't have such things in the UK."

"It's time to get comfortable," Mason said as he began showing Neville how to operate the weapon.

"A shell is in the chamber, so all you need to do to fire the first shot is to flick the safety off, here," he said, pointing to the tang where the receiver and stock meet. "After the first shot is fired, just rack the pump slide all the way back and then all the way forward again and it will be ready for the next shot. You only need to use the release button on the bottom when the gun has not been fired and you want to cycle through the shells to empty the weapon. This is the long-tubed, tactical version, so you have nine shots."

Handing the weapon to Neville, he added, "It's a shotgun, so pointing it is generally all you need to do since it's loaded with double-ought-buck, but to aim, look through this rear peep sight and hold the front side in the center of the circle. Oh, and hang on tight. This sucker will kick like a mule with those defensive loads."

Taking the shotgun, Neville looked it over carefully, saying, "Thanks, but I hope I don't have to use it. Oh, by the way, mate, what's double-ought buck?"

"Big lead balls," Mason responded with a smile.

Laughing and returning an uneasy grin, Neville said, "That's exactly what I need at the moment."

Turning and pointing to a door in the back of the room, Neville asked, "What's back there?"

Watching Neville closely as he spoke, Mason reached out and grabbed the barrel of the shotgun, stopping Neville from sweeping the others with the muzzle. "Whoa," Mason said, "I almost forgot. Don't ever point this thing at something or someone you don't want to kill or destroy. Pretend like there is a laser beam coming out of the barrel at all times. Don't let that beam touch any of us. And keep your finger off the trigger until you are ready to shoot. Guns don't just go off. People make them go off. And if it isn't pointing at any of us when it does, it won't hit us."

Jiggling the knob on the door in the back of the room, Dr. Hunter said, "It's locked." Knocking on it, he added, "This is a heavy door, too. I don't think we can just bust it in."

Walking up to the wall off to the side of the door, Vasily rapped on the walls with his knuckles looking for studs. Seeming to have found what he was looking for, he kicked the wall, putting his foot through the sheetrock. Pulling his foot back through the hole, he dusted himself off and peeked to the other side. He then began tearing away the sheetrock by hand, saying, "Door may be secure, but wall is not." Tapping the side of his head, he said, "Sometimes, smart people do not think."

Erebus

Once he created a hole large enough to fit his body through between the wall studs, Vasily slipped into the hole, appearing in the doorway when he opened the door from the inside. "This is it. This is what we were looking for," he said, gesturing for the others to step inside.

Chapter Fourteen

Crary Lab

"Jenny!" screamed Brett in horror. Running to her side, he turned and shouted in a panic-stricken voice, "Help! We need help!"

"I'll get first aid supplies," said Dr. Perkins as he turned and ran back toward the group.

Seeing horror and fear in her eyes, Brett knelt beside Jenny to render aid and to comfort her. Applying direct pressure to her open neck wound in an attempt to stop or slow the profuse bleeding, Brett whispered, "It's gonna be okay. He didn't get you too bad."

Unable to speak, Jenny responded simply with a look of fear and understanding in her eyes. Brett could see that she knew she wasn't going to make it. Or perhaps under the circumstances, she didn't want to make it. Reaching for his hand, Dr. Jenny Duval pulled his hand free of her wound, and as a rush of blood dumped from her throat, her eyes rolled back into her head and she took her final breath.

Hearing the others running up behind him, Brett turned to see the look of horror on Dr. Graves' face as she shouted, "Your hands!"

Looking at his blood-soaked hands, the realization set in that he may have allowed himself to become contaminated in his rush to render aid. Mumbling to himself in near disbelief, he said, "Son of a bitch."

"Walt!" shouted Dr. Graves, addressing Dr. Perkins. "Take him back to the lounge and get him washed up. Look for alcohol or something in the first aid cabinet. Clean him up the best you can, but don't touch it! Wear gloves and a mask!"

"Will do!" Dr. Perkins replied as he led Brett back to the lounge.

Looking down at Jenny Duval's body, Dr. Graves shook her head as tears welled up in her eyes.

Arriving in the lounge, Dr. Perkins quickly opened the first aid locker and handed Brett a package of sanitizing wipes. "Get started with these," he said as he searched the contents of the locker. Finding both hydrogen peroxide and isopropyl alcohol, the two mainstays of nearly every first aid locker, he began pouring one, then the other, as Brett scrubbed his hand feverishly with the wipes.

"I think I got it all," said Brett, pushing his sleeves, watch, and bracelet out of the way, showing his hands to Dr. Perkins for inspection.

"I see you've got a little nick right there on your finger." Handing him the alcohol, Dr. Perkins said, "Scrub that area extra well. Be aggressive. Make it hurt."

Seeing Dr. Graves and Dr. Bentley enter the room, Dr. Perkins looked up and asked, "Is she?"

"Yes. She's gone," replied Dr. Bentley.

Walking up to Brett, Dr. Graves asked, "Are you okay? Did he touch you? Did he..."

"No," Brett replied. "Dr. Perkins here took care of him right before he got to me. He was already on top of Jenny when we arrived. It appeared as if he was eating her neck."

Taking a seat on the lounge sofa, Dr. Graves put her face in her hands and gathered her thoughts. After a few moments, she raised her head, saying, "It's as if he was after her blood."

"Her blood?" Dr. Bentley replied. "What are you suggesting?"

"We've seen them develop in several stages. I've watched Jared myself, having been with him when he first started showing signs. At the onset, they feel sick. Fever and irritability seem to be the first signs. After a while, they begin to lose a grip on their own conscious thought, becoming more animalistic in nature as the infection progresses. By the time they reach a stage of uncontrollable violence, the visible signs of bloodshot eyes, heavy sweating, and what appears to be a colony of eukaryotes begins to become visible, shadowing the host's major arteries."

Struggling to maintain her composure, Dr. Graves continued, "In the more advanced state, such as when Jared attacked Jenny, they seem to be behaving in a strictly primal way as if feeding, rather than random acts of violence, is their true motivator. Perhaps the colony within them sees a need to expand their reach, or they simply see a future need for more food than their host can offer. Either way, Jared seemed to be feeding on Jenny's neck. Her blood was in his mouth as if he had been swallowing it. It wasn't merely an attack out of blind rage."

"Good Lord," Dr. Bentley replied. "Do you think such microbes would be capable of altering a host's behavior to such an extent? Inducing random fits of rage is one thing. We can see that in a virus such as rabies, but to turn a man into a vampire?"

"I'm not suggesting he was turned into a vampire," replied Dr. Graves. "Are you familiar with the fungus ophiocordyceps unilateralis?"

"Ah, yes. The zombie ant?" he replied.

"Exactly. Ophiocordyceps unilateralis is a mere fungus that infects the host ant, then alters its behavior by forcing it to leave its colony and attach itself to the underside of a leaf by clamping its mandibles on a leaf vein. The host ant then remains there, fixed in place while the fungus uses its body, eventually sprouting a reproductive spore from the ant's head.

"If a fungus can alter the behavior of an ant, repeatedly showing that the ant is, in fact, doing the bidding of the fungus in order for the fungus to grow and reproduce, then I don't think we can rule out such things here."

"Such a dreadful thought," he replied.

Turning to Brett, seeing fear and worry in his eyes, Dr. Graves said, "Don't worry too much, Brett. If that was only Jenny's blood flowing outward, there might not have been a transfer of the microbes to her yet. Also, any newly introduced microbes may have been washed away in her flowing blood. We are unsure of the specifics of that process at the moment."

"I can't believe I was so stupid," he replied.

"Don't say that," said Dr. Perkins sharply. "You were rushing to the aid of a friend and colleague. You put her safety ahead of your own. That was a very heroic move in my eyes. You did what any good man would have done. We learn as we go, but in times of crisis, sometimes we just have to act and think things through afterward."

"What about Jenny? We can't just leave her there," replied Brett, brushing off any notion of heroism.

"It's too dangerous to move her right now. The amount of blood that is present makes it too risky to move her, considering the potential for accidental contamination. We need to stick together. We need to remain here in the lounge until the others return."

"I agree," replied Dr. Bentley. "Jenny wouldn't have wanted us to risk ourselves just to move her in such a situation. She wasn't much for ceremony, anyway. As a matter of fact, I do believe she would have been the first among us to offer her body up for scientific discovery. I heard her discussing that once. Something about that 'Bodies' exhibition she saw at some art museum."

Walking toward the window, Dr. Bentley continued, "Besides, it's getting late out there. If I was with Dr. Hunter, Mason, and Neville, I would want to hunker down wherever they are for the night and return in the morning. It sounds like the winds are kicking up as well. They'd be in for a rough ride, trekking around in the dark in these conditions."

~~~~

For the next several hours, Linda, Gerald, Walt, and Brett sat quietly, listening to the pounding winds as they beat against the side of the Crary Lab. With thoughts of all that had happened, what the others must be going through to have kept them away so long, and of what may be yet to come, it was nearly impossible for anyone to sleep.

Breaking the silence, Dr. Perkins said, "Okay, before we all doze off and leave ourselves unguarded, I'll take watch so the rest of you can sleep. If recent events are any indication, tomorrow will be yet another trying and difficult day. We need to get some rest, so we're ready to face it."

"Wake me when you need a relief," said Brett eagerly.

"Nonsense," Dr. Bentley asserted. "You rest up. I'll take the next watch. Now, like Walt here said, let's get some sleep and prepare ourselves for the dreadful things that will surely come our way when the sun rises and casts its light over this dreadful place. Or perhaps, even sooner."

Chapter Fifteen

McMurdo Station Ops

Stepping into the small back room of the station manager's office, Dr. Hunter patted Vasily on the shoulder, and with a smile, said, "I'm sure glad you found the key."

Looking around the room, the men saw a rack of weapons with a cable lock running through the trigger guards.

Hearing Neville say something from his position standing watch at the outer door of the office, Dr. Hunter turned and asked, "What's that?"

"I said, I found you a new set of gloves, Mason. What did you chaps find?"

"We've got a rack of four M-16's."

"Well, they're the semi-auto versions. AR-15's," Mason said, pointing to the lack of a third position on the safety selector. "They're missing the happy setting."

"Saves ammunition," Vasily stated as he read the roll mark on the left side of the receiver. "Colt. Ahhh, the good stuff." Flipping the rifle over and reading the other side of the magazine well, he read aloud, "Restricted, military/government law-enforcement/export use only."

"That's crap," Mason said. "Colt left that on there long after the sunset to the so-called assault weapons ban was reached. I guess they thought it made them look cool. It always pissed me off to see one hanging in a gun shop with that on it, as if only someone in that special class could own one."

Pulling on the cable threaded through the trigger guards while looking for a way to free the rifles, Vasily turned to see Mason pick one up, pushing a small spring-loaded pin on the trigger guard in slightly, and then swinging the lower portion of the trigger guard open, freeing the rifle from the cable.

"Whoever set this up wasn't thinking," Mason said. "The trigger guards on these things flip open with just the tip of a bullet as a tool in order to make room for gloves or mittens. How they thought a cable running through the trigger guard was secure is beyond me."

Doing as Mason had done, Vasily and Dr. Hunter freed the other three rifles.

"You obviously know how to use one of these, Mason," Dr. Hunter said.

"Well, yeah. That tactical carbine class I mentioned used the AR-15 as the primary weapon."

Patting Mason on the back, Dr. Hunter said, "I sure brought the right grad student along. That's more evident every day."

"Are you good to go with that, Vasily?" Mason asked.

"I was Soviet military. I served during Soviet invasion of Afghanistan, as well as several," pausing to gather his thoughts, Vasily cleared his throat and continued, "I... I served in several, uh, 'unconventional' campaigns. We trained with your weapons. So, yes, I am familiar."

Pulling on a padlock secured to a steel security locker, Mason said, "This looks like a logical place to find ammo."

"If we can't find the key, I'd imagine it's clipped to the belt of our friend, the station manager," replied Dr. Hunter as he began sifting through the drawers, looking for keys."

"I found keys," said Vasily, holding up two open-end wrenches that he produced from a tool bag he found in the bottom drawer.

"Keys?" Dr. Hunter asked, confused by Vasily's statement.

Slipping the jaws of both wrenches into the hasp of the lock, Vasily pushed the handles toward each other, using the leverage of the opposing jaws on the wrench's open ends to break the hasp of the lock. "Keys," he said with a smile. "Locks do not keep people out. They tell you where things you seek are hidden."

Smiling at Vasily's response, Mason pulled the drawer open and said, "Jackpot," as he began removing loaded, thirty-round government-issue AR-15 magazines, placing them on top of the counter next to them. "Looks like we've got twenty. That's five mags per gun. That should be plenty for anything short of an armed conflict."

"Yes, very good," replied Vasily.

"Okay, guys," Dr. Hunter said as he slung his newly found rifle over his shoulder. "We need to get back to the group." Turning toward the door, he shouted, "Neville, come on back."

Seeing Neville walk into the back room, Mason gestured to him and asked, "Where's the shotgun?"

"It's on the desk," he replied.

"A lot of good it will do you there. Trust me, if you get in the habit of walking around without a gun when you have one available, the first time you need it, you won't have it with you."

"I'm guess I'm still not completely comfortable with the concept of carrying a gun," Neville replied. "Crazy, I know, given the situation, but years of conditioning are not easily undone."

"I'm personally not comfortable with the thought of being killed by a rabid psycho that's foaming at the mouth," Mason replied. "I suggest you get used to the concept and quick."

Nodding that he understood, Neville turned to retrieve the shotgun as Mason said, "Wait, we found these," as he pointed to the AR-15's.

Seeing Neville's hesitation, Dr. Hunter said, "Neville, why don't you just carry the shotgun? You've already been shown how to use it and it's far easier to hit what you're shooting at with it. We can give the other rifle to one of the others. Just grab the shotgun and get ready to move."

"Speaking of that," Neville replied. "The weather is becoming quite nasty out and the sun, what sun is left this time of year, is almost gone. Visibility is near zero in my estimation."

Looking to the others, Dr. Hunter said, "Thoughts?"

Scratching his chin, Mason said, "Maybe we should just hunker down here for the night. We can move to one of the rooms with a functioning door and a lock."

Nodding in agreement, Vasily said, "Is good idea. We stay. No use to your friends if we do not reach them."

"That, and I'm sure Brett would expect that. He'd take a look at the conditions and expect us to hunker down until morning."

"Okay, then. It's settled," Dr. Hunter confirmed. "Let's find a secure place to spend the night."

"That sounds like a plan," Mason replied. "But before we get going, have you fired an AR before?"

"No," replied Dr. Hunter. "I've hunted with my brother-in-law and shot rifles out at his ranch, but they were always bolt-actions. There was one semi-auto, but it looked like a hunting rifle. I can't remember what it was exactly."

Holding his rifle in front of Dr. Hunter, Mason explained the basic battery of arms, as well as a quick overview of how the AR-15's gas system functions.

Pulling back on the charging handle and locking the bolt to the rear, he explained, "After firing the last round, the magazine follower causes the bolt to be locked rearward, like this. When that happens, press this button with your trigger finger to release the old magazine, then insert a new one, tapping it firmly to ensure it's fully seated.

"Once the fresh magazine is securely in place, smack the bolt catch with your left hand to release the bolt, allowing it to travel forward, loading a round out of the new magazine into the chamber. You can also pull back on the charging handle to release it, but it's quicker to just smack the left side of the rifle with your left hand to get the bolt to go home when you're in the middle of a shit storm and need to get back on target. Either way, as long as the new magazine is in place, a round will be chambered once the bolt goes home, and you'll be back in the fight."

Pointing to the safety selector, Mason said, "Like I said before, these are semi-auto only. They're missing the fun mode. Safe and fire are your only two options. Keep it on safe when we're moving. I don't want to get shot in the leg or the back just because you bump into something. But keep this switch in your head, so you can get a shot off when you need to without fumbling around. When you bring the rifle to bear, your thumb should come up to the safety selector simultaneously. Locate your target, click it off, squeeze the trigger."

"Okay, I think I've got it," Dr. Hunter said. "Hopefully it won't come to that. We don't even know how many more infected are out there."

"I go first," Vasily said as he held his rifle at the low ready and worked his way to the front door of the station manager's office.

Falling in behind Vasily were Dr. Hunter and Neville, with Mason bringing up the rear to keep an eye on their six.

Working their way down the main hallway, Vasily paused and checked the knob to one of the rooms located between the two adjacent hallways. Feeling that it was unlocked, he knocked softly and listened with his ear just inches from the door. Hearing nothing, he nodded to the others as he began to slowly rotate the knob, pushing the door open as he peeked inside.

With a disappointed sigh, he opened the door to reveal a woman in her mid-forties leaning back in an office chair next to a computer. With her arms hanging to her side, the last few drops of her blood trickled onto the floor from the apparently self-inflicted wounds on her wrists.

"Good heavens!" Neville said as his eyes darted around the morbid scene.

"I guess it was all too much for her," Mason said. "Hell, this would be too much for most people."

Closing the door, Vasily continued down the hallway. Opening the next door on his left in the same cautious manner, Vasily placed his hand on the knob only to find it locked. Knocking gently on the door, he was startled by what sounded like a chair being knocked over. Stepping back, he motioned for the group to continue.

Reaching the end of the hallway, Vasily pointed to the placard on the door that read, "MAC COMMS."

Turning the lever-style knob with his left hand, he gripped the pistol-grip of his rifle with the stock under his elbow for leverage, ready for what might come on the other side.

As he slowly opened the door, he saw a man kneeling over a co-worker. He couldn't see what the man was doing, but could see a pool of drying blood on the floor beneath them.

"Hey," he said quietly to get the man's attention.

Turning slowly toward them, Vasily could see blood on the man's face, along with the tell-tale signs of the infection. As the man turned to stand, Vasily could see that the infected man was feeding on the entrails of his victim.

Through gritted teeth, Vasily said in his native language, "Боже, черт побери!" as he raised his rifle, firing one well-placed shot into the forehead of the infected man, dropping him on top of his victim.

Rushing into the room behind Vasily, Mason looked at the macabre scene and said, "Holy hell!"

With a look of disgust on his face, Vasily said, "He was feeding on him."

"What did you say—in Russian? What was that?"

Shaking his head, Vasily insisted, "I should not repeat." Looking up, he added, "Lord would not like."

"Let's go!" Neville insisted. "Others may have heard the shot."

"Wait," said Dr. Hunter. "The radios! Let's try to reach someone on the radios!"

Pulling the door shut behind them, Mason said, "Let's get with it then, so we can get out of here. Neville is right."

Walking over to the main communications desk, the men were bewildered by the complexity of the equipment.

"Well, who's the radio geek?" asked Mason.

"Black Island," said Neville.

"Huh?" queried Mason.

"All of McMurdo's communications are relayed through the radio facility on Black Island. Maybe we can reach someone there? They are very isolated and may not be suffering the same fate."

"That's right!" Dr. Hunter replied.

"I can work," said Vasily as he sat down at the console and began familiarizing himself with the radio equipment. Thumbing through a Standard Operating Procedures (SOP) manual he found on a small shelf off to the side of the desk, Vasily selected a frequency through the transmitter's preselect options, and handed the microphone over to Dr. Hunter. "You talk," he said.

Keying the transmit button on the microphone, Dr. Hunter said, "Black Island, or anyone else for that matter, are you there?"

Waiting for a brief moment, Dr. Hunter keyed up again, saying, "If anyone is there, please respond."

Seeing the RX light illuminate on the console, they heard a frantic voice say, *"Mac Ops, this is Black Island. What the hell is going on over there?"*

"Black Island, this is Dr. Nathan Hunter from MEVO. We are transmitting from Mac Ops, but..."

"MEVO? What the hell? Where is Keith, Rob, Luis, or Jessie? Where are the Mac Ops COMMS guys?"

"I don't know where to begin," Dr. Hunter replied.

"Look, I've been hearing a lot of shit over the radio and I'm about to lose my damn mind out here. What the hell is going on? After reports of some sort of attack on Mac-Town, I started hearing similar things from Christchurch. Then, the other major research bases, such as Palmer, Scott Base, Amundson, and others, started going dark. The only people I can raise now are at a few of the smaller, more remote facilities, and they are scared to death that no one is coming for them and that they'll soon starve. It's the end of the season, and they're not stocked with supplies to stay out any longer. What can you tell me? What the hell is going on?"

Clearing his throat, Dr. Hunter keyed up and said, "There's been an outbreak. People who contract the associated illness become extremely violent. Mac-Town looks like a horror movie. We too, couldn't get transport from MEVO and had to make our way back via snowmobile. Since we've made it, we've witnessed some horrible, horrible things."

After a moment of silence, the voice from Black Island said, *"Are you shitting me? This isn't a good time to be funny. You*

*can shove your practical jokes up your ass. We need a damn
ride out of here and so do the others at the outlying facilities. I
need to talk to someone there with a clue, and ASAP."*

"Look, we aren't shitting you. Like I said, this is Dr. Nathan
Hunter. I am the principle investigator at MEVO. We're in the
same boat as you. Now, what can you tell us about what you've
heard from Christchurch?"

With stress in the man's voice, they heard, *"They said the
same thing you did—that there had been an outbreak. They
wouldn't give details, but it was assumed to be a biological
attack of some sort that arrived via a transport plane. The last
report I heard before they went dark was that the military was
getting involved. The guy wished me luck, and I never heard
from them again. That was yesterday."*

"You're saying Christchurch, New Zealand, is no longer
transmitting?" Dr. Hunter asked, unable to believe his ears.

"That's right. We're all screwed," the man said, clearly
distressed.

"Are you there alone?" Dr. Hunter asked.

"Just me and..."

Before the radio operator could answer, another voice came
over the speaker. *"This is Black Island Station Manager Louis
Radcliff, what the hell is going on over there?"*

"Look," Dr. Hunter explained, "Like I was telling your
counterpart, this is Dr. Nathan Hunter, Principle Investigator
from MEVO. There has been an outbreak, and McMurdo has
been all but wiped out. You can ask him for the details once we
get off the air, but for now, can you tell us when and if help is
coming?"

"Hell no, it ain't coming," the man who identified himself as
Louis Radcliff replied. *"It sounded to me like they had too much
on their hands to worry about the likes of us. They didn't say*

that in so many words, but I got the gist of it. Like Chuck here was saying when I walked in the room, they also said the military was involved, which really tells me we're fucked. Whether the civil authorities have relinquished control of the situation, or it was taken from them, either way it says all we need to know. Since then, they've gone dark. I can still tell someone out there is sparking up, but it's nothing I can tune in.

"Chuck and I are gonna hunker down here. I suggest you do the same if you can. We're in for a long ride, boys."

Keying the mic to respond, Dr. Hunter's transmission was interrupted by the deafening crack of a shotgun blast. Turning quickly to see Neville standing there shaking, with smoke emanating from the shotgun's barrel. Behind Neville, he could see a dead, severely infected woman lying on the floor with her brains scattered in a fan-like pattern behind her.

"I killed her! Oh, God, no!" shouted Neville. "I had to! I swear!"

Putting his hand on Neville, Mason said, "She was sick. You're right, you had to. She would have infected one of us, or worse, if you hadn't. You did the right thing."

"We go now!" Vasily insisted. "More will come. My shot brought her, and Neville's will bring more."

Chapter Sixteen

Crary Lab

Unable to sleep, even with the assurance that Dr. Perkins was dutifully standing watch, Dr. Graves found herself staring at the ceiling, worrying incessantly over Brett's potential contamination during his encounter with Jared and Jenny. Looking over to him, seeing that he had finally been able to fall sound asleep, she relaxed, thinking, *surely, he would be showing signs by now.*

Awakened by what sounded like someone bumping into furniture, Dr. Graves's heart raced. She was disoriented, realizing that she had finally found the deep sleep that had seemed so elusive since the onset of the outbreak. Looking over to her left toward the source of the sound, she saw Brett walking across the room toward Dr. Bentley, who was standing watch after having relieved Dr. Perkins.

"Gerald!" she shouted, while rolling over to her side and struggling to her feet as fast as she could in an attempt to warn Dr. Bentley.

Startled by her cry, Dr. Bentley quickly turned to her, saying, "What is it, Linda? What's troubling you, my dear?"

"Brett!"

"Yes, what about him?" Dr. Bentley replied, as Brett turned to her with a look of confusion. "We're just having a pleasant conversation."

"Yeah," said Brett as he rubbed his forehead. "I've got one of those killer headaches that feels like it's right behind your eye. I couldn't sleep, so I figured I'd keep Dr. Bentley company."

Realizing her mistake, she placed her hand over her pounding heart and said, "Sorry. I... I woke up when I heard something and..."

Smiling, Brett said, "It's okay. I understand. Sorry that I bumped into the end table and startled you. I was pacing back and forth and wasn't paying attention. Don't worry. I'm not feeling anything but a headache. Headaches are kind of normal for me."

Shaking her head and chuckling at her own reaction, she said, "No, I'm sorry."

"Damn it, Linda. I had just fallen asleep," moaned Dr. Perkins from across the room."

Before she could reply, they heard a loud, metallic thud from the lower level of the building. The sound echoed through the empty hallways, as the winds outside still pounded the facility with what seemed to be a relentless assault.

"What the hell was that?" asked Dr. Perkins.

"If I were a betting man, I would say we are no longer alone in this building," replied Dr. Bentley.

"That's assuming we ever were," Brett mumbled as he listened carefully with his ear on the door.

As another loud thud reverberated through the building, the group looked at each other in the darkness, with only the flickering light of an emergency candle obtained from the lounge's kitchen cabinets to illuminate the room.

Hearing a door open, Brett said, "That was the door at the bottom of the stairwell."

"Maybe it's the guys," Dr. Graves said optimistically.

"Maybe, but I don't think so," replied Brett.

"What makes you say that?" asked Dr. Perkins.

"They wouldn't be making all that racket. They'd be moving quietly and methodically, not bumping around and violently opening doors."

Reaching to his belt for his ice axe, Brett said, "Shit!" as the realization set in that he'd left his ice axe on the mezzanine walkway after his encounter with Jared.

Holding his finger up to his lips, Brett walked over and extinguished the candle as the group listened intently to the sounds that appeared to be drawing closer.

Gathering around the corner in the kitchen area, next to the door to the second stairwell, the group heard a door swing open, banging into its stops. Nearly screaming out of fright, Dr. Graves held her own hand tightly over her mouth and kept her eyes closed, trying to paint a picture in her mind from the sounds she heard.

"That was the door to the mezzanine walkway," whispered Brett.

Hearing heavy, clumsy footsteps walk out onto the mezzanine, Dr. Graves whispered, "Jenny is still out there."

The sounds of the footsteps soon ceased, and then, sending chills up their spines, a loud animalistic roar emanated from the mezzanine.

Through the sounds of the pounding winds, they could hear similar shrieking cries outside the Crary Lab.

"Dear Lord," Dr. Bentley whispered, "Were those replies?"

The group sat silent in the darkness, their hearing being their only link to the world around them, painting a horrifying picture for their imaginations.

Hearing more noises from the lower floor of the lab, Linda whispered, "My God, you're right. They were replies. They're communicating."

"I must say, the rapid advancement of the condition of the hosts is quite concerning."

"Concerning?" replied Brett. "It's a bit more than concerning, don't you think?"

Hearing the stairwell door abruptly swing open once again, followed by the sounds of several sets of footsteps beginning to stagger their way up the stairs, Dr. Perkins whispered, "Holy shit! What the hell are we going to do?"

"We're gonna stop talking and stay put for now," Brett whispered.

~~~~

McMurdo Ops

Working their way down the stairwell on the northwest end of the McMurdo Operations building, Vasily led the way, followed by Dr. Hunter, Neville, and Mason.

Gently pushing the stairwell door open, Vasily looked out into the center hallway of the operations building, and said, "I see no threats," as he continued to push the door open, allowing the others to slip through and into the hallway alongside him. Carefully closing the door to avoid making a sound, Vasily motioned for the group to follow. Looking back at Neville as they began to move, Vasily whispered, "Do not cover me with your barrel, and take your damn finger off the trigger," reminding Neville to be vigilant in regard to his shotgun's muzzle and trigger discipline, as he had accidentally swept him with it on several occasions.

"Sorry," whispered Neville as he quickly repositioned the weapon.

Seeing a figure move across the hall in front of them, Vasily motioned for them to take visual cover as he ducked behind a stainless-steel drinking fountain. Quickly taking refuge in the recessed opening of a set of double-doors that led into the air traffic control facility, the other three men watched as the figure staggered and stumbled into a room at the end of the hallway.

Just as Vasily raised his hand to signal them to move forward, the lights throughout the building went dark, and the sounds of the building's environmental systems fell silent.

"I'm surprised it took this long," whispered Dr. Hunter. "Power generation was bound to need human input at some point before it fell offline."

"Things are gonna get really cold around here, really quick," added Mason.

"What the bloody hell are we going to do now?" Neville asked in frustration.

Hearing Vasily whisper, "Come. We move now," in the darkness, Dr. Hunter, Mason, and Neville fell in behind him and worked their way toward the rear entry doors in the center of the building.

Once the group was gathered at the doorway, Vasily whispered, "There are steps leading down on other side of door. Once we move, do not stop. Follow behind me, hand on shoulder of man in front of you. Do not become separated in darkness and storm. I have place to shelter until morning. Then, we find your friends."

With Dr. Hunter, Mason, and Neville all nodding in reply, Vasily pushed open the door against the force of the violent winds of the night's storm. Feeling Dr. Hunter place his hand on his shoulder, he moved forward, leading the men down the stairs, and off into the near-zero-visibility of the storm.

As the gusts of the storm intensified, causing their jackets to buffet violently from the pounding wind, Mason removed his hand from Neville's shoulder to adjust his goggles, in an effort to regain his sight.

Slipping and falling onto his rifle, Mason quickly stood, finding that he could no longer reach out and touch Neville. Spinning around while reaching out in all directions, Mason became disoriented as to which direction they had been traveling. The extremely poor visibility caused by the stormy conditions of Antarctica was something Mason had trained for when he first arrived at McMurdo with Dr. Hunter several seasons ago. He recalled his experience in the survival training course they affectionately known as the 'Bucket Head Challenge', where the students all wore plastic buckets on their heads to simulate a white-out condition, and were forced to navigate as a group without the benefit of sight.

He felt as helpless in this moment as he did when his training class became disoriented and failed to find the instructor, as was the course objective.

Feeling a hand grasp his left arm, he said, "Oh, there you guys are." As the hand clinched tighter and tighter and began to cause him pain, Mason heard an animalistic, spine-chilling roar come from the person who gripped him tightly.

"Shit!" Mason yelled as he attempted to pull away. Unable to break the man's grasp. Mason swung the butt of his rifle around with his free hand, smashing it into his assailant's face, knocking the man backward.

As the man fell, Mason was pulled toward him, falling on top of the him. Still unable to see due to the night's darkness and the blinding storm, and with his rifle now trapped between them, Mason quickly pulled his knife from his belt, flipped open the blade with his thumb and began stabbing at the man repeatedly.

As his attacker's struggles began to slow, Mason heard shrieks and cries drawing near, as more of the infected seemed to be communicating as they converged on his position.

With the dying man who lay beneath him releasing one more terrifying scream before succumbing to his wounds, Mason could hear the others begin to converge on his location more rapidly. Wiping his goggles with his glove, all he could see was darkness.

Feeling a hand grasp him by the shoulder, his heart still racing from the attack, Mason swung around, shoving his knife into his attacker as he heard a familiar voice scream, "It's me! Mason, it's me!"

To Mason's horror, his knife had already struck its' blow. He could feel the warmth of Neville's blood soaking into his glove.

Horrified, Mason released the knife and pulled his arm back just as Neville fell onto him in severe pain.

Standing up with Neville leaning into his shoulder, Mason picked him up and hurried away from the threats in the darkness with his rifle dangling from its sling, bouncing off his legs as he walked.

"Vasily! Doc Hunter!" he shouted, trying to find the rest of his friends.

"Mason!" Dr. Hunter shouted, reaching out to Mason. Still unable to see in the storm, but feeling that Neville was now being carried by Mason, Dr. Hunter pulled on Mason's parka, saying, "This way! Come on! Hurry!"

Closing a door behind them, Vasily lit the way into to the building with his flashlight. As the light shined across Mason's goggles, all he could see were streaks of blood illuminated by the light. Laying Neville gently on the floor, Mason pulled his bloody snow goggles from his face and threw them across the room. Quickly pulling off his crimson-soaked gloves, he turned his attention back to Neville, who was lying on the floor with both of his hands over a wound in his abdomen.

"What the hell happened?" asked Dr. Hunter as they began to remove Neville's parka to determine the extent of his injuries.

"I couldn't see!" Mason said in a trembling voice. "I fell, and when I was reaching out to find Neville, someone grabbled my arm. I thought it was him, until I heard the man scream as if he was possessed by the soul of a demon. I heard more screams from off in the darkness as if they were homing in on us by sound. I tried fighting the man off, but ended up on top of him on the ground. My only option was my knife, so I began stabbing him. The next thing I knew, I felt another hand on me, and fearing it was from one of the figures advancing on my position, I swung around and... My God, I stabbed Neville!"

Looking at Neville's wound, and then back to Mason, Dr. Hunter asked, "So, you stabbed him with a knife covered with the blood of your attacker?"

For a moment, it seemed as if time had slowed as the men looked at each other in horror, each of them realizing the implications of what had happened. Hearing Neville wince in pain, Mason looked down to him and said, "I'm so sorry, Neville. I'm so sorry."

"Don't fret about it, mate," Neville said, trying his best to talk through the pain. "You were under attack. I was foolish to reach out for you without identifying myself." Interrupted by a blood-filled cough, Neville continued. "None of this is your fault. We're surrounded by madness. None of us can help that."

Wincing in pain once again, Neville laid his head back onto the floor, and asked, "Is it bad?"

Looking over the wound carefully, Dr. Hunter said, "If we were back home at any other time, I don't think this would have been too big a deal. But given the circumstances, well..."

"I know," Neville said. "Don't worry, Doc. I know."

Changing the subject, Vasily said, "We must move him away from door to back room. Come."

Each of the men helped pick Neville up off the floor, then carried him in the direction that Vasily was leading them. Looking around, seeing the tall walls and majestic, timber-framed ceiling, Mason realized they were in the Chapel of the Snows.

"Fitting," he said.

"Huh?" Dr. Hunter asked.

"We're in the chapel. We all need to do a lot of praying right now."

Chapter Seventeen

Crary Lab

Huddling together in the Crary Lab's upstairs lounge and break room, Dr. Graves, Dr. Bentley, Dr. Perkins, and Brett listened as the shuffling footsteps of those they heard ascending the stairs worked their way out onto the mezzanine.

Making his way toward the stairwell next to the lounge's kitchen facilities, where they hadn't heard any movement, Brett whispered, "I'm gonna take a look. If this stairwell is empty, and if they are all on the mezzanine, this may be our chance to make a break for it."

"Make a break for it?" Dr. Bentley queried. "Make a break for what? Where will we go? Aren't we supposed to be hiding out until our colleagues return?"

"Brett's right," Dr. Graves replied.

"But Linda, you can't seriously be considering going out into the storm in the middle of the night. We'd be blind out there. We could be walking right into the arms of one of the infected and wouldn't even see it coming."

"They aren't going to stay on the mezzanine forever," Dr. Graves replied.

"She's right, Gerald," said Dr. Perkins. "Once they're done feeding, they'll be looking for more."

Feeling Dr. Graves punch him in the arm, Dr. Perkins recoiled away from her and said, "Linda, you know that's what they're doing. The first one to arrive called for the others. We heard that. We aren't imagining things. Then they arrived. What if they discover we are in here and call for more? How many more are out there? Two? Five? Ten? Twenty? Hell, there could be a hundred more for all we know. We need to be where they are not. Plain and simple. Dr. Hunter, Mason, and Neville will be able to find us."

"Yeah, they will," replied Brett. "Mason is sharp and has spent a lot of his days tracking big game. I'm sure a set of boot prints will be easy for him to follow."

"That is, of course, unless said boot prints are covered with snow during the storm," Dr. Bentley interjected.

"We'll leave them a note on the dry erase board," replied Brett. "We'll let them know we had to leave and are seeking shelter."

Just then, they heard the facility's heating system winding down, as well as the ever-present electrical buzz created by the research equipment throughout the building going silent, followed by the illumination of the facility's backup battery powered lights.

"Shit, the power's off," Brett said, noticing they could now hear the frenzy taking place out on the mezzanine even more acutely through the silence.

Speaking up, Dr. Perkins said, "If we're gonna get moving, we need to do it quickly. Wherever we end up needs to be a place with a stand-alone heating system that isn't connected to McMurdo's grid. We can't survive here long without heat. Any ideas?"

Pausing for a moment while they all thought through the situation carefully, Brett said, "Gallagher's Pub! Being a lover of all things beer, I got to know several of the bartenders there pretty well. When it was slow, we would often chat about the history of McMurdo. Sam mentioned to me once that Gallagher's had an old diesel heat-exchanger-style heating system."

"It sure seemed to me like the same forced air that the rest of the buildings have."

"Well, yes. It's been updated. But the old diesel system still remains."

"Won't the sound of a diesel engine attract unwanted attention?" asked Dr. Graves.

"It's not an engine," Brett explained. "There is a burner, like an old gasoline-powered VW bug heater from way back. The burner heats water that is circulated through the pipes in the facility. The water flows through heat exchangers, like the heater of your car, where a fan blows air over the fins of the heat exchanger, extracting the heat from the water. The cooled water then flows back to the burner to be reheated, continuing the cycle. In addition to ensuring they had heat, it also provided a guarantee of keeping the potable water warm enough to never freeze since there was a heat exchanger for a potable water loop as well."

"But what powers the fans?" Dr. Perkins asked.

Thinking for a moment, Brett asked, "Don't most buildings here have a battery bank for emergency power, just like Crary Lab? If I recall correctly, the batteries are charged by the grid while it is online, keeping them topped off for emergency conditions."

"Ah, yes," Dr. Bentley said. "I do believe you are correct. The wintering-over crew needs emergency power due to the lack of sunlight. If the power goes down, they need adequate lighting until they get things back online, as they have no daylight."

"So, you're saying we could use the battery power to run the fans?" asked Dr. Graves.

"I don't see why not," Brett said as he scratched his chin. "The fans may be twelve-volt already, but even if they're not, each of those systems has an inverter, or at least, they should. Either way, it's all theory until we give it a try."

"That sounds like a good option," said Dr. Bentley. "Especially since I feel it getting colder in here already."

"Okay, then," said Brett as he peeked down into the stairwell. Quietly closing the door after seeing that their path was clear, he said, "Okay, suit up for the cold. The wind is really pounding out there."

Walking over to the kitchen area, Brett began to look through the cabinets.

"What is it that you are looking for, if I may enquire?" Dr. Bentley asked as he watched Brett with curiosity.

"Ah, this will do," Brett replied, pulling an electrical extension cord from underneath the sink. "Visibility is going to be poor to say the least. We can each hang on to this cord to make sure we don't lose our way, just like the rope in survival school."

"Ah, yes, that was a quite the debacle, wasn't it?" said Dr. Bentley as he not-so-fondly recalled his time in survival school.

Once everyone was dressed in their outer layers and gloves, with their goggles on their heads ready to don upon exiting the building, Brett said, "Okay, let's go. Let's keep in mind that without the buzzes and hums that typically permeate this building, we have got to use extra diligence to move quietly. The last thing we want to do is turn this into a chase in the dark."

Leading them down the stairs, Brett paused at the first landing and stopped, listening before continuing. Giving them the signal to proceed, he heard a metallic clang that resonated throughout the stairwell. Looking back at Dr. Bentley, he saw him holding his makeshift spear, mouthing the word, *sorry*.

Continuing down the stairs to the lower landing, Brett heard commotion from the upper floor, followed by sounds of scuffling in the primary stairwell. "They're coming down," he said. "Let's go!"

Opening the door, Brett and the others were immediately pounded by the violent winds. Stumbling backward, he lowered his snow goggles and waved them forward as they stepped into the darkness of the night and into the unknown.

~~~~

Chapel of the Snows

With Neville's bleeding controlled from the use of fabric found in the back room of the chapel, as well as duct tape from one of the supply cabinets, Dr. Hunter sat next to him while Vasily stood watch and Mason searched the building for items of use.

"I don't feel so well," Neville said. "I'm starting to get the chills."

"We're all starting to get the chills, Neville. It's getting cold around here with the power being down."

"Thank you for your attempt at calming my nerves, but I can tell the difference. I'm not well. The knife had to have pierced my intestines. I know the outcome of such an injury without immediate emergency medical care, of which we have none, and none is coming."

"Nonsense, Neville," Dr. Hunter quickly replied. "I know only you can really tell how you feel, but I also know that a lot of people have survived a lot of things when others told them they wouldn't. You can't give up in your own mind. That's the most powerful weapon you have right now. You have to maintain the will to struggle through the pain and hang on until we can get help. You don't know that help isn't coming. The radio operator at Black Island told us the military was getting involved. They may be on their way here right now."

Wincing in pain, Neville began to speak, but was interrupted as Mason came through the door carrying a cardboard box.

Setting the box down next to them, Mason said, "I found some ceremonial candles. Also, in the emergency medical kit on the wall, I found a few space blankets. If we take the rest of that duct tape and use some chairs or other such things, we should be able to tape the blankets together and make a small shelter to keep the heat from the candles in to keep him warm. It'll be like a kid's blanket fort."

Looking up to see Vasily enter the room in the flickering light of the candles, Dr. Hunter asked, "Well, what did you see?"

"See?" Vasily replied. "I see nothing. Too dark. Too stormy. I hear though, and I believe one of them followed us."

"How do you know that?" asked Mason.

"I can hear it breathe between wind gusts. On other side of door. It breathes with—how you say it? Phlegm in chest. Is there. I am sure."

Reluctantly, Mason looked at Dr. Hunter and asked, "Doc, when I was out there with the one that grabbed my arm, it screamed out, bringing the rest to us. Do you think..."

"Yes," Dr. Hunter quickly replied. "I've been thinking the same thing. He was calling for the others."

"But how? How is that possible?" Mason asked. "How could microbial life take such control over someone's actions? I mean, I understand the rabies-like behavior, but communications and teamwork? It's almost like they're changing—or evolving—right before our eyes."

"We'll have to explain what we've seen to Linda when we get back. She's the astrobiologist. Having studied the strangest forms of life on Earth, if anyone has answers, it will be her. For now, let's just keep that in mind. We need to avoid being seen at all costs. We also can't afford to make any assumptions about their capabilities."

Looking down at Neville, who was obviously in severe pain, Mason said, "Maybe we need to get the others and bring them here? I don't think we can move him."

"Just go," Neville said through gritted teeth as he fought through the pain.

"You know that's not going to happen," Dr. Hunter replied. "Just get those thoughts out of your head."

Interrupted by the horrible shriek of one of the infected just on the other side of the window of the back room, Mason said, "Shit!" as he jumped up and pulled one of the space blankets over the already closed Venetian blinds that covered the window. "One of them must have seen flickers of light through the blinds. Damn it!"

Hearing replies off in the distance, Vasily said, "More are coming. We must go."

"We can't!" Mason said frantically. "We can't run with Neville. It would tear his wound back open."

"Those things will tear more than his wound open if we do not go," Vasily said with a look of seriousness on his face. "We go!"

"Just go," Neville said. "It hurts too bad. I can't run, and you can't run with me. You don't have a choice. Maybe they'll follow you away and I'll be fine."

"We can't do that, Doc," Mason said, giving Dr. Hunter a defiant look.

Hearing a thump against the back wall from where the shriek had come, Vasily insisted, "We go! We go now!"

Shouting through the pain, Neville said, "You do not understand! I feel it. I feel it growing inside me. I am not going to survive this, and before long, I will be like them. You have got to leave. You have got to follow Vasily and do what he says. There is nothing you can do for me now. All I ask is that you leave me the shotgun."

Holding the candle close to Neville's face, Dr. Hunter could see that what Neville spoke was the truth. He could see the swollen blood vessels in his eyes, as well as the beginnings of what appeared to be traces of gray on his skin near his jugular vein.

As beads of sweat ran down his forehead, Neville begged, "Go. Please."

Before anyone could answer, a fist smashed through the stained-glass window of the back room. The hand reached blindly into the room, dripping blood from the slicing action of the thick, jagged broken glass.

Handing the shotgun to Neville, Vasily said, "You are very brave man. I am honored to have met you. Godspeed."

Simply nodding in reply, as if he was unable to speak, Neville took the shotgun and held it close to his chest.

Pausing as the others ran for the front door, Mason looked at Neville, who was too consumed by his own pain and emotional agony to return the glance. Saying, "Sorry," Mason turned and ran, catching up with Dr. Hunter and Vasily at the front door.

Pointing, Vasily said, "Sun is beginning to rise and storm is subsiding. Crary Lab is that way. When door is open, run. Do not stop. I distract them if necessary. I catch up if fall behind. Get to your friends."

Nodding that they understood, Vasily swung open the door to see a crazed figure standing before them. It was a man in workman's clothes and a hard hat.

Mumbling, "Tom," Vasily raised his rifle and fired one shot directly at the man, causing his head to whip back violently as blood and brains sprayed onto the snow behind him. As the man's body fell back onto the ground, still and lifeless, his hard hat came to rest in the blood-splattered snow several yards away, revealing the name *Tom*.

Turning to Dr. Hunter and Mason, Vasily waved his arm and shouted, "Go!" sending the two men running in the direction of the Crary Lab.

Standing his ground for a brief moment, seeing another of the infected begin to follow Dr. Hunter and Mason, Vasily took aim and fired into the man's torso, dropping him to the ground.

Vasily's feeling of relief as he watched Dr. Hunter and Mason slip past the McMurdo Operations building and toward the Crary Lab soon turned to horror when he saw a horde of at least twenty of the infected as they began pouring out of Ops with their attention focused squarely on him.

Vasily's memories flashed through his mind. He remembered his earlier concerns that the shots fired in the air traffic control center would attract more of the infected. That concern was now validated as the operations building was now overrun.

"If this is how it ends, so be it," Vasily mumbled through a clenched jaw. "Lord," he said, looking high into the heavens. "Bless Dr. Hunter, Mason, and their friends. Help them. Help someone escape this evil that has been unleashed upon us."

Seeing the horde of the infected breaking into a run toward him, screaming with their teeth exposed and with hunger in their eyes as they ran, Vasily raised his rifle. Just as he began to pull the trigger, he heard a shotgun blast from over his right shoulder as one of the infected dropped to the ground. Turning quickly, Vasily saw Neville charging the horde, racking another shell into the shotgun's chamber, screaming, "Run Vasily! Run!"

Firing into the crowd again and again, taking out as many as he could, Neville's weapon soon ran dry. Stopping just shy of the horde, he slammed the pump action open, pulled a single shotgun shell from his pocket, slipped it in the chamber and closed the action. Just as the horde of infected reached him, Neville looked back to Vasily, raised the shotgun to his head, and fired as they overtook him and began tearing his body to shreds.

As Vasily began to run, he noticed that as quickly as they began attacking Neville, the violence ceased. It was as if they realized that he, too, was infected. He was one of them, or soon would have been.

~~~~

Crary Lab

Reaching the Crary Science and Engineering Center, Dr. Hunter and Mason began scanning the area for any sign of threats before attempting to make entry into the building.

Peeking around the corner toward the direction from which they had come to see if they had been followed, Mason said, "Did you hear those gunshots? There were quite a few as we ran."

"Vasily must have gotten into a bind," Dr. Hunter said. "That, or he was trying to create a distraction."

"Those weren't all from the same gun," Mason replied. "Some of them sounded more like shotgun blasts."

"Neville?" Dr. Hunter replied with curiosity in his voice.

"I dunno, but I hope Vasily got away."

Pulling his goggles off his face and resting them on top of his head, Mason knelt down and looked closely at the fresh snow from the previous night's storm. Pointing, he said, "There sure are a lot of tracks here. And most of these look as if they were made during or after the storm. They would have been covered up or at least filled in a little, otherwise."

Looking up at the second-floor windows, Dr. Hunter pointed and said, "That's the lounge, there." Looking around carefully, then taking a few steps back away from the building to get a better look, he said, "I don't see anything."

"You'd think they'd be keeping an eye out for us," Mason replied.

"Yes, but their night could have been as eventful as ours."

"There's only one way to know for sure," Mason said as he stood and placed his hand on the door.

"Well, there's still no sign of Vasily," Dr. Hunter said as he looked around the corner of the building once more. "I guess we better go in and see. Vasily knows where we were headed, so if he made it out of there okay, he can find us."

Nodding in agreement, Mason turned to the building, and said, "Here goes," as he pulled the door open slightly, taking a look inside. Seeing no threats, he opened the door and motioned for Dr. Hunter to follow. Holding his rifle at the low ready position, Mason worked his way up and around the steps toward the second floor. Reaching the upper landing, Mason pushed the door to the mezzanine open slightly to scan for threats.

"Holy shit," he whispered.

"What? What is it?" asked Dr. Hunter.

Pointing, Mason opened the door further to allow Dr. Hunter to see the macabre scene of blood and bits of flesh scattered on the mezzanine.

"Oh, my God," Dr. Hunter replied. "Do you think—?"

Closing the door, Mason interrupted, saying, "Let's just keep looking."

Moving to the lounge door, Mason waited until Dr. Hunter was in a position to provide covering fire if need be, then pushed open the door. Entering the room, they could see that it was in terrible disarray. Furniture was strewn about, the carafe from the coffee pot lay broken on the counter, and all the books from the casual reading corner had been pushed onto the floor.

"They didn't make this mess themselves," Mason said, dismayed by what they had found.

Looking around the room, Dr. Hunter said, "Well, I'll be damned," as he pointed to the dry erase board. "They left us a message."

Turning to the dry erase board, Mason saw the note:

Things got ugly here. Went to Gallagher's Pub. Graves, Bentley, Perkins, and Thompson are okay.

After taking a moment to digest the message, Mason said, "They didn't mention Jenny."

"I noticed that, too," added Dr. Hunter.

Looking around the room, attempting to process everything that had appeared to have happened, Mason said, "We'd better get a move on. If they had to leave, and with only the improvised weapons we'd made, they may need us sooner rather than later."

"Agreed. What about Vasily?"

"Let's leave him a message on the board like they left for us," replied Mason. "There isn't anyone on this base as capable as Vasily, even before this all went down. If he's still out there, he'll find us. I have no doubt of that."

Chapter Eighteen

Crary Lab

Slipping quietly out of the Crary Lab, Mason and Dr. Hunter were both caught off guard by the silence of McMurdo Station. Now that the storm had given way to a beautiful, calm morning, they heard nothing. The machinery noises and other sounds of the normally bustling research station were no more. They had felt this level of serenity while out in the field studying Mt. Erebus, but never here.

"Unreal, isn't it?" Dr. Hunter said as the two soaked it all in.

The week before, McMurdo was a thriving research station at the bottom of the world, buzzing with activity as the seasonal research teams packed up their gear for their return to their homes and universities, preparing to turn the place over to the wintering-over crew.

And now, here they stood, with their rifles held at the ready. Weapons were previously thought to be non-existent at McMurdo, a place virtually free of crime as everyone who made the journey to work in such a place, no matter how different, were all on the same sheet of music. Their love for their travels, their studies, and their work set them apart from most of the world's societies. Perhaps if McMurdo had been fully populated year-round, it would have regressed into what the rest of humanity had become. But here, with the temporary nature of their secluded and unique society on everyone's mind, it seemed to be an oasis, free from the dark side of human nature.

Freeing himself from his thoughts, Mason said, "You ready?"

"Yeah," replied Dr. Hunter. "Do you want point or rear?"

"Where is all that tactical talk coming from?" Mason whispered jokingly.

"I'm just trying to rise to the occasion, I guess," replied Dr. Hunter. "Like most people, outside of my profession I'm a product of the movies I've watched. Unfortunately, that's the extent of my tactical vocabulary."

With a smile, Mason replied, "In that case, I'll take point."

Carefully working his way around the corner of the building, Mason looked across the snow-covered area between Crary Lab and the cluster of buildings that held Gallagher's Pub. Signaling for Dr. Hunter to join up with him, he pointed at the ground and said, "This may be their tracks. It looks like they followed the shadow of the building to those pallets of gear. They probably cut across from there."

"If they crossed during last night's storm, that must have been tough," Dr. Hunter replied.

"Yep. Let's make our way to the pallets and see if we can pick up their tracks from there. Just because they set out for Gallagher's doesn't mean they didn't have to divert along the way. There's no reason to enter a building and deal with what may be inside if they aren't there."

"Agreed," replied Dr. Hunter, and with a nod, the two men moved carefully forward, scanning for threats as they went.

Reaching the pallets, Mason pointed at a cluster of recent tracks and said, "Right across the middle."

Taking another look around, he motioned for Dr. Hunter to follow as they continued across the empty expanse toward Gallagher's. Feeling vulnerable from being in plain view with no visual cover, they hurried as best they could without making noise.

Stopping half-way across, Mason pointed down in the snow, and said, "An extension cord. What the hell is an electrical extension cord doing way out here? It's on top of most of the snow, too, so it was dropped or tossed fairly recently."

"It looks like the tracks get a bit muddled up here as well," Dr. Hunter remarked.

"Someone fell here," Mason said, pointing several feet to the left. "I don't see any blood or obvious signs of trouble, though."

"It looks like their tracks veer off that way," Dr. Hunter said, pointing to the northwest. "Surely they didn't go toward the berthing buildings. The last place I would want to be is where everyone on McMurdo lived. There are bound to be infected there. You know people probably went to hole up in their rooms while waiting on help to arrive when it all started going down."

"Let's follow them and see," replied Mason as he continued, following the path of the tracks.

Looking up from the boot prints he was following, Mason's heart skipped a beat when he saw a figure standing directly in front of him, about fifty yards away. "Holy shit," he muttered as he quickly raised his rifle.

"Infected?" asked Dr. Hunter.

"Dunno," replied Mason.

"Where the hell did he come from?"

"Dunno," he again replied, holding his sights on the figure.

Waving his hand at the man in an attempt to determine his condition, Mason watched as the man continued to stand still. *What the hell?* he thought.

Hearing the pounding of footsteps behind him, Dr. Hunter turned to see three figures running toward him at a full sprint, "Shit!" he said as he quickly raised his rifle, unintentionally discharging it before getting on target, and striking one of his attackers in the knee.

Falling onto the snow-covered ground, the figure quickly got back to its feet, limping and bloody, but still moving forward.

The other two were nearing Dr. Hunter as he swung his rifle to meet the targets. He fired two shots into one before moving to the other, sending multiple shots into the attacker's chest, causing him to fall to the ground mere feet in front of him.

Hearing a shot behind him, Dr. Hunter swung around to see Mason firing into the man who had previously been standing alone, but was now almost upon them as well. "Come on!" Mason shouted, leading Dr. Hunter toward the cluster of buildings just ahead.

Running as hard as they could to find visual cover behind the buildings, Mason and Dr. Hunter knew their shots would attract more unwanted attention. Reaching the clusters of buildings, they ran between the fire house/telephone exchange building and Gallagher's Pub.

Seeing the side door to the pub open with a hand reaching out to wave them inside, they ran for the door, ducking inside as it was quickly closed behind them.

"Holy shit!" Mason shouted. "Am I nuts, or was that a trap?"

Leaning over and placing his hands on his knees to catch his breath, Dr. Hunter then stood up, removed his goggles, and said, "No, you're right. That was a coordinated effort."

Looking across the room to see Dr. Graves, Dr. Hunter ran to her, took her in a tight embrace, and said, "Oh, thank God you guys made it here safe."

"I take it you saw our message?" she asked.

"Yes. Yes, we did," he replied.

Looking into her eyes and with reluctance in his heart, he muttered the question, "Jenny?"

Shaking her head 'no' in reply, tears welled up in her eyes.

"Where is Neville?" asked Dr. Bentley.

"He... He..." Mason stammered.

Interrupting before Mason had to explain too much, Dr. Hunter said, "We were attacked. He didn't make it."

"Damn," said Brett as everyone in the room stood silently, soaking in the news that each group had received.

Breaking the silence, Mason asked, "Has anyone seen Vasily?"

"Who's Vasily?" Dr. Perkins asked.

"Oh, he works, or worked, rather, in the fabrication shop. He's Russian. He found us at Mac Ops and really helped us find the guns and get out safe. Last night, we were separated from him when we had to evacuate the Chapel. He knew where we were going and was supposed to meet up with us."

"We've not seen anyone but Tasha and Phillip," replied Brett, pointing across the room to a young woman, who appeared to be in her late twenties standing with a fit young man with a well-trimmed beard and glasses.

Introducing them, Brett explained, "Tasha and Phillip worked here in Gallagher's. They've each poured me quite a few beers over the years that I've been coming down to work out at MEVO."

"Have you been here in Gallagher's the whole time?" Mason asked.

Tasha answered, saying, "Yes, I was in the back doing inventory when Phillip heard the news that something was going on. He had just come from his room in the berthing complex and explained what he knew at the time. We hid in the liquor room in the back. It's got strong doors and good locks for obvious reasons."

After a few moments, with each of the groups sharing their stories, Mason sheepishly asked, "Tasha, may I have a beer? I need to calm my nerves."

"Of course," she said. "Help yourself. It's not mine, and I have a feeling Phillip and I don't work here anymore."

"This will be my last time down here, I promise you that," Phillip added.

Taking a sip of brown ale, Mason said, "Oh, I can feel it flowing through my nerves already. Doc, you should have a pint as well."

"No, thanks," replied Dr. Hunter. "And by the way, it's Nathan. Feel free to call me Nathan. I think it's time to dispense with the formalities. It's safe to say no one is working for anyone anymore."

"Sure thing, Doc," Mason said with a smile. "Uh, I mean, Nathan." With a chuckle, he added, "It may be a hard habit to break, though."

Changing the subject, Dr. Graves said, "So, Nathan, tell me about this trap you mentioned when you two arrived. We looked out the window when we heard the gunfire, but didn't see what had happened prior to that."

"Let me back up a bit first," said Dr. Hunter. "Over the course of the last day, we have observed that the infected seem to be advancing in some way. Last night, when we made our break for the chapel to wait out the storm, we were accosted by one of them. Instead of going for the kill, its reaction was what seemed to be a call for others, who quickly arrived on scene. It may sound crazy, but I swear I think they were communicating, and successfully at that. Then, later on that night when the chapel was breached, the same thing occurred. It was the same type of call and response."

Turning to Tasha, Dr. Hunter said, "On second thought, I'll have that beer."

Gratefully taking the mug from her, he continued, "Just now, when we were moving across the lot to get over here, one of the infected appeared in front of us. Unlike before, he didn't move. He merely stood there, silently. While we were focused on him, several more rushed us from behind. There were no calls, no screams, or sounds of any kind. I swear, it was like they were trying to attack while our attentions were elsewhere."

As Dr. Hunter took a sip of beer, Mason added, "And when our attention was turned to our attackers from the rear, the man out front launched his attack. It may sound crazy, but it was well coordinated and premeditated, if you ask me."

"We've noticed similar advancements in their behavior," Dr. Graves replied. "Not regarding pre-planning, as you described, but in terms of communication and teamwork. We, too, have witnessed the calls and responses that you have. That is the reason we had to flee the Crary Lab. One called, and others came in response. Then, as we were leaving, they all seemed to follow. Luckily, we must have lost them in the storm."

"We nearly got lost ourselves," Brett added. "Running blind isn't something I'm looking forward to having to do again anytime soon. About half-way across the lot, we became completely disoriented. We nearly froze to death while trying to fumble our way around to get our bearings."

Linda Graves spoke up, saying, "It's unlike anything I've ever seen before. Their rapid progression, that is. The microbes do have traits similar to others, but on a much different scale. Their ability to—take control—for lack of a better term, is startling. As we've discussed, other organisms have the same ability, in the realms of ants and flies, to take over a host, but to be able to control a highly evolved species such as humans, and to have perfected that control in such a short span of time? Well, that's something I simply cannot fathom. At least, not yet.

"Given the proper laboratory environment, I'm sure we could quickly observe and discover their methods and ways to combat it. But in the field, well, there's only so much we can do."

Pausing for a moment, she continued, "What's even more puzzling is that, although the infection seems to spread quite rapidly, Brett came in contact with what should have been infected blood, but he has yet to show any signs or symptoms of infection."

"Neville came down with it pretty quickly," Dr. Hunter replied.

"Oh, dear Lord," Dr. Bentley said, shaking his head. "Is that how the poor boy went?"

Avoiding a direct answer, Mason said, "He was a very strong-willed individual. He handled it with courage, poise, and grace. You would have been proud of him."

Walking over to Brett, Dr. Graves said, "Let me see your arm."

Rolling up his sleeve, he handed her his arm and she began to look him over. Examining his cut, she said, "I don't see any sign of the infection. Nothing at all. I was sure I would, given the scene at the time."

From across the room, Dr. Bentley stood up and asked, "What's that bracelet made of?"

Brett replied, "Copper."

Pausing, each of the scientists looked at each other for a moment, and then Dr. Graves said, "It seems unlikely, but it's possible."

"What's possible?" asked Mason.

"Copper has been used by civilizations for thousands of years as an anti-microbial remedy. It is possible, though how probable I am not sure, that the copper bracelet on Brett's arm repelled the microbes, if any were in fact present in Jenny's blood."

"And just how exactly could that be?" asked Dr. Bentley. "Not all of the potentially contaminated blood would have come in contact with the bracelet. In all probability, more came in contact with his flesh than the bracelet."

"As an astrobiologist, I've studied and searched for ways that life could function and exist throughout the universe by studying ways that it exists in the most extreme conditions here on Earth," Dr. Graves explained. "One of the things I have come to realize is that the Earth and everything on and in it, living or not, is made of the same materials found all throughout the universe. Every atom in your body was fused into the element it represents in a star before being scattered by a supernova, allowing those elements to coalesce into asteroids, planets, moons, and everything else we see.

"With that in mind, the universe itself behaves exactly the same way in all observable directions. There isn't one set of laws of physics in one part of the galaxy and a different set of laws elsewhere. I could go much deeper, but in a nutshell, if the universe is consistent, so should be life.

"Now, back to your question about the various conditions microbial life might have encountered when potentially transitioning from Jenny's blood to Brett. Let's take a look at honeybees for one possible example. When a beekeeper accidentally squishes a honeybee while servicing a hive, the other bees that instantly attack do not do so because they witnessed the atrocity and want justice. They do so because in the final seconds of the deceased bee's life, it emitted a pheromone to communicate the threat to the rest of the colony.

"In other words, they aren't consciously reacting to a self-made decision after analyzing a situation; they are reacting almost robotically, based on the communication from another bee in their hive. Though it is only one possible hypothesis, these microbes could react in such a way.

"We've already seen what appears to be an almost intelligent level of control over their host. Is each microbe capable of such thought? Probably not. It's probably more of a beehive reaction, where each microbe makes up a link in the chain, and together, function intelligently. In the human brain, for instance, one brain cell plays a very small role, but all of them combined make up an organ that is capable of intelligent thought.

"In this instance, if some of the microbes encountered a harmful substance such as copper, if that were to be the case, they could have possibly transmitted some sort of signal to the others to abandon the transfer. Again, this is far from something I would consider to be fact with the information we currently have, but based on how life in other realms has developed, it is a possibility."

Still having a tough time accepting Dr. Grave's proposed hypothesis, Dr. Bentley said, "But in the human brain, those cells are linked together and communicate via electrical signals generated by neurons. If those cells were separated and no longer connected, they could not communicate and transmit information."

"Honeybees aren't connected but they still communicate, using the air around them as the medium," she replied. "One of the most important things I have accepted as a scientist is that we have to shed ourselves of the modern concept of science as a religion. The modern concept of science is all too often a belief system, rather than a method of study. I consciously remind myself that I am not capable of understanding everything in the universe. I never will be and neither will you. If we don't keep our minds open, they will be closed to the answers that may be all around us."

Having satisfied Dr. Bentley with her rebuttal, Dr. Graves turned to the group and said, "So, what now?"

"How are we looking in the food department?" Dr. Hunter asked.

"There's still a large supply of snacks in the back," replied Phillip. "As long as our heat holds out, we should be able to survive in here for quite some time."

Looking at Mason and Dr. Hunter, Dr. Perkins said, "You two have another beer to help you sleep and get some rest. You've had a long night from the sound of it. The rest of us will need you on your game."

Seeing the same signs of fatigue on Dr. Hunter's face that he himself was feeling, Mason said, "I think we just might take you up on that."

Chapter Nineteen

Gallagher's Pub

Awakening to the sensation of warm breath on his face, Mason opened his eyes to see Neville kneeling over him. Neville's eyes were riddled with broken capillaries and the whites now had a grayish tint to them. The arteries in his neck and the corners of his mouth were traced with the microorganisms, indicating that they had fully taken over his body.

Afraid to move, Mason quietly muttered, "N... Neville. You..." as Neville viciously attacked him, lunging down and biting Mason's throat. Unable to breathe due to his crushed windpipe, Mason struggled to get the beast that Neville had become off of him as a searing pain like he had never felt before rushed through his body and the warmth of his own blood spilled over him.

Fighting off his attacker, Mason heard, "Mason! Stop! It's me, Nathan!"

Opening his eyes, Mason saw Dr. Hunter standing over him. Releasing his grip, Mason looked around the room to see Dr. Graves and the others all staring at him with looks of concern.

"You were having a nightmare, Mason," explained Dr. Hunter. "I was just trying to wake you. Are you okay? That sounded pretty bad."

Catching his breath with his heart still pounding in his chest, Mason sat up and looked around in embarrassment. "Um... It was Neville. I had a bad dream about Neville."

Turning to the others, Dr. Hunter said, "Let's give him a moment. We've all been through a hell of a lot, and we'll each have some things we need to work through."

Patting Mason on the shoulder, Dr. Hunter said, "We'll leave you be. Just come on in the other room when you feel up to it."

Nodding his head, Mason said, "Will do, Doc."

Watching the others leave the back room where he had been sleeping, Mason sat up and placed his face in his hands. "Holy shit, that was real," he mumbled to himself.

Regaining his composure, he stood and stretched. Walking across the room, Mason lifted the corner of the curtains that were drawn shut over the window and looked around. As his eyes scanned the area around Gallagher's Pub, he started to lower the curtain after having seen no threats, but paused when something caught his eye. "What the...?"

Looking closely at the Joint Space Operations Center (JSOC) to the west, he saw a figure that seemed to be standing motionless, directly facing Gallagher's Pub. Rubbing his still sleepy eyes, he looked again, and it was gone.

"I'm losing it," he mumbled as he yawned and turned to go and join the others.

"Mason," Brett said as he entered the bar area of the pub. "Glad to see you up and about."

"I'm sure glad to see you, too, man. I'm glad to see every one of you. That dream was too real."

"We've all been through a hell of a time," replied Dr. Perkins. "I'm surprised any of us are holding up as well as we are."

"I'm sure that'll all come to a screeching halt as soon as we get out of here. We'll have our own floor in a mental hospital somewhere," Brett added.

Walking over to one of the front doors, Mason pulled back the blind slightly to look outside.

"What is it?" asked Dr. Hunter.

"Oh, nothing. I just thought I saw something from the other room. It's probably just my paranoia getting me prepared for that room in the mental hospital," Mason replied, only half-joking.

"Maybe you need another beer to calm your nerves, mate," Dr. Bentley said jokingly.

"No, thanks," Mason replied. "I want to keep what few wits I have about me."

Laughing from across the room, Brett said, "Yeah, I never understood the guys in a horror movie who would find a bottle of whiskey somewhere, crack it open, and start drinking. An alien invasion or zombie apocalypse is the last place I'd want to be drunk."

With a half-hearted laugh, Mason said, "And here we are, in our very own horror movie. Only, in the movies, I can usually guess where the ending is going. Here, though, I have no clue. I just can't see it. It's not like there is safety on the outskirts of town. There is nothing on the outskirts of town here but a cold, frozen death. And beyond that—more cold."

"Just imagine how the others at the smaller research stations are doing," said Dr. Perkins. "Those who didn't leave for the season before everything started falling apart, that is. They have even fewer resources. At least Mac-Town is set up for the wintering-over crew to make it all the way through the winter. The smaller, seasonal research stations scattered about are probably finding their cupboards beginning to look bare, just like we were out at MEVO while we were waiting for a ride. They've got to be getting desperate by now."

In a grim tone, Dr. Bentley said, "Some are out there starving with nothing to eat but each other, and here we are, trying to avoid being eaten by our fellow man. It seems we have the same problem."

After a moment of awkward silence, Tasha screamed, pulling back from the window.

"What? What is it?" Dr. Graves asked.

"I saw something go past the window just now," she replied, pointing.

"Was it one of them?" Brett asked, running to the window.

"I see something," said Dr. Perkins from another window across the room. Separating the blinds with his index and middle fingers, he said, "Someone seems interested in the pub."

Joining Dr. Perkins, Dr. Hunter looked out the small opening in the blinds, saying, "It's one of them for sure."

"Why the bloody hell is he just standing there staring at us?" Dr. Bentley asked.

"We've seen that behavior several times before," replied Dr. Hunter. "My guess is it's either a distraction, trying to get us to focus our attention on that one individual, or it's a marker of some sort, pointing us out to the others. Either way, I think our comfortable stay here at Gallagher's Pub is nearing its end."

Turning to the group, he then said, "Everyone, get your cold weather gear on. You may have to get out of the building in a hurry, and you won't last long out there without it."

Looking to Mason, he said, "Only fire your rifle if you must. We don't want to attract more attention than we're already receiving. Everyone else, get your improvised weapons ready as well. Brett, you take the extra rifle we brought back. I know you can handle it."

Turning to Phillip, Brett asked, "Phil, where's the exhaust outlet for the diesel burner?"

"It's back here," Phillip said, leading Brett into the spirits storage room. Walking to the back of the room, Phillip opened what appeared to be a closet door. Inside was the diesel-fired water heater, surrounded by thick layers of insulation along the walls, with piping going in several directions.

With the door open, the sound of the burner and the water flowing through the piping could be heard clearly. "Wow," Brett said. "That thick insulation really dampens the sound. So, is that the exhaust for the combustion chamber?" he said, pointing at a six-inch section of tubular duct work that appeared to exit the side of the building through a heat shield.

"Yeah, the dumpster is right on the other side of this wall. It comes out above that."

Looking around, Brett asked, "Are there any windows where you can see the dumpster area?"

"There are no windows here because it is secure storage, but if you go into the staff restroom just off the kitchen, there is a small window that lets in some sunlight. It's not transparent glass, though, but privacy glass."

"Show me," Brett said as the two men began working their way toward the kitchen.

Entering the restroom, Brett looked up to see the small window that Phillip had been referring to. Stepping up and onto the toilet to reach the window, Brett attempted to look through the frosted glass. Unable to see at first, he wiped off the dust buildup that had apparently been accumulating for quite some time. With a clean spot now on the window, he looked again, this time seeing several figures moving around near the exhaust outlet of the diesel-fired boiler.

"Yep, they found it," he said as he stepped down from the toilet. "Let's go tell the others."

Reaching the main bar room, Brett said, "They found us, or they found a source of heat, that is."

"All living creatures have the same needs," said Dr. Bentley. "When the power went down, they too must have been forced to find a heat source."

"That's exactly right," said Dr. Graves. "There is a reason they were confined to the fumaroles of Erebus. They need heat just as much as we do, and just outside of there was a frigid, unrelenting cold. They were kept captive deep within the mountain until we freed them."

"The god of primordial darkness," Mason said, referring to the ancient Greek root of the volcano's name.

"Yes, very fitting, indeed," replied Dr. Bentley.

Interrupted by the sound of an impact against the back door, Dr. Perkins said, "What the hell was that?"

"I would imagine they are probing the building and looking for a way in," replied Dr. Hunter.

"They may not even know we're in here," said Tasha. "If they are seeking warmth, that is. Maybe they just found a source of warmth and haven't caught on to our presence, yet."

"I doubt it," Mason said, looking out a crack in the blinds toward the lone figure that still stood approximately fifty yards in front of Gallagher's. "If he's a distraction, which is one of our two known possibilities for his behavior, it's because they know there is someone who needs distracting."

"Either way, we need to move on," replied Dr. Hunter. "Whether they are on to us or not, they'll eventually get inside, and when they do... well, you all know how that's gonna go."

"What's the plan?" asked Dr. Graves. "What are our alternatives that will provide us with a source of heat that they won't be able to discover yet again?"

"Black Island!" answered Dr. Perkins. "If we can get out of here unscathed, we can take a PistenBully to Black Island. You guys said you spoke with the staff out there, right? Those guys are set up for long-term stays, with food, water, heat, and everything they need to safely remain isolated during times of inclement weather. They were isolated enough not to be exposed."

"That's a damn fine idea," replied Dr. Hunter. "But we'll need to take as much food as we can carry from here. We can't show up at Black Island potentially needing to spend the winter there on the supplies they have for two or three people. I'm sure they won't appreciate facing an early starvation because we ate too deeply into their supplies."

"What's a PistenBully?" asked Tasha.

"It's one of those red, tracked vehicles you see going out into the snow. They're made to travel in this sort of extreme cold across snow and ice," replied Brett. "I've gone out in them before, and they're quite cozy inside. Bumpy, but cozy. They can fit a driver and eight passengers, too."

Dr. Perkins added, "They only average around eleven miles per hour, but they'll get us there. They've got onboard GPS as well, which will help if visibility stays as low as it has been lately."

"I'm all for getting the hell out of Mac-Town," Tasha replied, satisfied with their answer. "Especially if no one has been infected out there."

"I think the debate is settled," said Dr. Graves. "Let's do as Nathan recommended and gather as much food as we can carry."

Working their way through the shelves in Gallagher's walk-in pantry, the group filled several sacks with everything they could find that could be seen as having nutritional benefit.

"I guess we're gonna survive the winter on bar food," said Mason, shoving a bag of sweet southern barbeque-flavored pork rinds into his sack.

"Surviving is the key word," replied Phillip, as he too filled a sack. "That's all that matters at this point."

Interrupted by the sound of an impact against the front door, Mason said, "What the hell?" as he ran back into the bar room.

"They definitely know we're here," said Dr. Hunter with his AR-15 held at the ready, facing the door.

As another impact hit the door, nearly busting it open against the lock and hinges that appeared to be weakening with every blow, Dr. Hunter said, "There is a group of them outside, ramming the door in unison. It's a coordinated effort. There's no doubt about that anymore."

Hearing a thump against the back door as well, Brett asked, "So, how do we get out of here?"

Looking around, Dr. Hunter replied, "Any ideas?" as the back door violently smashed open.

"They're in! They're in the building!" Tasha screamed.

Running toward the back door, Mason raised his AR-15 and fired several slow, deliberate shots, dropping each of the infected that entered the building.

Another smash against the front door came as the assault appeared to intensify.

Just then, the roar of a diesel engine could be heard barreling toward them. "What the hell is that?" Brett said as he approached a window to get a look at the source of the sound. His investigation, however, was brought to an early end as the bloody fist of one of their attackers came smashing through the window, followed by several more windows throughout the building.

"Shit!" Brett shouted as he attempted to hold them off with one of the group's makeshift spears, having left the extra rifle in the other room.

As the high-velocity 5.56 NATO rounds from both Mason and Dr. Hunter's AR-15's began discharging simultaneously, the noise was deafening in the enclosed confines of the building.

As Tasha screamed in horror, Phillip ran to her side, picked up a nearby bar stool, and held off one of the infected that had breached the building through one of the windows.

Hearing a crashing noise overhead, the group turned to see the roof of Gallagher's being peeled away by the bucket of a large, Caterpillar articulated bucket loader. The gigantic machine tore away the building's roof as if it was merely paper mâché.

Once a large section of the roof had been removed, the enormous bucket was lowered inside as the machine shoved against the building's front wall.

Hearing a familiar voice shout in a thick, Russian accent, "Get in! Get in bucket!" Mason motioned for the group to do as instructed. While standing by the bucket, he fired shots at the attackers who were now getting to within feet of them, overrunning the building like a swarm of locusts.

Dr. Graves, Dr. Bentley, Dr. Perkins, Dr. Hunter, Brett, and Phillip were all inside the bucket as it began lifting upward. As Tasha struggled to climb inside, one of the attackers grabbed her boot, pulling her onto the floor. Without hesitation, Phillip leaped down to help her, lifting her to the bucket, securing her safety just before being overwhelmed by the infected.

As the bucket was raised out of harm's way, Tasha held on for dear life as the others pulled her to safety. Looking down at Phillip as he screamed in terror, being consumed alive by the infected, Mason aimed his rifle at Phillip while Tasha screamed in agony, reaching out in vain for her beloved friend.

Unable to pull the trigger, Mason lowered his rifle as a shot rang out, striking Phillip directly in the forehead, exploding his head and ending his misery.

Looking over to Dr. Hunter, with the smoke from the shot still emanating from of his barrel, Mason simply nodded.

Dr. Hunter lowered his rifle, and said, "It was the only choice. It had to be done."

Chapter Twenty

Bouncing in the large, steel bucket of the Caterpillar articulated bucket loader as it raced away from Gallagher's Pub, Dr. Graves asked, "Is that your friend?"

"Yeah, that's Vasily," Dr. Hunter replied.

"Where is he taking us?"

"I have no idea, but that man has proven himself to be very resourceful and capable. I would gladly go anywhere he felt was safe," replied Dr. Hunter in a confident tone.

Speeding past Crary Lab, heading southwest toward the thick ice that covered the Ross Sea, Vasily swerved between buildings, running over or through a few pallets of pre-positioned freight that never made it aboard the transport to its intended destination.

On the outskirts of McMurdo Station, Vasily drove the large, industrial yellow Caterpillar down a gently sloping incline and onto the ice of the Ross Sea. Continuing out onto the ice while paralleling the shoreline, Vasily tilted the bucket in an attempt to shield its occupants from the sub-zero winds blowing in from the ocean just beyond the ice.

Making a turn back onto land after approximately one mile, Vasily made an arcing turn to the left and proceeded back toward McMurdo Station. With Mac-Town now visible once again through the snow and ice-covered windshield of the loader, Vasily began to slow and brought the heavy machine to a gentle stop, lowering the bucket to the ground.

Climbing down from the heated cab of the machine, Vasily rushed to the bucket. "Quickly, climb inside. Is warm. Get warm," he shouted, pointing to the steel steps leading up to the fully enclosed cab.

As Dr. Graves, Dr. Bentley, Dr. Perkins, Tasha, and Brett rushed to the cab, squeezing themselves inside, Dr. Hunter and Mason both greeted Vasily with gratitude.

Patting Vasily on the shoulder with his heavy winter glove, Dr. Hunter shouted through the howling winds, "We are damn glad to see you, old friend."

"How did you know where we were?" asked Mason.

"You were making enough noise for everyone to find you," replied Vasily. "Crack of rifle travels far. Cuts through wind. I hear clearly."

Looking up to the cab where his friends were desperately trying to warm themselves, Dr. Hunter shivered and asked, "What now? Where are we going?"

"I told you. I have safe place," replied Vasily. "Once everyone has chance to warm, I take you. Had to get away from infected. Now, we sneak back in."

Once everyone had their turn in the heated cab of the huge Caterpillar, they once again climbed into the safety of the bucket as Vasily proceeded closer to McMurdo. Once on the outskirts of the station to the southeast, he lowered the bucket to the ground, shut off the engine, and climbed down to join the others.

"Hope we not need again. Engine will not start in cold after shut down for long time," he said, pointing to the huge machine.

"How did you get it started to get to us?" Mason asked.

"Propane engine warmer," he replied.

Pointing to McMurdo, he said, "Come, we go before we freeze."

~ ~ ~ ~

Reaching the edge of McMurdo on foot, the group stopped in the cluster of diesel and jet-fuel storage tanks reaching out to the southeast from the station. After a few moments observing and looking for potential threats, Vasily motioned the group to move forward, following along behind.

Pausing, he pointed to the rifle that he still carried, saying to Dr. Hunter, Mason, and now Brett, "Use only if you must. Like I found you, so will they." Pointing to the makeshift weapons carried by the others, he said, "Use first. Use rifle only if no other choice."

Seeing that everyone understood, Vasily led the group forward, past the paint barn and the cold food storage buildings to building 637, the construction storage warehouse. "Follow in my footsteps. Do not step outside of them," he said insistently.

Looking around both sides of the building and seeing that they were alone, he opened the door and led the others inside.

Once inside, the group saw the storage of construction supplies and materials of every sort. From metal sheets, tubing, and wood, any of McMurdo's building projects could be supplied from there.

Pointing to a large section of sheet metal with an X pattern cut in several places, Vasily explained, "I make these and put underneath snow outside. If you step on X, your foot slips through, pushing the triangular cuts downward. When you try pull foot out, metal holds you, cutting leg. Is good trap."

Walking over to a large, roll-around metal supply cart, Vasily began pushing it out of the way as Mason noticed a piece of cord running from the cart and into a gap in the floor between two wooden planks.

Leaning down and working his fingers into the gap, Vasily lifted what they saw to be a hidden door, leading into a chamber beneath them. Pointing, Vasily said, "Quickly. Inside."

Climbing down a ladder fabricated from scrap pieces of metal tubing, the group found a six-foot by ten-foot space beneath the floor stocked with food, water, and medical supplies, as well as cots for sleeping.

Once everyone was safely inside, Vasily closed the panel overhead and pulled on the cord, causing the metal supply cart to once again roll into position over the entrance to the compartment.

"Wow," Mason said, looking around. "How did you know this was here? And why is it here?"

"I know, and only I know," Vasily responded. "I built myself."

"How did you dig out a hole underneath a building with no one noticing?"

Sitting down on a supply crate, Vasily ignited an indoor-safe kerosene heater, illuminating the space with a soft, red glow, and said, "I work many late nights. I also worked as winter-over crew. During winter, when only two-hundred people here, it easy to slip away and work on project. As fabricator, I have all tools necessary to do what I wish."

Speaking up, Dr. Bentley said, "If I may be so bold as to inquire, why on Earth would you dedicate so much time to doing such a thing? And here, at McMurdo? You had no way of knowing this would happen."

Nodding and taking a moment to gather his thoughts, Vasily said, "In Soviet military, I experienced many things. Many things in places people such as you never hear of. I see many bad things. I do many bad things that haunt me to this day. Most important lesson of this was that comfort and security very fragile. Is not rule of things, but the... how you say it? Exception. Yes, not rule but exception. Suffering is always on other side of corner. You may walk around corner any time. You do not know when."

Clearing his throat, still clearly haunted by his memories, Vasily continued, "Even in Soviet Union, my home, I see many people starve."

"After the collapse?" Dr. Bentley asked.

"Some, yes, but not all. Soviet government used food as weapon against own people. My parents did not die of old age. They died from hunger. They starved to death, victims of iron fist of government and chose to starve people to secure power over others. Government controlled all food. Government controlled everything. I not let that happen to me. I control me. No one else.

"I come here to escape rest of world. I did not want reminders of past. Rest of world haunt me too badly. Everywhere I looked, I saw suffering that had yet to come, but would... someday.

"Here, my mind could be free of nightmares. People here different. People here come, like me, to escape, or like you, to learn. Feeling of safety soon felt like trap. Global politics soon worked way into science, reminding me that I was at mercy of someone else, somewhere safe and warm, pulling strings of rest of world like marionettes. Maybe I'm just paranoid? If so, I have reason to be."

Looking around, wiping a tear from his eye, Vasily moved his hands around in the air like a puppet master, and said, "Dance, puppets, dance."

Regaining his composure, he continued. "I knew place such as this not protect me forever. Is only place to hide. Knowing it here gave me sense of security. Having control over one little place, one little hole in ground gave me peace."

Snapping out of his dark memories, Vasily said, "We rest now. All have long day. Wake tomorrow and make plan."

Looking around nervously, Dr. Graves said, "Um, what about a bathroom?"

Pointing at a five-gallon bucket in the corner of the small space, Vasily said, "Bucket half-full of oil-absorbing material. Is toilet for now. Put lid on when done for smell."

With a grimace, Dr. Graves nodded and said, "I guess I should just be thankful someone like you thought of everything in advance, including the toilet."

With a smile, Brett looked to Vasily and said, "There are people like you back home in the states. They're called preppers. They're prepared for anything that may come, and like you, they see the fragility of the world around us. Society likes to paint them as crazy nut jobs, but I bet if things are getting ugly back home from all of this, those people are getting the last laugh now."

"I'm sure they no laugh," Vasily replied. "They hurt for those who are not prepared. When you are haunted by fears of what you see coming, you do what you feel you must, not for pride."

Chapter Twenty-One

Vasily's Bunker

Awakening to the smell of warm, fresh coffee, Mason felt as if he must be dreaming. Opening his eyes, he looked across the small room to see Vasily brewing coffee over a small, backpack-style camping stove in a small, stainless-steel container.

Rubbing his eyes in disbelief, Mason said, "Coffee? Really?"

With a smile, Vasily poured a cup of the piping hot brew. Handing it to Mason, he said, "No cream, but is good."

"Thanks," Mason said, taking the cup and savoring the aroma.

As everyone in the room began to stir and get ready for the day, Dr. Hunter graciously accepted a cup of coffee as well, and asked, "So, Vasily, what did you see while you were out there? After the chapel, that is."

"This I have been needing to tell you," he replied. Looking to Dr. Graves, he asked, "Are you biologist?"

"Why, yes," she replied with a puzzled look, perplexed at how he would know such a thing. "How did you know?"

"Dr. Hunter speak of your group when we met. You will want to listen to what I am about to say."

"Okay, I'm listening," she replied.

"When separated from Mason and Dr. Hunter, after Neville sacrifice himself to save me, my only option was run toward berthing complex. All other routes blocked. I entered building and find something terrible."

"Neville sacrificed himself?" Dr. Bentley asked, smiling and proud of his former student for his bravery in the most adverse of conditions.

With a nod, Vasily continued, "On second floor of building two-eleven, I find nest."

"Nest? What do you mean, a nest?" Dr. Graves enquired.

"Many bodies weaved together with gray fiber. Bodies seem to be alive, but not move."

"Alive?" she asked.

"Could not move," he explained. "Sticky gray fiber wrapped them like cocoon. Other infected come and go. They attach themselves to cocoon, but not like others. They attach for time, then detach and leave. People in center of mass not move. Trapped, as if being used by group."

"But they're alive?" she asked again. "The ones in the middle of the mass are still alive?"

"Yes. Can see chest rise and fall with breath, but not try to leave like others."

Thinking through what he was saying, Dr. Graves turned to the others and said, "It sounds as if he is describing a hive or a colony-like structure."

"The ones that come and go," she asked. "How do they look?"

"Like ones at Pub. Capable of fighting. They come in from outside covered with ice from sweat. After being with cocoon, they seem to warm and leave again as if refreshed. Skin is covered with gray material. Eyes bulging and bloodshot."

"That's why their actions are beginning to seem coordinated," she said. "Once the power grid failed, the organisms must have sensed that their source of heat was gone. By clustering tightly together in a confined space, they could use the heat of the bodies woven into the hive, or nest, alive, generating heat for the others. The fibers could simply be a source of insulation, or it could be a way to transmit information throughout the hive as if each organism is functioning as the cell of a brain.

"Their coordinated actions are obviously from some form of collective thought. That may be the source where they can come together and communicate."

"Linda, at any other time I would call you raving mad," Dr. Bentley said, looking directly at Dr. Graves. "But considering all that is going on, I can't honestly find it in myself to argue the possibility of anything. However, how could something as simple as a eukaryote have advanced so quickly into a colony with collective intelligence? This entire thing baffles me."

"Like I said before," she replied, "These things may have a rapid generational cycle, allowing the information they've obtained to pass along to new generations, giving them the ability to adapt to their new environment far quicker than we could have imagined. Also, you've got to remember; this continent hasn't always been covered with ice. They could have been highly developed long before this world became what it is today. The fumaroles of Mount Erebus may have simply been a life-support system for them while they were in a semi-dormant state, awaiting their chance to escape their frozen prison."

Cutting to the point, Brett spoke up, bluntly saying, "So, what's our plan? We know we can't stay here—at McMurdo, that is. We're cut off from the world in a place that cannot support us on its own with no supply chain, with organisms that are rapidly developing to kill or assimilate us. The clock is ticking. Hiding out only works when you're waiting for a storm to pass. This storm isn't going anywhere."

"Black Island," said Dr. Perkins from across the room. "Once again, Black Island is our only rational option. We know they have comms to the outside world, and they are isolated

Steven C. Bird

from this mess with facilities to support long-term habitation. What other choice do we have?"

Looking around the room, Dr. Hunter said, "I'm in for a trip to Black Island, unless anyone else has any new or better ideas."

"Is good option. Is very good option." Vasily confidently agreed.

Seeing everyone nod in agreement, Dr. Hunter said, "Well, that's it. I guess we're setting out for Black Island." Turning to Vasily, he asked, "Based on what you saw while you were out there, how likely are we to make it to the heavy vehicle facility to acquire a PistenBully?"

Looking at the group, Vasily replied, "Maybe two or three, but not everyone. We take small group, get machine, then come back for others."

"I'm not so sure I'm keen on us splitting up again," said Dr. Bentley with concern in his voice. "We lost several people the last time something like this happened. Why do such a thing again?"

Hearing Dr. Bentley's dissension, Vasily's face tightened as he scrunched his forehead and said in a frank tone, "Lose more if not split up."

"Gerald," Dr. Hunter said, trying to dissuade Dr. Bentley from further protest, "You've not seen what he's seen. Mason and I are alive right now due to the actions of Vasily at Mac Ops. We are all alive right now due to his actions at Gallagher's Pub. He's been out there in the middle of the shit storm we're surrounded by more than anyone else in this room. What kind of fools would we be if we didn't use his experience-based advice?"

"I agree," replied Dr. Graves.

"Of course, you would agree with Nathan, Linda," Dr. Bentley quipped.

With her facial expression quickly turning to a scowl, she asked, "What the hell is that supposed to mean?"

"We're going with Vasily's recommendation, and that's that," Mason said firmly. "Unless, of course, anyone wants to strike out on their own. Where are you sitting right now, all safe and warm, Dr. Bentley? You're in a secure location created solely by the foresight and efforts of one man. Look around you and realize that your options are limited. Take advantage of the strengths of those you are blessed to be surrounded by, before either your fear or your pride get you killed."

"Hey, hey," Brett said while holding up his hands, trying to calm the obvious escalation of Mason's temper. "We'll send a small group to get the PistenBully. That's settled. Let's not let the situation get to us. We've all had a lot happen to us and those we love, without having the ability to deal with any of it properly. Let's not start to unravel now."

Looking Vasily in the eye, Dr. Bentley said, "I'm sorry, Mr... um, what was your family name again?"

"Fedorov. My name is Vasily Fedorov."

"I apologize, Mr. Fedorov. My mouth stepped ahead of my brain there for a moment. I sincerely apologize," Dr. Bentley said in a humble and reconciled tone.

"No need," Vasily replied. "Every person here free to do as he or she wishes. I hold no special place. I do what I must; you do what you must. No room for feelings in struggle to survive. Survival important, not pride."

Standing, Vasily said, "I go. I take Mason and Dr. Hunter. Good team. If not back by dark, another group set out in morning."

"Brett, that should be you and Dr. Perkins," added Dr. Hunter. "That would leave Dr. Bentley, Dr. Graves, and Tasha to hold down the fort while you're gone."

"Wait," Dr. Graves interjected. "What do you mean, if you're not back by morning?"

Sharing a look of understanding with Vasily, Dr. Hunter said, "If we don't make it, you can't stay in here forever. You'll eventually run out of food or freeze to death when you're out of kerosene for the heater. You'll need a second attempt to get to a PistenBully."

Scrunching her eyebrows, she replied, "*And if they* don't come back?"

"Then the three of you set out," he said. "What other choice do you have?"

With a smile, Vasily said, "Don't worry. Each group get easier. We take many with us if we die. Fewer infected to fight for next group."

Chuckling under his breath, Dr. Hunter said, "I doubt that's what she wanted to hear." Turning to Dr. Graves, he said, "But he's right. It is simple math."

"And Black Island will have to share less of its valuable resources, if it is only the three of us," she said while giving her best attempt to seem nonchalant about the whole thing.

"We go now," Vasily insisted. "Days are short now. We go while we have light, before extreme cold of night."

As the three men began donning their extreme weather clothing for their trip to the heavy vehicle facility, Dr. Graves put her hands on her hips and approached Dr. Hunter. "Nathan," she said. "Why is it that in your divine wisdom, you assigned me to be in the last group. Is it because you see the women as less capable than the men? Both Tasha and I are in that group."

"Not at all," he quickly replied. "I put you in that group because I knew someone had to be around to protect Gerald."

Speaking up from across the room, Dr. Bentley said, "You do realize I'm in the room, don't you? I can hear you."

Responding to Dr. Bentley with only a smile, Dr. Hunter looked at Dr. Graves and said, "Actually, it's because if anyone is going to be able to come up with an answer to this biological crisis we've found ourselves in, it's you. You need to survive to help the rest of the world deal with it. Not only are you a brilliant astrobiologist, but also, you've been at ground zero. You've been inside the mountain from which they came. No one else has your first-hand perspective. The world will need you."

Pausing, seeing a slight look of disappointment in her facial expression, he asked softly, "Was there something else you wanted to hear?"

"No. No, that answer will suffice," she replied sharply.

"Well, there's more," he said. "Just stay safe and take care of Gerald," he said, winking at Dr. Bentley. "Maybe I'll find an appropriate time to share the rest of it with you if we all get out of this."

With a smile, Dr. Hunter turned to the group and said, "Okay, we've got four rifles in total. Our group will take two with us, then I want the other two to stay behind, one for each potential group trekking out to the heavy vehicle facility. Brett, do me a favor and make sure everyone knows how to use them. In the unfortunate event that it actually comes down to the third group, I want to make sure they have every chance the rest of us did."

Turning to see Vasily climb the short ladder and remove the overhead door, he said, "Well, I guess we'd better get going. Stay safe."

As the group watched Mason close the door above them, tossing the cord tied to the metal cart down to them, they heard the cart roll over top the door to hide the entrance.

Looking at the cord as it dangled in the light of the faint red glow of the kerosene heater, Dr. Perkins said, "So, we just pull that cord and the cart rolls out of the way?"

"I believe that is the setup," Brett replied. "It's not heavy, though. In an emergency, we could shove it off the door. That would make a lot of noise, though. Hence the roll-away setup."

And with that, the group settled in to silence as each of them got lost in their own thoughts of what their fates might be.

After a few moments, Brett said, "It's plenty warm in here. How 'bout we save some fuel and shut the heater off for now."

"It'll be dark, won't it?" Tasha asked.

"Yeah, but we can do without the light," he replied. "If you're okay with that, of course."

Hesitating for a moment, she replied, "Yeah. That's fine. Save the fuel. We may need it."

~~~~

Breaking the silence of the underground hideaway, Dr. Bentley spoke up, and said, "I wonder what the current state of things back home is? Based on what that chap on the radio said, they are having quite the kerfuffle there as well."

"Don't worry, the government will handle it," Brett said with a chuckle. "But seriously, I've been wondering the same thing. There is a reason we seem to have been abandoned here. If the outbreak was isolated to McMurdo, or even to the continent of Antarctica, we would see some sort of support coming in. My guess is, they have their own crisis to deal with, and we're just not on their priority list."

"How did it get off the ice?" Tasha asked.

"A sample from deep within Mount Erebus, my sample," Dr. Graves said, assigning herself blame, "was damaged during the pack-out here in McMurdo. One of the cargo handlers was injured, and the sample was damaged. My assumption is that he was the first to become exposed."

"Patient Zero," Brett said in the darkness.

"Yes, if you want to use such terms," Dr. Graves replied. "Anyway, the source or extent of his illness was unknown at the time. Emergency medical care was given to him before placing him on a U.S. Air Force transport plane on its way to Christchurch, New Zealand. Soon after, medical professionals and those who were on the scene of the accident began to show signs of the infection, or rather, of being hosts.

"It's natural to conclude that the injured man who was transported to New Zealand was the vessel in which the microbes traveled. Now that they are unleashed in a warmer climate, more hospitable to life, I shudder to think of how fast it must have spread."

Putting her head in her hands, Dr. Graves began to weep, and said, "If I had only—"

"That will be enough of that," Dr. Bentley interrupted. "Placing blame on yourself will not help us in our situation, nor will it help those in New Zealand and elsewhere. Thousands of samples of bacteria, ice cores, and rock have been taken from Erebus for study in our laboratories back home. Any of us could have been the root cause for such a thing along the way. There was no way you could have foreseen this. This is the stuff of Hollywood science-fiction movies, not day-to-day science. None of us could have foreseen such a thing."

Wiping a tear from her eye, Dr. Graves took a deep breath, gathered her composure, and said, "Thank you, Gerald. I do promise to devote what's left of my life to the eradication of those microbial bastards. My complicity in their release from

Erebus may have been accidental, but my devotion to sending them back to Hell where they belong will be unrelenting."

Chapter Twenty-Two

Vasily's Bunker

As the day passed, the group hidden away beneath the construction storage warehouse began to fear for their friends who had ventured out in search of a PistenBully, which was their only hope for reaching Black Island.

"They should have been back by now," Dr. Graves said with anxiety in her voice. "I'm going nuts just sitting here waiting, doing nothing."

"There's no way to know how long it should take them, given the circumstances," replied Dr. Perkins.

"He's right," Brett said. "They may have to hole up in several spots along the way, looking for windows of opportunity. We can't assume they could just stroll right up to the heavy vehicle facility, fire one up, and drive away. All we can do is rest up and wait. Speaking of which, have you eaten anything?"

"No," Dr. Graves replied. "My stomach is in knots right now."

"I'm sure it is," he said. "But you'll need your strength for what lies ahead. All of us will."

Igniting the kerosene heater, sending a puff of fumes and the soft glow of red light throughout the room, Brett searched Vasily's supplies and quickly produced an unopened case of snack crackers. "Who wants peanut butter and who wants cheese?"

"Peanut butter!" Dr. Perkins quickly replied, catching a pack of crackers tossed to him by Brett.

"I'll take peanut butter, as well," replied Dr. Bentley.

"Tasha, what would you like? Peanut butter or cheese?" Brett asked, holding up a pack of each.

Reluctantly, Tasha replied, "I'll have cheese."

"Dr. Graves? If you want peanut butter, you'd better claim some before these two pigs scarf it all up," Brett said in jest.

Exhaling loudly, Dr. Graves replied, "Peanut butter, I suppose."

Handing her the pack of crackers, Brett set the case aside and said, "It could be worse," as he began devouring a pack of cheese-filled crackers."

"Yes. Yes, it could," Dr. Perkins replied.

"So," Brett said, working his way up to saying something.

"So, what?" Dr. Perkins replied.

"Are you ready to set out? If it becomes necessary, that is. Perhaps we should work on a game plan—a route or something?"

"They'll be back!" Dr. Graves snarled.

"I... I'm sorry. I was just..."

"No, I'm sorry," she said. "My mind is running rampant. I don't think I've ever felt so stressed in my life. When I was a child, my mother was seriously ill for quite some time. My father had to work two jobs to keep us financially afloat, as well as to pay for her medical care. I was only twelve, but the responsibility of running the household and caring for my mother fell to me while my father worked.

"At first, it nearly broke me. The stress of it all, a stress no twelve-year-old girl should ever feel, piled up on me with a weight I thought I could not bear. Then, one day, my father sat down to tell me that the doctors had done all they could, but my mother would soon leave us and this world forever.

"That night, I cried as I had never cried before. All of the stress came flowing out in my tears like an unrelenting flood.

The next morning, I woke up a different person. The fragile twelve-year-old of the previous day was gone. She had been replaced in the night by a strong young woman who would dutifully care for her mother until her end, and for her father, who would pass just a few years later.

"The stress I feel right now is reminiscent of the stress felt by that little girl when she first learned her mother would soon die. Only now, I can't see into the future. Back then, my fears of a world without my mother chewed on my stomach with ferocity. Now, though, I can't even fathom a world in the future at all. All I see in my future is darkness, empty darkness."

As the group sat in silence, contemplating the depth of Dr. Graves' feelings and the bleak picture she painted for them all, they heard a rumble off in the distance.

"Is that them?" Tasha asked.

"That's not a PistenBully," replied Dr. Perkins. "That sounds like Ivan."

"Ivan?" she asked.

"Ivan the Terra Bus!" he replied with excitement in his voice, referring to the near sixty-thousand-pound bus, fitted with six huge tires that are nearly six-feet in height. The massive bus with a personality of its own was used to transport passengers to and from the transport aircraft that would come and go on McMurdo's nearby ice runway.

Scurrying up the ladder, Dr. Perkins shouted, "Pull the cord!"

Pulling the cord as requested, Brett felt the cart begin to roll away from the door as Dr. Perkins shoved it open, and hurried into the building overhead.

Following close behind, the group ran to the door of the storage building, opening it to see the large, red and white, fat-tired bus barreling toward them. As it approached their location, its six large tires locked up, causing the massive vehicle to slide to an ungraceful stop.

As the door opened, Mason shouted, "Come on! Hurry!"

Doing as he asked, everyone rushed on board as Dr. Bentley said, "Careful! The traps! And Provisions! We need to bring our provisions!"

Turning to assist him, Brett and Dr. Bentley retrieved their pre-packed provisions from down below and rushed onto the bus, just as a horde of the infected could be seen off in the distance to the northwest.

Running up to Mason, Dr. Graves frantically asked, "Where is Dr. Hunter? Is he okay? What happened?"

"He's fine, and so is Vasily," Mason replied. "They're both fine."

As the door closed behind them, Brett and Dr. Bentley tossed their sacks of food onto an empty passenger seat and sat down as Mason sped away, leaving a cloud of white mist behind them as the three-hundred-horsepower Caterpillar turbo-diesel engine moved the great bus with authority.

Speeding away, Dr. Graves worked her way to the back of the bus and observed the infected in their futile attempt to give chase. Joining alongside her, Dr. Bentley sat in the seat across the aisle from her.

"Their body mechanics seem to be improving," she said.

"Yes, I do believe so," he replied. "It's quite a different scene from the stumbling beasts we encountered at the beginning of it all."

"Their motor skills, their organization, their obvious ability to work in unison with one another in coordinated efforts that all seem pre-planned—it's shocking."

"Terrifying is more like it," Dr. Bentley replied. "Just how does one contain such a thing? Especially back in the unfrozen world where life has every opportunity. I've often wondered if we were back in England right now, would these buggers be able to infect and control a fox in the same way that they control humans here? Or heaven forbid, a bear? Would humans be their vehicle of choice if this place was not so frozen and desolate?"

"You're not alone in that line of questioning," she replied. "Here, you can go for miles without seeing life. That's what kept them contained deep within Erebus. They themselves couldn't survive outside of the fumaroles, much less anything else. That kept them from making the leap. There are places on this Earth where there isn't a square inch that doesn't contain life. Can they take it all over? Can they control a simple caterpillar or field mouse? The possibilities are maddening."

"Dr. Graves! Dr. Bentley!" Brett shouted from the front of the bus.

Turning to see Brett motioning for them, Dr. Graves said, "We'd better go see what they want. Ivan the Terra Bus wasn't part of the plan, so who knows what changed?"

With a nod, Dr. Bentley followed Dr. Graves to the group gathered at the front of the bus.

Gathering around Mason, who was still driving the bus at a rather quick pace, Brett, Tasha, Dr. Perkins, Dr. Graves, and Dr. Bentley listened intently as Mason explained, "We ran into a little trouble. There must have been a hell of a lot of those bastards hunkered down in the berthing buildings. When we fired up the PistenBully, they came pouring out toward us like fire ants."

Swerving to miss the above-ground pipeline leading from the diesel storage tanks into Mac-Town, Mason continued, "Ivan fired right up. You've just gotta love a Cat diesel. Anyway, I charged at the group and then swerved away, leading them off behind me, giving Dr. Hunter and Vasily a chance to get the

PistenBully out of there. PistenBullys aren't all that fast. They could have been overrun without a diversion. They probably still had to fight off some of them, but at least the herd followed Ivan. I guess they instinctively went after the bigger target."

"Ivan has the potential to fit a lot more of their meals inside," added Dr. Perkins.

With a crooked grin, Mason chuckled and said, "Yeah, I guess so. Anyway, we're gonna meet up with the PistenBully just outside the southeast corner of Mac-Town. They've gotta take the long way around to avoid being followed, so it may take some time for them to meet up with us. For now, just enjoy Ivan's warmth and comfort. The PistenBully will be cramped with all of us onboard, and it's a rough ride compared to Ivan. Spread out and relax while you can."

Approaching their planned rally point, Mason brought Ivan the Terra Bus to a stop and kept the engine running at idle, both to be ready to depart in an emergency and to provide power for heat.

Joining the rest of the group in the passenger seating area, Mason sat down as Dr. Bentley asked, "If Ivan has so much more room, why not take him to Black Island?"

Speaking up, Brett said, "The trip to Black Island is way too rough for Ivan. There is a reason they only use helicopters and PistenBullys to routinely travel that way."

"I don't get it," Tasha asked. "Why do they keep all of the communications equipment so far away from McMurdo? I mean, doesn't that just make things harder for them?"

"It's the location of Mount Erebus in relation to McMurdo," Mason replied. "Being nearly twelve-thousand-five-hundred feet tall, the mountain creates too much of a barrier, considering our low southern latitude of seventy-seven degrees. At this latitude, communication satellites are visible very low on the horizon, not straight up, which means Erebus is directly in the path between Mac-Town and the satellites. Black Island is situated in a place that gives it the ideal line of sight to the same satellites."

Shaking her head, Tasha replied, "This place is nuts."

"Which is why it's filled with nuts like us," he replied with a smile. "There is a reason so many of us feel at home down here on the bottom of the world."

As the conversation began to wind down, Mason looked at his watch and said, "I'd imagine they'll be here any time now."

"How much fuel is in this thing?" Brett asked.

"About a quarter of a tank," replied Mason. "We didn't really have time to check off all the boxes before we got the hell outta there."

"What's plan B?" Dr. Perkins asked.

"Plan B?" Mason queried.

"Yes, plan B. You know, if they don't arrive. We can't assume anything around here anymore."

Thinking it over in his head, Mason replied, "Well, it will be dark before we know it, thanks to these damn short daylight hours. Once it is, we will be required to keep Ivan running to keep the heat going, or we'll freeze to death. If it runs all night on a quarter tank, we won't have enough to make it very far. We'd better hope they make it. I sure would hate to have to return to Mac-Town in search of fuel after seeing those things pour out of those berthing buildings like that."

"Based on what Vasily said, the berthing buildings were serving as their hive or colony," Dr. Graves replied. "It makes sense that a major concentration of them would be located there."

"Yes, but now that we know the sheer numbers of them, I'd rather not tangle with them again, if I can help it. We don't have enough ammo to deal with them all. Evidently, a lot more people were left behind at Mac-Town than we initially thought."

Shaking his head, not wanting to think about how many of the infected or the digested are, or were, friends of his, Mason said, "I'm gonna stand watch for a while. Someone relieve me in a couple of hours if nothing happens."

Standing up, Mason took his rifle and walked quietly to the back of the bus where he leaned back against the side of the bus with his legs outstretched across the seat, and simply began gazing out the rear window toward town.

Chapter Twenty-Three

The Outskirts of McMurdo Station

As the last remaining rays of the day's sun disappeared over the horizon, Dr. Graves folded some of her research notes she had been carrying, placed them securely in her pocket, and mumbled, "Where are you, Nathan? Where the hell are you?" as she looked into the darkness beyond her frost-covered bus window.

Tasha, looking nervous as she cuddled up in one of Ivan's bench seats, asked, "So, what's to keep those things from just walking up on us in the middle of the night?"

"Well, the cold, I would imagine," Dr. Graves replied. "We're quite a distance from any source of heat out here. When you factor that with the extreme cold of the nights this time of year, or any time of year here for that matter, the human hosts that the microbes, or parasites, or—whatever we choose to call them in the long run—have limitations. The bodies of their hosts would freeze solid before reaching us. Remember, that's what kept them confined to the fumaroles of Erebus. The lifeless expanse of cold was their prison."

"I still can't help but wonder what's standing on the other side of this window right now," Tasha replied.

Answering with only a reassuring smile, Dr. Graves closed her eyes and attempted to fight off the demons of her mind.

~~~~

Startled by a tap on the shoulder, Brett sat up quickly as Mason said, "Shhhh. I was just hoping you could relieve me for a while. Everyone else is asleep, and no one has offered to give me a break."

"Oh, yeah, man. Of course," Brett replied, rubbing the sleep from his eyes. "I hear that the engine is still running. I guess that's a good thing."

"Yep, but we're down to an eighth of a tank of fuel. The prospect of Ivan running into the morning isn't looking all that good. He's using more fuel at idle than I had guessed. To make things worse, it's so cold out, if we shut him down to save fuel, he may not start back up, regardless of fuel quantity."

"Better just keep him running, then," Brett said as he stood and stretched.

With a yawn, Mason said, "Yep, I don't think we really have a choice. We'll freeze without the engine, or run her, uh, I mean him, out of fuel if we keep it running."

"If we run out of fuel, hopefully, it will be after sunrise," Brett replied, taking the rifle from Mason. "Get some sleep, bud. Tomorrow probably won't be any easier than today."

"If recent history is any indicator, it will be worse," Mason said as he lay down on an empty seat, pulling his parka over him for a blanket.

After several hours of dutifully standing watch, Brett heard a crunching sound coming from the darkness of Ivan's interior. Looking to the source of the sound, he stood to look, and heard, "Sorry," from Dr. Perkins' familiar voice. "Crackers. I couldn't sleep with a rumble of hunger in my gut."

Laughing quietly, Brett replied, "Okay, I was just making sure it wasn't something eating one of you."

"It's insane that such a thing could even be a reality," Dr. Perkins replied.

"We humans have been sheltered for too long," Brett said, turning back toward the window and admiring the brilliant, colorful glow of the aurora australis.

"I mean, every other creature on Earth, with a few exceptions at the top of their respective food chains, is always in fear of being eaten. And those that are at the top of their food chain are in fear of being killed by us. We've just been spoiled, sitting at the top for so long. And that is only due to technology. There are still plenty of things out there, besides the infected, that would be more than glad to have us for lunch. Yes, we are spoiled."

Pointing to the sky, he continued, "Take the aurora australis here, for example. Both the northern and southern lights are a reminder of just how lucky we are. If the Earth didn't have its gigantic rotating iron core, creating the magnetosphere that protects us from the constant bombardment of energized particles blasting through space, our atmosphere would have been stripped away long ago, much like Mars. We are spoiled in many ways, or were, at least. It appears our luck on this planet may be running out, though."

Hearing Dr. Perkins continue to crunch his crackers in the darkness, Brett said, "Oh, well, I guess I should be happy I've had the chance to see both the northern and southern lights in my lifetime. It's been a good run."

Swallowing his crackers, Dr. Perkins said, "You sound as if you're giving up."

"No, not giving up, just accepting our reality for what it is," Brett said. "Don't get me wrong. I'll struggle and fight for survival until the end, but I'll be at peace when that end comes."

"Well, don't give in to the peace too soon. The rest of us need you," Dr. Perkins replied. "Are you ready for a break?" he added. "I'm already up. I may as well sit and look at the lights for a while so you can sleep."

"Sure thing, Doc. And thanks," Brett replied as he gratefully accepted the opportunity to put his busy mind to bed.

~ ~ ~ ~

Feeling Ivan shudder to a stop, Mason sat up and looked around. Seeing light coming from over the horizon, he felt somewhat relieved that the relative warmth of daylight would soon be upon them as Ivan fell silent, finally running out of fuel.

Walking to the front of the bus, Mason tapped on Ivan's fuel gauge in a ceremonial act of futility, and said, "Yep, he's bone dry."

"They never came," Dr. Graves said in a somber voice. "Nathan and Vasily never came."

Changing the subject, Mason said, "Okay, everyone," as the group crawled out of their sleeping positions. "I know some of you may feel the urge to go to the bathroom, but we really can't afford to lose any of our heat. We can't open the door for any reason. We need to retain what heat we have inside, as well as any greenhouse heat that we may be blessed with from the sun, until Dr. Hunter and Vasily arrive."

"But what if they don't arrive?" asked Dr. Perkins.

"We'll cross that bridge when we get to it," Mason replied.

Dr. Bentley spoke up, saying, "We appreciate your positive attitude, but I do believe we are sitting in the middle of that bridge at this very moment. Crossing it is no longer a future proposition."

"There aren't many options left," Mason replied. "Which is why I feel it in my gut that we have to stay the course and have faith that Dr. Hunter and Vasily will arrive."

"And if they don't?" Dr. Perkins again asked.

"What is your suggestion, Doctor?" Mason retorted. "I'm just a lowly graduate student here to assist Dr. Hunter, yet you look to me for leadership? My, how quickly that title reverts to nothing when the shit hits the fan."

"Dude," Brett said, attempting to get Mason's attention before his temper could get the best of him.

Looking toward Brett, the two shared a look of mutual understanding as Mason said, "I'm sorry. This is all just getting to me. I never set out to be the rock for other people to lean on. I've just been being me."

Clearing his throat, Dr. Perkins said, "You have no reason to apologize. You are right. Everything you said is right, and so far, everything you have done has been right, or at least, the best choice given the circumstances. You have become a rock on which other people lean because that is who you are. Title or no title, you are that kind of man, and I admire you for it."

With a half-hearted smile, Mason said, "Thanks. I appreciate the vote of confidence."

As silence fell throughout the group, the temperature felt as if it dropped with each passing moment that Ivan was no longer generating heat. Soon, everyone was shivering and huddled into a group in the center of the bus.

"I've got an idea," Brett said. "Let's pull the cushions off the seats and build a shelter out of them. The padding in the cushions will provide some insulation. It will be like a seat-cushion igloo. Hopefully, it will be enough to retain some of our collective body heat."

Following Brett's recommendation, the group removed each seat cushion from its frame and began stacking them around two rows of seats. Squeezing into the area, Dr. Graves, Dr.

Perkins, Dr. Bentley, Tasha, Brett, and Mason all huddled together.

"I think it's working," Tasha said. "A little, at least."

"We'll still be cold, but not *as* cold," Brett replied. "Just think about how much shivering someone does in a snow shelter when they're trying to survive a cold night. They never truly feel warm, but they have a better chance in there than they do out in the open, exposed to the elements."

Brett's remarks echoed through the minds of the group as everyone conserved their energy and held tightly to one another, awaiting whatever fate may come their way.

Chapter Twenty-Four

The Outskirts of McMurdo Station

After a half-hour of being huddled together underneath their seat-cushion shelter, Tasha perked up and asked through her chattering teeth, "What's that?"

Hearing a rumble off in the distance, Mason stood up, knocking a section of their pillow fort to the floor as he rushed to the back of the bus to get a glimpse of what might be heading their way.

"It's them!" he shouted. "It's a PistenBully! They made it!"

The seat cushion shelter toppled like toy blocks as the group rushed to join Mason in the back of the bus.

Pulling alongside Ivan the Terra Bus, the driver's door of the PistenBully opened to reveal Vasily behind the controls and Dr. Hunter riding along with rifle in hand. Exiting the vehicle, Dr. Hunter was immediately met by an anxious and relieved Dr. Graves, who embraced him with a warm hug.

"Oh, thank God you made it," she said with relief in her voice.

"We almost didn't," he replied.

"What happened?" asked Mason. "What the hell took you guys so long?"

"Is long story," Vasily replied. "Tell later. We go now. Long trip ahead."

Walking up to Dr. Hunter, Dr. Perkins said, "You guys arrived just in time. We ran out of fuel last night keeping the heat going. It was starting to get awfully damn cold inside. Ivan was starting to feel like a deep freezer. Brett and Mason here did a damn fine job of holding down the fort while you were gone, too."

"I wouldn't expect anything less," Dr. Hunter replied, glancing a smile at both men.

Squeezing into the crowded PistenBully, the group quickly got underway on their journey to Black Island. Soaking in the warmth from the Pistenbully's very effective heating system, Dr. Bentley asked, "Might I ask how long our trek to Black Island will take?"

Brett spoke up, saying, "I've been there several times while on past assignments. I never actually had a working reason to go, but I had friends who took me along for the fun of it. Black Island is actually only twenty or so miles from here, but the only passable route is far from being a straight line."

Turning back to Dr. Bentley, Vasily added, "We go on ice shelf. Only way."

"It's about five hours because the long way around ends up being over fifty miles, and this thing isn't a speed demon," Brett added. "Just sit back and relax, and rest assured you won't come across any living beings between here and there."

"It could take all week and I wouldn't mind as long as the heater keeps working," Dr. Perkins replied with a chuckle.

Smiling, Dr. Graves flipped through her notes that she had been carrying with her. Tucking them neatly back into her jacket pocket, she said, "I agree with you on that."

"What's that?" Dr. Hunter asked.

"Oh, it's just something I've been working on since the beginning," she replied. "I'm just trying to make sense of..."

Interrupted by an ominous thud coming from the direction of McMurdo Station, the group crowded the rear window of the PistenBully to see large, black plumes of smoke emanating from

McMurdo as several more thuds were both heard and felt, followed by several high-speed jets screeching overhead.

"What the hell!?" Brett shouted as the jets arced back toward McMurdo for what seemed to be another pass.

Several more explosions erupted as the jets passed overhead and turned back to the north, disappearing out of sight. Before anyone could speak, another wave of aircraft began pounding the station, this time hitting the fuel storage tanks, sending plumes of fire and dark smoke high into the sky.

"Whose are they?" Mason shouted.

"No way to tell," Brett said. "They may be F-18's, or F-16's. I dunno."

"Why? Why would they be doing this?" Tasha asked frantically.

"Eradication," Dr. Hunter replied as he watched in horror at the scene that was unfolding back at McMurdo.

After a few more minutes of bombardment, more impacts and explosions could be heard and seen off in the distance, with the thick, black smoke contrasting against the icy, white color that blanketed the continent.

"My God," Dr. Bentley said quietly, as if in disbelief. "They're hitting all the research stations."

"That's Zucchelli, the Italian base at Terra Nova," Dr. Perkins said, pointing at a billowing black cloud off in the distance.

Rubbing his face with his hands, Dr. Hunter wiped his lips and said, "Things must be worse than we thought out there. If they are resorting to this—"

"Yeah, the only way governments could justify such actions is if the crisis had reached epic proportions!" Brett interrupted with excitement. "They could only do this when the public no longer gives a shit about touchy-feely political correctness and the opinions of the talking heads of the twenty-four-hour news cycle. This is all-out war against the outbreak! That tells us everything we need to know."

"Get out of vehicle!" shouted Vasily as he leaped onto the snow, waving frantically for the others to follow.

"Wait, what?" questioned Tasha. "But...why?"

Shoving her out the door, Brett took her by the hand, helped her to her feet, and led her away from the PistenBully as an F/A-18 arced across the sky, turning toward their position as if it were positioning itself to target them as well.

Bearing down on them at a high rate of speed, the group stopped and began waving frantically to the aircraft, as if getting the pilot's attention could somehow thwart the attack.

As the jet streaked toward them, it pulled up and banked hard to the right, arcing around and away from them as if it was about to make a second pass.

"He didn't shoot!" Dr. Graves shouted. "Why didn't he shoot?"

Bearing down on the PistenBully once more, the pilot flew by at a mere fifty-feet above the ground, rocked his wings, and then pulled away, quickly disappearing into the smoky haze of the distance.

"What the hell just happened?" Dr. Perkins asked.

"He had a conscience," Dr. Hunter replied. "Our actions, recognizing him as a threat and then running away while trying to get his attention, must have clued him in that we were free from the infection. My guess is his finger was brushing the trigger, twitching and ready to fire, but he couldn't bring himself to kill innocent people. I guarantee that level of discretion wasn't in his orders."

"He killed us anyway," Vasily said in a cold, even voice. "We just die slow, now.

~ ~ ~ ~

Black Island Telecommunications Facility

"What's wrong?" Charles Koch, Black Island electronics and radio communications technician, asked.

Staring blankly at the radio transmitter for a moment, and then scanning the racks of microwave, satellite, and HF radio equipment, Black Island Station Manager Louis Radcliff, or Lou, replied, "I don't know. I just don't know."

Leaning back in his chair, running his fingers through his hair as his hat fell to the floor, Lou said, "Alaskacom is down, the microwave link to Mac-Town is down, and our HF radios are picking up nothing but dead air. At this point, if I went to the kitchen to nuke a burrito, the damn microwave oven probably wouldn't work, either. I've never seen anything like this. I mean... sometimes, we'll see disruptions in one system or another due to natural phenomena, but not all three. Not all at the same time, and certainly not at this level. We're—for the first time in my twenty years coming down to Black Island— completely in the dark."

Walking over to the rack of HF radios, looking them over in an act of futility, Charles said, "Do you think we're being affected by some sort of catastrophe up north? With all the chaos that's going on due to the outbreak, do you think a nuclear facility has been compromised or something? Maybe even an intentional nuclear blast detonated to contain the virus or whatever the hell it is?"

"I... I just don't know," Lou said, placing his forehead against the table. "I don't even wanna think about that shit right now. We're fucked, Chuck. That's all I know. We're fucked."

"Ah, man, don't give up on us so fast," Charles said.

"I'm not giving up at all, Charles," Lou replied. "I'll man this facility until the end. The people at Mac-Town may desperately need to contact the outside world. Whether it's to transmit vital scientific information that may be related to what's going on, or if they just need to call for help. I'm not sure what help we could wrangle up for them, but we can't just walk away from our responsibilities here."

"Not that we have anywhere to walk to," Charles replied.

"Regardless, I'll be right here," Lou assured, lifting his head off the desk. "Like a captain going down with his ship. I'll keep this place running no matter what, just in case. B.I. has been good to me. I owe it to her to keep her running. I... I just need to stay. I have responsibilities."

"I'm getting kind of hungry," Charles said, trying to change the subject. "How 'bout we try out your microwave-oven theory and nuke up something to eat? Unless, as you theorized, it's down as well," he said with a grin.

"Nuke? Hell, let's cook up something right. How about a homemade pizza? I need to cleanse my mind with carbs."

Hearing a thud off in the distance before Charles had a chance to reply, the two men shared a look of concern as Lou said, "What the fuck was that?"

Donning their parkas, gloves, and goggles, the two men ran to the door, pushing it open against the fierce winds that consistently pounded the facility at Black Island. Running outside, looking toward McMurdo Station, they could see black smoke billowing up over the horizon.

"What the hell?" Charles said, shouting over the strong, pounding winds.

Before Lou could respond, they started seeing plumes of black smoke rising from other locations in the distance. Speechless, they stood there, unable to grasp the situation fully.

After a few moments of bewilderment, Lou said, "If something happened at McMurdo, with fuel storage or the like, it would all be coming from right there," he said, pointing. "But that's Zucchelli, and that's Amundson-Scott, that's Casey Station, that's..."

Before he could finish, a jet appeared from over the horizon, streaking toward them.

"There's help!" Charles shouted. "They're sending help!"

"That's not help," Lou replied. "They jammed us. They've been fucking jamming us with electronic countermeasures."

"But why?" Charles asked, looking at Lou in bewilderment as an AGM-88 High-Speed Anti-Radiation Missile (HARM) detached from the outboard pylon of the approaching EA-18G Growler.

"Fucking bastards! They fucking lied to me!" shouted Lou as the HARM smashed into the eleven-meter Intelsat ground station, sending debris crashing into the men, hurling them both into a world of darkness as their bodies fell to the icy, cold ground of Black Island.

Chapter Twenty-Five

McMurdo Ice Shelf

Standing in shock and disbelief, the group gazed across the frozen landscape of Antarctica at the black towers of smoke, billowing up from what used to be research stations sponsored and maintained by countries from all over the world.

"I... I can't believe it," Dr. Graves said, breaking the silence now that the bombing had stopped.

Pivoting around, looking at each plume, Dr. Perkins said, "Well, that's it."

"What do you mean, that's it?" Dr. Hunter asked.

"We're out of options, Nathan," Dr. Perkins replied. "I mean... Well, hell, man. You've got eyes. Every option we had before us has just been taken away from us. We can't survive in this place on our own. We need shelter, supplies, resources, and most importantly, a source of resupply. It's only a matter of time, and I fear our timeline just got shorter."

Seeing Brett comforting Tasha, who was now crying in disbelief, Dr. Hunter said, "Okay, we're all a little shocked at what we just witnessed, but that doesn't mean we're out of options." Looking over to the PistenBully that still sat there with its engine idling, he said, "Come on. Let's get back in the PistenBully and warm up while we work this out."

"I certainly hope the bombardment is truly over," said Dr. Bentley. "It would be a pure shame to have survived such a thing only to be killed in some sort of second wave."

"I'll stay out here and keep an eye out," Mason replied. "I'll signal you if you need to bail out in a hurry."

Nodding to Mason, Dr. Hunter said, "There you have it. Let's warm up. I'll swap out with Mason soon, and we can keep rotating the watch while we work things out."

"I just don't see what there is to work out," Dr. Perkins said with frustration in his voice.

"It's never over," Dr. Hunter said, looking to Vasily in hopes of seeing an answer, hidden somewhere in his resourceful mind.

"There is place," Vasily said while stroking his bearded chin, deep in thought. "May be still there." Shrugging, he said, "Depends on bomb."

"Where?" Dr. Hunter asked. "What do you mean, depends on bomb?"

"Type of bomb. Is at Black Island," Vasily replied.

"But... Black Island is that way, toward the smoke. It looks like they hit it just like everywhere else."

"There is one place that, perhaps, they did not hit," Vasily replied.

"How do you know that?" Dr. Hunter asked.

"Is chance it not destroyed. We go, and I show you," Vasily replied confidently.

Turning to the others, Dr. Hunter said, "Okay, folks. Everyone pile in. Let's get going to Black Island."

Suppressing a flurry of protests and questions, Dr. Hunter assured everyone that Black Island was still their best chance, and to have faith.

~~~~

Arriving at Black Island several hours later, the PistenBully came to a stop at a scene of what, just hours before, had been a world-class telecommunications center. Reduced to rubble, with pieces of the structure blowing across the rocky, ice-covered landscape with every gust of wind, the group began to grumble at what they saw.

Looking at the sky, Dr. Bentley said, "Well, we sure burned a good portion of the daylight taking on this futile journey. We're likely to freeze to death on our way back when we run out of fuel or whatever the next disaster to unfold is."

Looking at Dr. Bentley with a cold, icy stare, Vasily turned and walked toward the site of the Intelsat system, finding the bodies of Black Island's caretakers. Kneeling down, Vasily looked them over and said, "This one die from wound. This one freeze. Leg looks broken. Could not get to shelter."

"Do they look infected?" Dr. Graves asked.

"No," he replied. "Never leave. Stay here during outbreak."

Looking down at Lou, Dr. Hunter said, "This must be the colorful fellow I spoke with on the radio. Damn, I wish we could have gotten here just a little bit sooner. We may have been able to save him."

Seeing Vasily walk toward the rubble, Dr. Hunter asked, "What are you looking for?"

Holding his hand up as if to stop the questioning, Vasily sifted through the debris. Seeing something of interest, he began pulling on a large piece of metal tubing that was once used to help support the eleven-meter Intelsat ground station.

Looking to the others, he motioned and said, "We pull. Pull out of way."

"Pull out of the way of what?" Mason asked as he walked over to comply with Vasily's request.

Heaving the fragment of the ground station's structure to the side, Vasily pointed to a metal, vented piece of tubing beneath more of the debris. "Is under here."

"What is under here?" Mason asked.

"Shelter," he replied.

With their interest peaking, the group all lent a hand, clearing debris from Vasily's area of interest. "Here," he said while pointing.

"Get tow chain and hook to PistenBully," he said to Brett. "Back PistenBully to there, then bring chain."

Doing as instructed while the rest of the group continued to clear debris, Brett moved the PistenBully into position, attached the chain to a tow cleat, then dragged the chain to Vasily.

Running the chain through what appeared to be a steel handle of some sort, Vasily slid the tow hook on the end of the chain around one of the links, and said, "Now, you pull. Slowly. Watch for signals."

Once Brett was in place in the PistenBully, Vasily motioned for him to begin moving the PistenBully forward. As slack in the chain was taken up, the heavy, tracked vehicle began applying significant force on the handle, bending it slightly. Motioning for Brett to continue, Vasily watched nervously as the handle began to creak under the stress.

Just when he thought the handle would break, the door swung open, having broken the hinges. "Stop!" he shouted, holding his hand up in a fist to signal Brett to cease all forward movement with the PistenBully.

"Holy shit, what is this?" Mason asked.

"Is bunker," Vasily said calmly as he began descending a steep set of metal steps that seemed to be a heavily-made ladder, such as that aboard a ship. Poking his head back up out of the opening, he motioned for the others to follow. "Come."

Waiting for them on the first level below the surface, Vasily waited patiently for Dr. Perkins, the last of the group to make it down, and said, "We get hatch back into position to keep in heat, then spend night here."

"Where exactly is 'here'?" asked Dr. Hunter. "What is this place?"

"Is bunker," Vasily explained.

"That part is obvious," Dr. Hunter replied. "The stairs seemed to descend through at least five feet of concrete."

"This is why I told you it depended on bomb. They did not bring big enough bomb."

"But... How did you know about this place?" Dr. Hunter asked, still bewildered by the find.

"I once tell you I was in Soviet military. I tell you I was involved with unconventional operations. I serve here once."

"Here?" Dr. Hunter said, pointing at the floor.

"No. At Vostok and Mirny," Vasily replied.

"The research stations?" Dr. Graves asked, having been listening intently to Vasily, a man who seemed to grow more mysterious with every turn.

"Everything in Soviet Union had multiple roles," he replied. "During height of Cold War, both U.S. and Soviet Union felt need to have contingency operations outside primary kill-zone of nuclear weapons. They needed sites to survive attack, that could act as critical communications relay for surviving troops. What better place than peaceful research station working only in name of science and world peace?" he said with a grin.

"Why—that's appalling," Dr. Bentley said, offended by the idea of using scientific research as a cover for military activities.

"What? You think governments around world spend money on you to expand their textbook knowledge?" Vasily replied sarcastically. "No, they fund research to increase government power. Nothing more. They do that to obtain science and technology to use as weapon, or to use as excuse for political action. They not care about causes or good deeds for planet.

"In some cases, they use science as cover for... what is word? Ah, yes. Clandestine activities. Yes, Black Island served as important communications station for McMurdo, supporting research, but government willingness to spend come from own interest."

Seeing the look of disgust on the group's faces, he added, "If makes you feel better, Black Island never used by military. Only in waiting. Very few knew of existence."

"How the hell do you know all of this?" asked Dr. Hunter.

"I tell you repeatedly, I served doing unconventional things. When part of special unit that functioned as civilian organization with authority of Kremlin, I served at both Vostok and Mirny. We work as support staff, but really act as security force in event war break out. Vostok location contains underground, fortified communication facilities with antenna arrays that could be brought to surface in few hours.

"Later, when my service was complete, I felt disgust in my heart for things government does in name of people. Things you never see. People are sheltered from true nature of government. Is like puppet show. They pull strings, you dance. You not know who really pulls strings."

Looking off for a moment to gather his thoughts, appearing to become choked on his own emotions, Vasily said, "After I leave service, friends began to die."

"Friends you served with?" Mason asked.

"Yes. I fear they were killed because of what they knew. What they knew about places like this. Huge problems if world knew about military activities on Antarctica, especially as signatory of Antarctic Treaty.

"USA and USSR both signed Antarctic Treaty in 1959, for sake of international scientific cooperation, of course," he said with a wink.

"But how did you know about Black Island?" asked Brett. "If you were Soviet, that is. I mean… wasn't it all top secret?"

"Not all men can be bought, but many can," Vasily replied. "We purchase information from man who, if memory serves correctly, is now in grand position in one of your political parties. I do not remember name, but he is dastardly man. He has done you great harm, yet those around him keep his position safe. Politics are work of devil."

Shaking his head, he continued, "As I say, government sickens me. Now, back to question. We paid informant to supply operational and structural plans of this station. We learn much from information obtained. Helped improve facilities at Vostok."

"This facility looks mothballed to me," said Dr. Hunter as he looked around.

"It is," Vasily replied. "However, one man remains to begin activation if need be. Or, one man did remain."

With a nod of understanding, Dr. Hunter said, "I presume that was the station manager? Hence his long tenure here?"

Seeing Vasily nod in reply, Dr. Hunter then asked, "What about Vostok and Mirny? Are they still staffed, or are they mothballed as well?"

"I not involved in long time," replied Vasily. "If I had to guess, I would say yes. Soviet Union, I mean, Russian Federation, does not abandon plans easily. Doctrine of staying course leads me to believe they are still here. I also believe they not bombed like rest. Russia would not allow that. The person who authorized Black Island on target list probably not know about its secrets, or too stupid to understand benefits in future. Russia not give up one inch.

"Perhaps," Vasily said, shrugging his shoulders, "they allow symbolic attack, only hitting non-military interests at locations, giving advanced warning to certain personnel, but they not allow facilities to be destroyed."

"Why didn't you want to go there, then?"

With a smile, Vasily said, "First of all, they would kill us on sight. Is very serious business. Second, Vostok too remote and Mirny too far. Too far and too rugged to travel in PistenBully. Why do you think they put Vostok facility in such isolated place, far from coast? Was not for scientific advantage, but for strategic advantage.

"Mirny station is on coast for logistical reasons, to supply and access Vostok."

Dr. Bentley spoke up and said, "The irony of it all is Mirny in Russian, or Мирный, means 'peaceful.' They named a station of war, 'Peaceful Station'."

"You know Russian?" asked Vasily with a raised eyebrow.

"Just a bit," Dr. Bentley replied. "Life can't be all about volcanos. Besides, I dated a young beauty from Russia in my younger years. I felt obligated to pick up some of the language. It turns out, what I gained from those language classes was the only thing that would stick around over time."

"I don't understand," Dr. Hunter said while stroking his beard in a moment of confusion. "You served on Antarctica in some program so secretive that it was getting your friends killed after retirement... and you came back to Antarctica? Isn't that getting a little too close?"

"One thing I learned during tour in Vostok and Mirny, is it good place to hide. On McMurdo, PhD's working as cooks in your galley, and philosophers working as heavy equipment operators. Why? Why did they come here? It was not to work in their craft, but because there was something about being free from outside world that they felt was value to them inside. This was one of few places one could escape world and simply be.

That's what I wanted, to simply be. I put my hands to work, fabricating what scientist like all of you needed for research, and tried best to forget past."

"Is Vasily your real name?" Mason asked. "I mean, if you had to hide, wouldn't you have changed that?"

Looking down at his feet, Vasily said, "The person I was is dead. That name will stay dead with him. I am Vasily now, and for rest of life I will not utter different name."

"Well, Vasily, we're sure glad to have you here with us right now." Dr. Hunter said, placing his hand on Vasily's shoulder and looking him in the eye. "Your experiences, although troublesome to your heart, are what has kept us alive all this time. We're very thankful to have you."

Responding with only a smile, Vasily said, "We rest now. In morning, we work on plan for future. Our options are becoming limited. We need everyone thinking of possibilities. Come, I show you bunk room."

Chapter Twenty-Six

Black Island Strategic Bunker

Early the next morning, unable to sleep, Dr. Hunter crept out of the bunk room and began to explore the underground bunker. Standing outside a room with warning placards for the threat of electrical shock and radiating equipment, Dr. Hunter moved the large, steel lever that operated mechanisms that surrounded the door, holding it equally tight all the way around, and pushed it open.

The weight of the door was obvious as it took a substantial shove to get it open far enough to step inside. Inspecting the door, he thought, *Was this supposed to be waterproof? Or radiation proof? Either way, it looks like it seals up tight.*

Hearing a cough behind him, he turned to see Mason standing there. With a smile, he said, "You couldn't sleep, either, huh?"

"I slept fine, but I guess I woke as curious as you did," Mason explained. "What's this?"

"It looks like the transmitter room," he said, stepping inside.

Mason and Dr. Hunter were impressed by the racks of transmitters and electronics cabinets, each fitted with large cooling fins and seemed to be made for extreme ruggedness.

"It all looks pretty old school, but sturdy as hell," Mason remarked as he ran his hands over several large glass insulators supporting massive power cables that ran between cabinets.

"Everything in this place was built for World War Three," Dr. Hunter said. "Even the light bulbs are encased in metal screens to prevent breakage. It's like a scene from an old sci-fi movie or something."

"Or the scene from a Cold War-era nuclear-war movie," Mason quipped.

Sharing a laugh, the two men continued working their way through the facility. "It's a shame we can't use all this equipment to call for help," Mason said.

"Yeah, the only help you would get would be in the form of bunker-buster bombs. We're on our own in this mess, that's for sure. Like we were saying before, if the governments of the world have resorted to the eradication of the offending microbes by the total, unfettered destruction of the source, regardless of the presence of potential survivors, things must be pretty bad. I can't even imagine that order being given, or that consensus being reached, if things didn't look so dire that public opinion either no longer mattered, or didn't exist."

"Do you have any ideas?" Mason asked.

"None that doesn't require long, dangerous scouting trips in search of resources," Dr. Hunter replied.

"That's what I've been thinking. We can survive here, but not forever. We've got to find some sort of mode of transportation to get away from this place—off this frozen continent. But the question is, was it all destroyed?"

"Gentlemen," Dr. Bentley said, entering the room and looking around, admiring the equipment in amazement. "Everyone is gathering in the little mess hall by the bunk room. I guess no one felt up to sleeping in today."

"Let's get to it, then," replied Dr. Hunter.

Entering the tiny mess hall with Dr. Bentley, Dr. Hunter and Mason squeezed inside, taking a place against the wall behind the two dinette-style eating tables.

"Well, then, what have your brilliant minds come up with?" Dr. Perkins asked.

"Well, Walt, you go first. I insist," Dr. Hunter replied smugly.

"Since you asked," he said confidently. "I think we should hunker down in here for the winter. It's coming upon us fast. We have food, water, shelter, and heat. What more could we ask for?"

"We can ask for a future, that's what," Mason replied.

"And just what do you mean by that?" Dr. Perkins quipped.

"I mean, when we crawl out of here like bears waking from their hibernation in spring, will the PistenBully start after having sat in such extreme weather for the entire season? If not, we're dead. If it does start and we use our fuel resources to travel in hopes of finding transportation resources left undamaged by the attacks, will they still be viable after having gone through the harsh winter without shelter and winterizing? Again, if not, we're dead. I don't think taking any unnecessary delays in getting off this iceberg is in our best interest."

"First of all, young Mason, this is not an iceberg..." Dr. Perkins replied in a condescending manner, before being cut off in turn by Mason's quick retort.

"No shit, doc! It's a fucking continent! I know that! Are you unable to think like a regular human being using common sense, or does that doctoral-level degree you have, hanging on a wall somewhere in your cushy university office, override your ability to think? Or, at the very least, does it override your ability to see those of us without it as being capable of intelligent thought, just as you are?"

"Hey, now," Dr. Hunter said, holding up his hands and urging calm. Looking at Dr. Perkins, he said, "You, drop the attitude." Turning to Mason beside him, he said, "And you, relax and stop letting your testosterone get the best of you. We all need to remain civil and use our brains, not our emotions, to figure out the best course of action to take."

"Mason is correct," Vasily said calmly. "Waiting will not yield any new benefits that do not exist today. It may erase them."

"Well, then," Dr. Bentley said in an upbeat manner. "My money is on Mason and Vasily. Based on Vasily's experience alone, the man knows how to keep on living in the most adverse situations, and that's precisely what I want to do. My physical comfort today does not outweigh my desire to still be breathing in the future."

"We can't wait!" Dr. Graves said, nearly bursting with emotion. "We just can't. There's too much at stake."

"What do you mean?" asked Dr. Hunter.

"I... I've been quiet about this because I didn't want to speak up before I could see something in it, something of value that might be worth risking the lives of anyone else."

Walking over to Dr. Graves, Dr. Hunter knelt down, and softly asked, "What is it, Linda?" He had seen a change in her lately. She had been more closed off than normal. He wasn't sure if the stress and despair of the situation was getting to her, or if it was something more. Placing his hand on her shoulder, he waited patiently for her answer.

"As you all know, while I was at Crary Lab, alone, before you made it off Erebus and left MEVO for McMurdo, I had Jared locked away. I confined him with his blessing. He had witnessed the changes that others who were infected were going through. He didn't want to contribute to the spread of the outbreak, so he agreed to a confined quarantine."

Clearing her throat and wiping a tear from her eye, fighting back the memories of her dear friend Jared and the suffering he had gone through, Dr. Graves continued. "Anyway, while he was still—well, himself—he allowed me to take samples of his blood and other fluids, as well as of the organic material that began forming around the corners of his nose and mouth."

Turning to Dr. Hunter, she said, "You remember the slides? The slides I showed you in the microscope room?"

"Yes, of course," he replied.

"That's when I discovered the connection between my samples from deep within Erebus, and the outbreak. That's when I was able to put two and two together to pin down the source as being the accident in the Ship Off Load Command Center and the injured worker who came in contact with the disturbed sample. Ever since then, ever since I knew I was to blame."

"Now, Linda," Dr. Hunter said, getting immediately cut off.

"Don't 'now, Linda' me!" she snapped. "I know the truth. Whether or not I played any knowingly negligent or careless role in the events that began to unfold after I left the mountain or not, I am the root source. I know that. I accept that.

"Carrying that burden with me has given me a never-ending desire to figure out a way to stop this. When we left Crary Lab, I took my notes and data with me. I've been studying them relentlessly. Brett's bracelet gave my thought process a turning point that has led me to what I now believe is a possible answer."

"My bracelet?" Brett asked, looking down at the copper bracelet on his arm.

"Yes," she replied. "Whether or not Jenny's blood had been infected in the attack that took her life, the thought of the antimicrobial effects of your bracelet gave my mind a turning point that it so desperately needed. It may be too early to tell without a real lab environment to test my theories, but I feel strongly in my heart that if I can get to a place where I can obtain living specimens and run a battery of trials based on my current theories and real-world observations and analysis, we just might be able to beat this thing before the entire world is lost."

Looking to Vasily, she said, "We have to get out of here. We must get out of here now. We can't wait. You've seen how fast this thing spreads. We have all seen the reactions of governments who have a strong reason to fear the spread of these microbes. It's getting awfully damn bad out there, and we know it. If we wait—well, there may not be a world to escape to, if we wait out the winter."

Turning to the others, she said, "We can beat this thing. I know it deep down in my heart. But now that all of the scientific facilities here have been destroyed, we can't do it without getting to a suitable laboratory environment. We need to get to a proper research facility where I can put my theories into practice."

"I'm in," said Dr. Hunter, nodding to the others. "If you need a reason to dig down deep inside to press on, there it is."

"Me, too," said Brett.

"I'm going where he's going," Tasha said, pointing to Brett. "His job as a guide and survival expert is to help people survive in harsh conditions, and if he agrees with them, so do I."

"You're welcome to come with us, Walt," Dr. Hunter said to Dr. Perkins. "But no one is forcing you."

"Of course, I'm coming," he replied. "It's die here or die out there, and I'd rather not die here, alone. Besides, Linda makes a very convincing argument. And based on her work in the past, I have every reason to have faith in her."

"I will not let you drag us down," Vasily said in a flat, serious tone.

Looking into Vasily's eyes, Dr. Perkins could see a man who had gone to hell and back, and had no plans of returning anytime soon.

Summoning the strength to reply, he said, "Yes, sir. You shouldn't tolerate such a thing, either. You'll get these people to safety. You'll get Dr. Graves to a place where she can try to end this madness. I can see that in your eyes. I will go with you, and I promise you, I will give it everything I have as well."

Following a moment of awkward silence, Dr. Hunter said, "So, we need to determine what resources could be helpful to us, and where those resources may be. Many of the research stations are spread far and wide, making it a one-shot deal either in fuel range or in the possibilities of getting stranded in the weather, or both."

Looking around the room, he said, "Does anyone have any suggestions?"

Vasily replied, "The Italians keep trawler-type boat on large trailer. It would take equipment to move, if not destroyed, but such journey may be for naught, given the accumulating sea ice as winter approaches. It may already be too late for such things. Would not know for sure unless travel to Zucchelli."

Shaking his head, and then thinking of another idea, he said, "The Brits kept Twin Otters on peninsula, but is too far," he added, as if he were merely brainstorming aloud.

"Otters?" Tasha enquired.

"Otters are airplanes," Brett replied. "Twin Otters are good passenger bush planes. They can get in and out of rough, mountainous strips with ease. A Twin Otter would be a godsend, but like Vasily said, that is way too far to travel over land, especially this time of year."

"What then?" Dr. Graves asked. "Do we even have any real options? If we found a plane, could anyone here even fly it?"

"I could handle an Otter," Brett said. "When I was working at Mount McKinley, or Denali, whatever you want to call it these days, I flew the old single-engine DHC-2 Beavers and DHC-3 Otters on skis, hauling our clients to and from the base of the mountain. Bush flying is what got me into mountaineering in the first place. I was envious of those guys I was hauling around."

"Why is it that you guys with doctoral-level degrees and professorships never have such interesting resumés?" Dr. Graves asked jokingly, cracking a smile for the first time in days.

Blushing, Dr. Hunter replied, "I guess we were too busy studying to actually get out and live a little. Maybe that's why we're drawn to crazy places like MEVO once we get the opportunity. That is, to catch up on the life unlived, I suppose."

Patting him on the arm, she smiled and said, "I guess my life was put on hold in pursuit of university goals, as well. I can't give you too hard of a time."

"What about Concordia?" Dr. Perkins asked. "That's a relatively new facility, only open for a decade or so. What do they have there?"

"That's the deep ice-core drilling project," Dr. Hunter replied. "I don't think there is much there but isolation."

"Concordia is over eleven-hundred kilometers from here," Vasily replied. "Is seven to twelve-day traverse from Dumont du'Urville Station." Shaking his head, he said, "Too far."

"Damn it! Every possibility we present has some sort of disqualifier," Mason replied. "I don't want to give up on things because they might not work out. Everything might not work out, but something might. I say we go to Zucchelli. If we know for a fact they had a boat there, we might be able to get it to the water and slip out before the ice is solid. What else are we going to do? We have to give something a try."

"We could arrive to find that the boat was destroyed in the airstrikes," Brett said. "Don't get me wrong. I'm not saying we shouldn't go. I just think we need to consider the reality of the situation. Whatever we decide to do, it may be a one-shot deal. If we arrive to find nothing is left, we may run out of fuel in the PistenBully and be killed by the elements. What about Scott Base?"

"Wouldn't Scott Base have been hit, too?" asked Mason.

"I'm sure everything was, but the strikes were most likely anti-personnel, not anti-material," Brett explained.

"Then why did they hit Black Island so hard? There were only two guys here and the place was all but erased. Well, above ground, anyway."

Shrugging, Brett said, "Dunno. It could have been ordered because Black Island had been in communication with them, and because Black Island had the ability to transmit globally. Perhaps they didn't want what they were doing down here relayed to the rest of the world? Their 'eradication at the source' plan may not have been well received by countries who had personnel in the line of fire."

"What would Scott Base have to offer?" Dr. Perkins asked.

"Arrival Heights," Vasily replied.

"What? What's Arrival Heights?" Dr. Perkins asked, confused by Vasily's vague, short statement.

"Arrival Heights is satellite ground station for Spark New Zealand. Is three kilometers away from base. Perhaps it was not targeted in strikes. If so, communication could be possible."

"With whom?" Dr. Hunter asked.

"Not at that bridge yet," Vasily replied. "Worry about crossing later." Raising an eyebrow, he added, "There may be resources outside government control that could give assistance. Especially with potential of Dr. Graves' work." Turning to

Mason, he said, "Zucchelli risky. Is past Ross Ice Shelf. Travel overland dangerous due to coastal terrain. Must travel inland and around. Take too long. Too many risks. Scott Base is logical choice between two. If Scott Base no work, continue on toward Zucchelli and accept risks. Nothing left to do at that point."

Looking around the room, reading everyone's faces, Dr. Hunter said, "Well, I guess it's unanimous, then, since no one will speak up with an objection. We're setting out for Scott Base."

Chapter Twenty-Seven

Black Island Strategic Bunker

Once the PistenBully's engine was adequately warmed by its electric block heaters and urged to life, the group loaded it with food, blankets, and other items they would need, taken from the long-term storage deep within the bunker. With everyone prepared to begin their journey toward Scott Base in hope of finding a way out of their once-beloved, seasonal home, Mason closed the passenger door as he took his seat, gave Vasily the thumbs up, and said, "Let's roll."

With a nod and a glance in the rear-view mirror, Vasily urged the PistenBully forward toward their new destination.

After a few miles of having only the drone of the diesel engine and the mechanical clanking of the vehicle's tracks to listen to, Dr. Perkins spoke up and asked, "So, if Scott Base ends up being a wash and we end up pressing on to Zucchelli, who is the skipper of the boat? If we find it intact and can get it in the water, that is?"

"I vote Linda for Captain," Dr. Hunter said. "Argh, Captain Graves, what be ye orders?"

"Oh, now," Dr. Graves replied. "The only boats I've been on are Washington State Ferries. Most of the time when on them, I just stayed in my Subaru. I'm not the nautical type at all. I definitely shouldn't be the captain."

"It's your mission, Doc," Mason said, giving her a wink. "The rest of us are just along for the ride. It's only fitting that you call the shots."

"I did some time on a fishing boat in Alaska," Brett said from the other side of the passenger cab.

"What haven't you done, Brett?" Tasha asked.

"Acquire a penny to my name," Brett said. "I've worked my whole life, but always seemed to have just enough to feed myself, clothe myself, and recreate."

"Well, Mr. Thompson," Dr. Bentley replied. "You seem to be the winner in the game here. You've been out living. You've had a quite fabulous life. You've seen and done things others have only dreamt of. If you had pursued other, loftier goals in life, what would that have gotten you? What good would your bank account do you in a world that is reeling and in turmoil as we speak? You've managed to have a life while making a living. That's an accomplishment most people will never be able to lay claim to."

With a crooked smile, Brett said, "Well, for one, I would have been thousands of miles from ground zero, instead of fighting off zombie hordes with an ice axe at the bottom of the world and at the epicenter of the outbreak."

Chuckling, Dr. Bentley said, "And what fun would that have been? You, sir, are a part of history. Whether it goes down as an historic failure, or a triumph of humanity, you are a part of it all. That is a grand life, in my most humble opinion."

"Where did your upbeat and positive attitude magically materialize from?" asked Dr. Perkins.

With a sly look, Dr. Bentley said, "I looked at you and asked myself, is that how I'm behaving? Heavens, I've got to snap out of it."

Watching to see the full expression of bewilderment and confusion on Dr. Perkins' face, Dr. Bentley said, "I'm only joking. No, I've finally come to realize anything that in this world I thought was important, isn't important at all. All my life I have been in pursuit of the esteem of my colleagues. I managed to climb my way to the top of my field. I've published many papers. I've received numerous accolades from my peers. But all of that is really quite useless, if you think about it."

Turning to Brett, Dr. Bentley smiled, and said, "Young Mr. Thompson here, has lived less than half of my years, yet has lived more than twice the life as I. He doesn't need prestigious titles, accolades, or peer acceptance. No, he's been more than that. He's been happy."

Turning to Dr. Graves, he continued, "And this brilliant scientist and wonderful human being has set out on a quest to single-handedly save the world. Why, I'm in the company of gods, riding along in this bumpy, noisy machine, yet when I was in the halls of Cambridge, I was merely in the presence of unjustified pride and a false sense of superiority."

Looking around at everyone, Dr. Bentley said, "You people have taught me more than I have learned in decades at the university. Whether I live or die on this foolhardy mission we are undertaking, it's of no consequence. I'll die having known each of you, and that makes my life truly fulfilled."

With a warm smile, Dr. Graves said, "I'm hardly doing anything single-handedly. Without each and every one of you, I would have died in the airstrikes at Crary Lab, and that's if I would have even survived that long, which I doubt I would have. We're a team."

Beaming with pride, Dr. Bentley replied, "And a damn fine team at that."

~~~~

After a long day of traveling, with the sun now far beyond the horizon, the PistenBully pulled up on a ridge just outside of Scott Base. Turning to the others, Vasily said, "Scott Base downhill toward ocean. Is on peninsula. We stay here for night.

No need for surprises in dark. Too cold to explore, and wind getting dangerous."

Feeling the PistenBully continue to rock back and forth after coming to a stop, it was clear to the group that Vasily was right. After a few moments of small talk, everyone shifted around, trying their best to get into position to sleep for the night while the purr of the diesel engine provided them the warmth they would need as it soldiered on, idling into the night.

~~~~

As the sun peeked above the horizon behind them, shining down on the remnants of Scott Base below, Vasily stepped out of the PistenBully, wiped his goggles, and looked down on the tremendous toll the airstrikes had taken on the peaceful Kiwi research station. Hearing a door close behind him, Vasily turned to see Dr. Hunter joining him outside.

"Is it a total loss?" Dr. Hunter asked, stepping up alongside him.

"Is not good," Vasily replied. "We can search for anything of use down below, then make our way to Arrival Heights. It should be warmer by then. Make wind at ground station not so bad."

Climbing back into the PistenBully, Dr. Hunter relayed the news to the group while Vasily drove the machine down the hill and onto the peninsula where Scott Base now lay in ruin.

Sifting through the debris, Dr. Graves found a concentration of human remains. Turning to Vasily, she shouted, "Mr. Fedorov. Can you come here for a moment?"

Joining her, he said, "Yes, ma'am. What can I do for you?"

Lifting up what used to be part of an insulated wall, she said, "Mason, hold this." She then turned to Vasily, and asked, "Is this what you saw in the berthing buildings?"

Looking at the bodies that had suffered catastrophic blows during the airstrikes, Vasily could see the web of grayish material stretching from a severed arm to the chest cavity of another corpse. Pointing, he said, "Yes. Yes, this was stretched all around, like web—no, like cocoon. The bodies in center of mass appeared alive, but wrapped so tight they could not move. Had no chance of escaping web. The ones on outside were still mobile. They would attach and detach after period of time. This one," he said, pointing, "looks like one in middle."

"My guess is the ones in the middle were livestock," she said. "Producing heat to keep the cluster warm, while also serving as a source of nutrients and energy. Look here," she said, pointing with her pencil. "See how the extremities of this one appears to have been dissolved away, yet the core of the body remains intact? It's as if they wanted to use them for resources while keeping them alive."

"Are you sure that isn't damage from the attacks?" Dr. Hunter asked.

"No, this is definitely the result of a chemical process and not of trauma," she replied. "I'm going to take some more notes and try to find a jar or container of some type that I can use to take a sample."

"Sample?" Mason asked, taken aback by her statement. "You want to take some of those bastards with us?"

"It's necessary for my work," she replied. "I need to study them in all stages of development. What may be a vulnerability in one stage of development may not be so in another," she explained.

Nodding that he understood, Mason went on about the business of searching Scott Base for anything they may find of use.

"Do you hear that?" Tasha said, tugging on Brett's arm as he was lifting a piece of one of the building's outer walls.

Stopping to listen, he turned to see the silhouette of an aircraft coming toward Scott Base with the sun at its back. "Plane!" he shouted, pointing at the approaching threat.

"Take cover, everyone!" shouted Dr. Hunter as he took Dr. Graves by the arm, pulling her toward the remnants of a small, green storage building. Lifting up on a sheet of metal siding, he hurried her underneath and followed close behind.

Watching to see that the aircraft appeared to be heading directly for them, with the morning's sun still obscuring the view as it approached from the east, Dr. Hunter could see Dr. Bentley frantically searching for a place to hide. "Damn it, Gerald," he said to himself as the aircraft got within range.

"Wait, that's not military," he said. "It sounds like a turbo-prop." As the full silhouette of the plane became clear, he said with excitement in his voice, "That's a Twin Otter! That's the Brits! It's one of the Otters from the British Antarctic Survey!"

Scurrying out from underneath the debris, Dr. Hunter began waving his arms and was soon joined by the others as the De Havilland Twin Otter, with skis mounted to its landing gear, banked to the right, circling around for another pass. Watching as the aircraft slowed and lowered a notch of its flaps, it made a low pass, rocking its wings and blinking its landing lights.

Arcing to the left, the aircraft made its way toward nearby Williams Field, the snow-covered, ice runway that served both McMurdo Station and Scott Base.

"He's going to land! Everyone, get in the PistenBully!" Dr. Hunter shouted.

Rushing to their trusty, red tracked snow vehicle, Vasily ensured everyone was inside, then shoved the throttle forward, hurrying toward Williams Field and their potential rescuer.

"It's coming back," Mason said with his head pressed against the side window of the PistenBully, struggling to see the aircraft ahead and above them.

Making another low pass and circling overhead, the aircraft once again rocked its wings and blinked its landing lights.

"He definitely wants us to follow him," Brett said with excitement in his voice.

Pulling just out of sight, unable to match the slow speed of the PistenBully, the twin-engine turbo-prop disappeared from view as it descended toward Williams Field.

Arriving at Williams Field a short time later, Vasily brought the heavy PistenBully to a stop as they saw a lone pilot standing alongside the aircraft, wearing British Antarctic Survey gear.

Dr. Hunter anxiously stepped out of the PistenBully, waved at the man, and said, "Well, hello, there!"

"Good morning," the pilot replied. Holding his hand up, seeming to urge the group to stop, he asked, "Is anyone sick or infected?"

"No, none of us," Dr. Hunter replied. "I'm Dr. Nathan Hunter. I'm the Principle Investigator for the Mount Erebus Volcanic Observatory." Turning to his group, he gestured and said, "This is Dr. Linda Graves, Dr. Gerald Bentley, Dr. Walter Perkins, Mr. Brett Thompson, Mr. Derrick Mason, Mr. Vasily Fedorov, and Ms. Tasha... uh, what's your last name, Tasha?" he asked, embarrassed that he didn't know.

"Roark," she replied. "I'm Tasha Roark. Nice to meet you, sir."

"How nice to meet you all," he replied. "What took you to Scott Base if you're from MEVO?"

"It's a long story," Dr. Hunter replied. "We've been through quite a bit."

"I'd imagine so," the pilot replied.

"And your name is?" Dr. Hunter asked.

"Of course," the pilot replied. "How rude of me. My name is Mark Robinson. I'm a pilot with the British Antarctic Survey. We managed to get most of our personnel off the continent before... How do you Yanks say it? The shit hit the fan? Anyway, we'd managed to evacuate a large portion of our personnel when most of the chaos began. I stuck around to retrieve several of our researchers who were working on joint research missions with other nations at other research stations. I was on my way to Concordia when the airstrikes began. Concordia was destroyed before I was even half-way there. I put her down on the plateau to wait things out. I didn't want to get shot down. This has all been madness, and I didn't know what else to do.

"When it all seemed calm and the radios were quiet, I took off again and headed back this way. Luckily for me, we carry an engine heater or I would have never gotten her started again. I nearly froze to death sleeping in the plane.

"I overflew McMurdo before I came here, hoping to find other survivors, but saw none. I then flew toward Scott Base, and there you were."

"We were on our way to Black Island when the airstrikes began. We've been hoping to find a way out of here," Dr. Hunter said, pausing for a moment to feel the pilot out. "Might you be that way out of here?" he asked.

"Certainly. If we can find fuel, that is. If I would have made it all the way to Concordia, my fuel would have been completely exhausted, as I had planned to fuel up there before returning. Stopping halfway and then flying back put me on fumes. I was getting ready to call it quits when I saw you. I'm afraid I don't have enough fuel to get us anywhere at the moment, and the fuel-storage facilities at both McMurdo and Scott seem to have been destroyed."

Vasily nodded to the pilot and asked, "Do you have way to heat fuel?"

Looking at Vasily with a semi-confused expression, Mark replied, "If you mean heat-exchangers in our fuel system, yes. In fact, due to the nature of our operations, we have retrofitted an auxiliary heat-exchanger for good measure."

"Are you willing to run kerosene?" Vasily asked.

"Kerosene?" Mark replied. "Well, I suppose. I mean, it's basically the same thing as JET A and the JP5 we generally use down here.

"If survived bombs, I have kerosene," Vasily replied.

"How much?" Mark asked.

"Three thousand liters," Vasily replied.

A look of shock and amazement swept through the group.

"But how could it have possibly survived the bombardment?" Mark asked with skepticism in his voice.

Dr. Hunter smiled and said, "Vasily here, is a very resourceful man. He never ceases to amaze and surprise us."

With a smile, Mark reached out his hand and said, "Well, then, I do believe we have entered into a mutually beneficial relationship."

Chapter Twenty-Eight

Williams Field

After an in-depth discussion, sharing the plights of each of their groups during the crisis they all had faced, as well as details of Dr. Graves' work and her potential for a breakthrough that could lead to a turning point for humanity, British Antarctic Survey pilot Mark Robinson thought deeply about what was said. After considering what he had been told, he said, "As part of our evacuation, we relocated several of our scientists and researchers to a secure location on the Falkland Islands. They have laboratory facilities there. It has been used as both a jumping off point and a fall-back research facility during winter months when a departure from our Antarctic Peninsula locations was required due to severe winter conditions.

"Several of the researchers that have been evacuated to our site there are in fields similar to yours and may be able to lend a hand in your research. Dr. Simon Kelly is a brilliant microbiologist, Dr. Winston Harrison is, I believe, a biochemist and Dr. Samantha Gibson is a molecular biologist. There may be a marine biologist or two on hand as well. It was such a frantic scene I couldn't take note of it all. All three of the aforementioned are quite terrific people, and with the global travel ban in place, will more than likely not be able to leave the Falklands anytime soon."

"Global travel ban?" Dr. Hunter asked.

"Yes, well, after my final departure from the Falklands en route to the Rothera Research Facility on Adelaide Island, we were informed that a global travel ban had been put in place to help prevent further spread of the outbreak."

"That won't do a damn bit of good," Dr. Hunter replied. "Borders are just a make-believe line drawn on a map. Governments can't stop the spread of this by mere executive action and mandates."

"I imagine they want to at least limit the spread of the outbreak via mass transit or air travel," Mark replied.

"I suppose," Dr. Hunter begrudgingly agreed.

"So, as I was saying," Mark continued. "We received word that all international travel had been restricted as a result of a meeting of the United Nations and a consortium of nations around the world, formally not part of the UN, and that the ban would remain in place until further notice."

"How rapidly had it been spreading?" Mason asked.

"My only exposure to the outside world was in the Falklands," Mark replied. "Most media sources, as well as the Internet, were down. Most communication had reverted to ground-based radio and some limited satellite communications. Whether or not those other methods of mass communication have been physically compromised, or if they were simply left unstaffed, I do not know. The people in the Falklands were basically on lockdown, only receiving information as disseminated by the British Government."

Pausing for a moment, Mark looked at the group and said, "The situation was changing so rapidly, I really don't know what the conditions are like at this point. It seemed each day that the world had changed to a state that was unrecognizable from the previous day. I could have never expected the world to begin crumbling so fast."

"This is unlike anything we've ever dealt with," Dr. Hunter replied. "It's going to take a lot of hard work, and perhaps a miracle, to put the genie back in the bottle."

"That's the perfect analogy," Brett said as he thought about the magnitude of what they were being told. "The bottle being Mount Erebus. It's as if God put those microbial demons in the most remote place on Earth, deep underground, inside the walls of a gigantic volcano whose lava shafts reach to the center of the Earth, and then, we unwittingly uncorked the bottle. It's as if we freed the demons from the fiery depths of Hell."

Changing the subject, Mark said, "So, tell me about this kerosene you fellows have stashed away."

"We travel to McMurdo," Vasily said. "I show you. We bring back with PistenBully, pull on sled or trailer. Without front-end-loader, we will not be able to put on top on rack. Barrels too heavy to lift high up."

Looking around, Mark said, "It will be far too cold in the Otter for anyone to stay behind without the engines running to provide heat. Everyone will have to travel to McMurdo to retrieve the fuel."

"Let's get to it, then," said Dr. Hunter as the group began to mentally prepare themselves for a return to McMurdo Station.

~ ~ ~ ~

Approaching McMurdo Station, the PistenBully chugged on as the occupants surveyed the devastation of the airstrikes. A thick, black cloud of smoke still filled the air, emanating from what remained of the above-ground fuel storage tanks.

"Damn," Mason said. "They really hit this place hard."

"It was the root of the evil," Brett replied.

"They didn't leave a building untouched," Dr. Perkins noted.

Scanning the area for threats, the groups saw that several of the buildings were partially burned and had collapsed, yet still maintained some form of their previous structure.

Driving past the remains of the above-ground fuel storage tanks, the smoke was so thick, several in the group began coughing as they each tried to cover their mouths with their scarves or parkas.

"There," Vasily said, pointing to the remains of an unheated storage shed that now lay nearly flat, its walls having been blown over by the devastating explosion from the fuel storage tanks. "Is not burned, just damaged," he said, pulling the PistenBully to a stop.

Tugging on Dr. Hunter's arm, Dr. Graves said, "Nathan, Brett and I are going to try and find tissue samples from the remains of the infected. We will need to travel toward the berthing area, since that was where the mass concentration was, including the hive-like mass that Vasily described."

"Absolutely not," Dr. Hunter replied. "We need to get the fuel and get out of here."

"What good is escaping if we can't answer the questions we need to answer once we reach the Falklands? I need samples from the microbes in their most advanced form to fill in the gaps in my research."

Looking at Brett, Dr. Hunter knew he wasn't going to talk them out of it, as Brett said, "We're going, Doc. That's that. I was with her when we discovered these microbial monsters, and I'm gonna be there with her until we see it through."

"Okay," he said, going against his gut. "But make it quick."

"We will need everyone else to help lift barrels from below," Vasily said. "Are underground. Like bunker."

"We'll be fine," Brett said as he and Dr. Graves turned to begin working their way toward the remains of the berthing buildings.

In a firm tone, Dr. Hunter insisted, "Well, then for God's sake, take a rifle. Brett, you just stand watch while she works.

You can't afford for both of you to get distracted out there alone."

Looking to each other, Dr. Graves and Dr. Hunter shared a look of uncertainty. As Brett took one of the AR-15's from the PistenBully, Dr. Graves gave a final nod to the group and turned to follow along with Brett. Disappearing into the thick, black smoke that emanated from the burning debris that was now casting an ominous shadow over McMurdo Station, the two were gone in an instant.

Watching Linda and Brett walk away, disappearing into the haze of the smoke, Dr. Hunter's stomach was in knots with the fear of what may come. In this new world, he had learned that death was around every corner. Unlike before, when he and his friends and family lived in the relative safety and security provided by the seemingly permanent protection of living in the first world, he and the friends alongside him faced a never-ending threat. Would they die from exposure to the extreme elements of Antarctica? Would they die a violent death at the hands of the infected, or even now, at the hand of the world governments that sought to eradicate the source of the outbreak? Or would they simply starve to death, stranded on the ice, after having successfully survived the myriad dangers they had encountered?

Watching her and Brett walk away left him feeling vulnerable, as if the outcome of the group was now more uncertain than ever. Now that they had met Mark Robinson, they had a chance, a hope of getting off the ice and returning to a more habitable climate, even if it wasn't home. He didn't want anyone else to succumb to the dangers that constantly presented themselves, but he knew she was right. Without risks and without taking chances to gain what she must in order to achieve her goals, all of their efforts might be for naught. If they couldn't help save the world from the doom that was sweeping across it like a wildfire, what would be the point of living, anyway?

Shaking his head, snapping out of his momentary trance-like state, Dr. Hunter heard Vasily talking with the others. Vasily said, "We move debris, then dig."

"Dig?" Mason asked.

"Yes. Dig. Thirty to forty centimeters of ice and snow over entrance," Vasily replied, pointing underneath the former storage building's wall panels that now lay flat on the ice.

Pulling the emergency pickaxe and shovel off the PistenBully, Mason and Mark began to chip away at the frozen surface while Vasily, Dr. Perkins, and Dr. Bentley began dragging the remnants of the building out of the way.

Seeing Tasha shivering in the extreme cold, Vasily said, "You stand lookout. Keep us safe. You can do that from inside PistenBully. Bang on window if see something."

Nodding in reply, shivering too hard to speak, Tasha quickly took Vasily up on his offer and climbed back inside their vehicle.

Reaching approximately one foot in depth, Mason's pickaxe struck something, causing his pickaxe to bounce off, making a metallic thud sound. "Is door," Vasily said. "Keep digging."

"Mason," Mark said. "If you chip away at it, I'll shovel your bits of ice out of the way. It'll go faster if we work as a team, instead of randomly digging away."

Nodding in agreement, Mason followed Mark's request and the two began to make steady progress, uncovering an industrial yellow metal door.

"Was door of old diesel generator housing," Vasily said. "I use for roof and door of storage."

"How did you dig this?" Mason asked.

"Many hours working in cold," Vasily replied. "Weather in winter-over bad, but very few people. Get much work done if willing to freeze and work in dark. Also, no one around to see what I do with equipment."

"You're something else, Vasily," Mason said, smiling under his extreme weather face mask.

Feeling the sweat they had worked up begin to crystallize on their skin, Mark said, "We've got to get back inside the PistenBully soon. We're going to get frost bite."

"I hope Dr. Graves and Brett are okay out in this," Dr. Hunter said, still distracted by their absence.

"Maybe they'll luck out and find a bit of warmth from a still smoldering building," said Dr. Bentley, trying to ease his friend's worries.

Taking the pickaxe from Mason, Vasily began prying on the door, breaking it free from the frozen grip of the ice around it. Lifting the door open, the men could see fifteen, fifty-five-gallon steel barrels down in the crude, icy pit.

"How long have you been storing this?" Mark asked.

"Since last winter-over," Vasily said. "Is stabilized. Is good," he said, nodding to assure Mark that it would be suitable for their needs.

"How in heaven's name do we get it back to the airplane?" Dr. Bentley asked.

"Make skid out of building walls," Vasily said, pointing at the debris. "We pull with tow chain. Use straps to keep barrels on."

"Well, let's get to it, then," Dr. Hunter said as he turned to retrieve the tow chain and straps from the PistenBully.

Chapter Twenty-Nine

McMurdo Station

As they worked their way through the blinding smoke, Brett and Dr. Hunter stuck closely to one another to avoid being separated in the eerie, low-visibility conditions.

"Of all the times I cursed the wind, I wish it was blowing now to clear some of this smoke," Brett said with a cough.

Clearing her throat, irritated by the bitter fumes, Dr. Graves asked, "Do you recognize anything?"

"It's hard to make anything out. They really hit this place hard."

Nearly stumbling on a piece of a curved, white structure, Dr. Graves said, "What is this?"

Looking around, trying to focus his eyes as they burned from the fumes of smoldering insulation and building materials, Brett pointed to the side, and said, "That looks like the siding material that was on Mac Ops. I would assume that's a piece of one of the large antenna-dome structures that was mounted on the roof."

"I guess we have a rough idea where we are, then," she replied.

"So, what's our goal?" he asked.

"I want to get to the berthing complex. I need to get a sample or two from the hive-like area Vasily described. That's probably the peak stage of their development."

"One can hope," Brett replied, hesitant to assume the microbial menace wouldn't continue to rapidly evolve and adapt past what they had already witnessed. Regaining his bearings, he pointed and said, "If this is, or was, Mac Ops, we need to head that way, if I am oriented correctly."

Continuing along the path he directed, Dr. Graves and Brett worked their way through the debris. Pointing down, Brett said, "This looks like the heating ductwork that led to the dormitory, or, um, berthing buildings. I forget they use Navy lingo since this used to be a U.S. Naval facility."

Following along the trail of debris, the smoke began to clear as the two got further from the burning residue in what used to be the station's fuel storage tanks.

Exiting the smoke, Brett grabbed Dr. Graves by the arm as she began moving forward with urgency in her steps.

"What? What is it?" she asked, anxious to get her samples and get back to the others.

"Let's not be too hasty," he replied. "Let's observe for a minute. The dorm buildings were not completely destroyed. They were hit, but it appears not as directly as the rest of the station. There are plenty hiding places in that rubble."

Standing there, still and silent, Brett and Dr. Graves visually scanned the area. The berthing buildings, formerly the lodging facilities for the researchers and staff of McMurdo Station, were mostly destroyed, yet heaping piles of debris still stood at the structures that had received only indirect hits.

Brett's eyes darted all over the areas where he felt there was sufficient room for a man-sized threat to remain sheltered from the elements. Not seeing any signs of movement, he said, "Well, what do you think?"

"The hive-like mass would be toward the center of a building, based on Vasily's accounts."

"Logic would dictate, assuming of course, that logic was involved, that the main colony would want to be located in not only the center of a structure but also the center of the complex.

Let's start with the rubble in the center and go from there," she said, pointing.

Taking his rifle off his shoulder, Brett checked to ensure a round was in the chamber and that the magazine was fully seated. Positioning it at the low ready, he followed alongside Dr. Graves, continuously scanning their surroundings for movement.

Standing on the edge of a pile of debris as Dr. Graves began climbing through it, looking for what she needed, Brett dutifully stood watch. Turning toward her, he asked, "Do you see anything?"

"Too much heat went through here. Everything is charred. Let's look at the one that's partially standing."

"I was afraid you were gonna say that," Brett replied.

"What? What's wrong?" she asked.

"If I were a host for an army of man-eating microbes, that's where I'd be looking for shelter from the elements."

Thinking his statement over, she replied, "It looks to me like the airstrikes did their job. There's nothing left alive. This may be a bust for us."

Following Dr. Graves to the next building at the far end of the complex, Brett scanned the area as she approached the remains of partially standing structure. As she began to climb through the debris on the outer edges, she said with excitement in her voice, "Come look at this!"

"What is it?"

"It looks like a mass of that sticky, web-like structure that Vasily described."

Retrieving a sample jar from her bag, Dr. Graves used a piece of metal debris to tear a piece free. Scraping the sticky material into her container, she tossed the now-contaminated piece of debris aside and screwed the lid on tight. "The webbing in that material seems to have a very high tensile strength for an organic material, which I assume is made of living, or formerly living, cellular structures."

Climbing further into the debris, Dr. Graves began looking for other types of samples when she heard Brett say, "You're making me nervous."

Looking back, she said, "Nervous, why?"

"Because the further you go into that pile of rubble and beams, the longer it will take you to get out in a hurry."

"Let's just hope I don't have a need to get out of here in a hurry," she replied.

~ ~ ~ ~

Meanwhile, at Vasily's underground fuel storage location, the men were feverishly working to fashion a drag sled out of the building materials they had available.

"Walls make good skid," Vasily said. "Mason, use pickaxe to poke holes for chain along this edge."

"That should work nicely," Dr. Bentley said, admiring Vasily's resourcefulness. "The corrugation of the metal sheeting will do nicely to both help reduce drag by reducing the surface area making contact with the ground, as well as aiding in directional stability. We wouldn't want our last hope to be flailing about behind us uncontrollably."

Pulling the pickaxe free from the metal, Mason said, "Here ya go."

"Good... Is Good," Vasily replied as he began weaving the chain in and out of the holes across the leading edge of the wall material. Bringing the hook on the end of the chain out of the final hole, he pulled the chain, adjusting it to where it could be hooked onto itself in the center of the width of the metal sheeting, forming a coat-hanger-type shape that would provide even load distribution throughout the skid. From the hook where the chain met at the neck of the coat hanger, Vasily then ran the remainder of the chain in a straight line toward the PistenBully, and said, "Dr. Hunter. Please back vehicle to chain."

Replying with a nod, Dr. Hunter climbed aboard the PistenBully and backed it into position following Vasily's hand signals.

Bringing the vehicle to a stop upon seeing Vasily's clenched fist, Dr. Hunter reached for the door handle as he heard Tasha ask, "Do you think this will work?"

With a reassuring smile, Dr. Hunter replied, "If you're going to have to go through a catastrophic event such as this, there are never any guarantees. But if you must, it's best to be with a man such as Vasily. I have every faith that we'll pull it all together and make it out of here in one piece."

Responding with only a smile, Tasha turned her attention back to the world outside the Pistenbully's window, dutifully scanning the area for threats.

Joining the other men behind the vehicle, Dr. Hunter approached as Vasily pointed and said, "Climb down in hole and help lift barrels out."

Doing as they were asked, Mason and Dr. Perkins climbed down into the hole, and said, "Um, guys. We're gonna need some help down here."

"Oh, of course," Dr. Bentley replied. Climbing into the hole alongside them, Dr. Bentley looked to the others and said, "Hand me the end of one of those straps. Young Mason, Walt and I will work it around the barrel and tie it off, then as we begin to lift, you chaps can pull. Perhaps with such a joint effort, we can lug this heavy bastard out of here."

Lifting as hard as they could, Mason, Dr. Perkins, and Dr. Bentley got the barrel to begin tilting upward as the others began to pull. "There we go, mates!" Dr. Bentley said. "I do believe it is working."

As the heavy barrel of fuel slid onto the surface above, Dr. Perkins quickly climbed up, removed the strap, and with the help of Mark, began rolling it to the skid. Tossing the strap back down to Mason and Dr. Bentley, Vasily and Dr. Hunter helped them ready the next barrel for retrieval.

Looking up to Vasily, Mason asked, "How in the hell did you expect to get these out of here by yourself?"

"I never plan to be alone," he replied. "Also, I assumed I would have front end loaders and other vehicles if I ever needed to recover fuel. I not anticipate bombs from planes would destroy equipment. In the event I alone, would use pumps, not lift barrels."

Once the last of the barrels had been pushed and heaved to the surface, the men rolled it into position and began strapping them together on their makeshift sled with the ratchet straps from the PistenBully.

Tugging hard on the straps, then shoving on the barrels, Vasily said, "Is good. Will work."

Placing his hands on his hips, Dr. Hunter looked around and said, "I think I had better go look for Linda and Brett."

Shaking his head, Vasily said, "No! Absolutely not. No sooner than you would leave, they would return. Then we would have to send help to find you. No. We wait. Wait for their return or sign."

"Sign of what?" Dr. Hunter asked.

Pausing before he replied, Vasily said, "We will all know when and if it comes."

~ ~ ~ ~

Looking around nervously, Brett mumbled to himself, "Come on. Come on. You're taking too long," as he looked back over his shoulder to see Dr. Graves climbing and sifting through the rubble.

"I think I've got it!" she said.

"Got what?"

"There's a body. I believe she was infected. She's frozen stiff, so the material I need for a host sample during the advanced stage should be well preserved."

Turning to Brett, she shouted, "Come give me a hand."

Placing his index finger over his lips, he replied, "Okay, but don't be so loud."

"From the looks of it, the airstrikes were quite successful in eradicating them," she said as she turned back to the body to find that the hand was no longer there.

"What the hell?" she mumbled as her boot was pulled violently into the pile of broken timber and building materials.

Seeing her body suddenly jerk down against the rubble, Brett slung his rifle over his shoulder and ran straight for her, leaping from beam to beam, scurrying up the jagged, wire-and-pipe riddled debris pile as fast as he could.

Screaming, Dr. Graves shouted, "Brett! Help me! Oh, dear God, help me!"

Arriving at her location, Brett looked into the debris below and saw the hand of one of the infected pulling on Dr. Graves' boot. Her leg was bending against an obstruction, causing her intense pain as her knee was being hyperextended to a very unnatural position.

Being out of reach from his knife or axe, Brett aimed his rifle at the creature's hand and squeezed the trigger, striking it in the wrist. With the hand still gripping firmly onto her boot, he fired another shot, severing the hand, freeing her from the creature's tight embrace.

Frantic and in pain, Dr. Graves did not waver from her mission. Tossing her bag to Brett, she said, "Get me a sample dish," as she pulled out her knife and began removing a portion of the hand which was still gripping her boot. "Luckily, being nearly frozen, there wasn't much material splatter from your shots. We may not have been exposed. I'll remove my boots and toss them as soon as we make it back, just to be sure," she said.

Once her sample was safely inside her container, she tossed her contaminated knife into the debris pile and said, "Okay, we've got it. Let's go."

Standing next to her, Brett reached out his hand to help her to her feet as she winced in pain. "Shit! My knee," she said, unable to put weight on it.

"Suffer through it," he said. "When we get to the ground, I'll carry you, but I need you to help me get you off the heap."

Working their way down, she winced and cried out in pain with every step and every movement.

"Come on," he said. "We're almost there."

Looking up, Dr. Graves saw the infected bodies of the residents of the dormitory building working their way out of the rubble. "Shit!" she screamed, "Hurry!"

"There must be a pocket or area under the rubble where they've hived back up," he replied.

Realizing they wouldn't make it to the ground at their current pace, he leaped toward Dr. Graves, landed on a broken beam, and threw her over his shoulder with his rifle in one hand while holding on to her legs with his other.

Leaping to the ground, his legs collapsed under the weight of the impact, causing the two of them to roll on the soot-covered ice and snow. Quickly sitting up, aiming his rifle at the closest of their pursuers, Brett aimed and squeezed off several shots as he realized they were quickly being surrounded. The infected were crawling out of the debris like cockroaches, some of which were missing arms and showing signs of severe trauma from the attacks.

"Fuck!" he shouted. "I don't even have enough ammo to deal with all of them."

~~~~

Warming themselves in the cozy passenger compartment of the running PistenBully, the group patiently waited for Brett and Dr. Graves' return.

"How long will be flight?" Vasily asked Mark.

"It depends on the winds aloft, but it should be approximately—"

With the conversation interrupted by the sounds of gunfire in the distance, Dr. Hunter jumped up, banging his head against the low ceiling of the vehicle. "It's them!" he shouted. "We've got to help them!"

Opening the door and jumping out, Dr. Hunter slipped and fell in his haste. Quickly getting up and dusting the snow off his rifle, he heard Vasily say, "Dr. Hunter, I go. You stay with others."

"Hell, no, I'm not staying! They need us! They need all of us!" Dr. Hunter shouted frantically.

"I'm going, too!" demanded Dr. Bentley.

Looking to the others as they exited the vehicle, Vasily said, "Pilot! You stay with Tasha." Pointing to Dr. Perkins, he said, "You stay as well. Mason, you make sure they get out of here if we do not return."

"Hell, no, I'm going!" Mason shouted.

With a serious look on his face, Vasily said, "No! Someone must survive. All of this cannot be for nothing! Dr. Graves left notes and data behind. See that they get put to good use wherever you go. I trust you to get them out of here if we do not return. Do not let me down."

Nodding that he understood, Mason and Dr. Perkins watched as Vasily, Dr. Hunter, and Dr. Bentley ran toward the sound of the gunshots, disappearing into the smoke.

Nearing the area from where the gunshots had come, Vasily handed his rifle to Dr. Bentley, and said, "Go! Hurry! I catch up!"

"What are you doing?" Dr. Hunter asked, confused by Vasily's sudden change of course.

"Go!" Vasily demanded.

Running on ahead, Dr. Hunter and Dr. Bentley emerged from the smoke to find Dr. Graves sitting on the ground while Brett stood beside her, firing into the advancing crowd of the infected.

"Come and get me, you sons of bitches!" Dr. Hunter yelled as he began firing into the group.

While some in the group turned their attention to Dr. Hunter and Dr. Bentley, others ignored their distraction and continued advancing toward Brett and Dr. Graves.

Firing their rifles as best they could, dropping many of the infected, Dr. Bentley, unfamiliar with firearms, shouted, "I'm empty! I'm out!"

Dropping the spent magazine from his own AR-15 to the ground, Dr. Hunter quickly reloaded, chambered a round, and handed it to Dr. Bentley, taking his empty weapon and quickly reloading it as well.

With both of them back in the fight, they once again fired continuously, dropping many of their attackers. Looking to Brett when they heard him shout, "I'm out! I'm empty!" a feeling of helplessness swept through Dr. Hunter and Dr. Bentley as they watched the group close in on their two friends.

"Damn it! What do we do?" shouted Dr. Hunter, realizing they were severely outnumbered.

Just then, from out of his peripheral vision, Dr. Hunter saw Vasily running full force toward the horde of infected.

"What the hell does he have?" Dr. Bentley asked.

"Looks like a pipe," Dr. Hunter replied. Thinking quickly, he shouted, "Cover him! I don't know what the hell he is doing, but cover him!"

Firing at the infected getting within reach of Vasily, the two were in shock to see him run directly into the center of the horde. Swinging his pipe wildly, knocking many of them out of the way, Vasily looked at Dr. Hunter, and with calm in his voice, said, "Get her out of here. Get her to where she can help stop this."

"What are you doing?" Dr. Hunter shouted as Vasily ignited something at one end of his pipe. As the end of the pipe began to smolder, Vasily looked into the crowd before him, let out a primal scream, and dove straight into them.

Almost instantly, before any of the infected could sink their teeth into him, a violent explosion erupted, sending Vasily and at least twenty of the infected to their deaths.

As the smoke cleared, with his ears still ringing from the explosion, Brett saw a gap in the horde. Picking Dr. Graves up, he tossed her over his shoulder, and ran with every ounce of effort he could muster, narrowly avoiding the outstretched hands of the surviving infected.

Following along behind, Dr. Hunter and Dr. Bentley provided cover as the group disappeared into the thick, black oil-fired smoke from which they had come.

~ ~ ~ ~

Hearing the explosion, Dr. Perkins stepped back out of the PistenBully and said, "Dear God. What the hell is going on out there?"

Turning to Mark, he said, "Get this thing ready to move. I hear something coming."

As Mark familiarized himself with the controls of the PistenBully, Dr. Perkins saw a figure emerge from the smoke. "It's Brett!" he shouted as Brett collapsed on the ground, dropping Dr. Graves as he coughed violently from smoke inhalation.

Running to her side and attempting to get Dr. Graves to her feet, Dr. Perkins heard her cry out in pain. Realizing the extent of her injury, he quickly picked her up and carried her to the PistenBully, placing her inside where Tasha could begin to care for her.

Turning back, he saw Mason helping Brett to his feet, followed by Dr. Hunter and Dr. Bentley emerging from the smoke. Hurrying them inside, Dr. Perkins looked back toward the smoke and asked, "Where is Vasily?"

"Just go!" shouted Dr. Hunter.

Seeing a massive horde of the infected emerge from the smoke, he climbed in, shut the door, and patted Mark on the shoulder as the PistenBully began making its way toward Williams Field where their aircraft waited.

As the vehicle rumbled on, Dr. Bentley stared out the front window in disbelief of what he had just witnessed. That strange man. The Russian with a past very few men could have lived through, who had helped them all survive up to this point, had given his life to save them. Unable to understand such an act, he wiped a tear from his eye, and said, "Fedorov."

"What?" Mark asked from the driver's seat.

"Fedorov. Vasily Fedorov. That was his name."

"Where is he? What happened?" Mason asked, still confused.

Looking at the expressions on the faces of all who had been at the scene, he knew Vasily was gone.

Dr. Bentley continued, "Vasily Fedorov. All names have meanings. Do you know what Fedorov means in Russian?"

"What?" Dr. Graves asked as Tasha inspected her leg for injuries.

"It means 'a gift from God'." Pausing, mustering the strength to maintain his composure, he said, "And that's exactly what he was. A gift from God."

Chapter Thirty

Williams Field

Reaching the airfield, Mark pulled the PistenBully alongside the Twin Otter and said, "Okay, gentlemen. I've got a hand pump on board for such occasions. Fueling out of Antarctic research stations has always been a bit of a challenge. It will take a while, but we need to top off the tanks and then place the remaining barrels in the cargo area. We will barely have enough fuel to make the Antarctic Peninsula, where we will have to stop, refuel with what we have left in the barrels, and then try to make it to the Falklands from there. She's got the long-range tanks, as well as an additional ferry tank, so we should make it if we fly as efficiently as possible, but it will be pushing it."

"And if it doesn't work out?" Dr. Perkins asked.

"Then we divert to the southern tip of South America. We won't have friends waiting for us there, but it will be dry land. That's better than the alternative of ditching."

With that, the men got busy following Mark's directions while he supervised and began preparing the aircraft for departure.

"It's almost dark already," Dr. Hunter said, sitting down beside Dr. Graves, who was keeping warm in the PistenBully with her leg elevated.

"We're getting out of here in the nick of time," she replied with a smile that quickly turned to tears of sadness.

"Did you get what you needed?" he asked, referring to her specimens.

Nodding as she wiped her eyes, she replied, "Yes, at the cost of Vasily's life."

Embracing her, Dr. Hunter said, "Now, Linda. You saw what I saw. Vasily knew what he was doing. He knew he was sacrificing himself so that you and your work could go on. He knowingly gave himself so that others, possibly even the rest of the surviving world, might live. We all must die sometime, but most of us won't get the choice to go in such a noble and valiant way. All we can do at this point is honor his memory and work to find a solution to all of this, so that he did not die in vain."

Wiping her tears, she said, "I know. And Nathan," she said.

"What?" he asked.

Seeing Mason approach the PistenBully, they heard him shout, "Okay, everyone. We're ready. Let's go!"

Turning back to Linda, he said, "What? What is it?"

Shaking her head, she replied, "Nothing," as she wiped her tears and regained her composure. "Let's get going."

~ ~ ~ ~

Following the long flight to the peninsula and a successful refueling stop, the De Havilland DHC-6 Twin Otter made its way toward the southern tip of South America and the Falkland Islands. Flying into the sunrise, Mark looked over to see Brett, his co-pilot for the flight, dozing off to sleep. Turning his head, he saw that only Dr. Bentley was still awake.

Making small talk, Mark said, "Well, Professor. I stuck it out to retrieve as many of my fellow Englishmen as I could, and at least I'm not going home empty-handed in that regard."

"Do you honestly think we'll ever see England again?" Dr. Bentley asked. "I used to long to return home, but now... now I feel as if I will never see her again. Our beloved island nation is ludicrously far from the Falklands, considering the state of the world."

"Just remember," Mark replied. "You probably never thought you'd get this far, either. And here we are."

Replying with only a smile, Dr. Bentley looked out the window at the vastness of the ocean as the distant sun began to shine over the eastern horizon.

Nudging Brett awake, Mark asked, "Did you get a good nap?"

"Oh, man. I'm so sorry," Brett said, regaining his bearings.

"No trouble at all," Mark replied. "It's not like I needed you to respond to radio calls or the like. The usual chatter has gone completely silent."

Pointing out the window, Mark said in a hushed voice, "Do you want the good news or the bad news?"

"Dude, just say it," Brett replied.

"That speck on the horizon is the Falklands." Pointing at the instrument panel, Mark then said, "This is probably not enough fuel to get us there. I've already run the other tanks dry. We're pumping from the ferry tank now. If we make it, we'll be on fumes. If we are lucky enough to make it to the runway, there will be no go-arounds or do-overs. We put her down no matter what. And to be honest, that's a pretty big if."

"I thought you calculated that we'd make it?" Brett replied. "I mean... well, I'm not criticizing you, but..."

"I said we'd *probably* make it, depending on numerous factors. The winds aloft seem to be a tad bit higher than I'd hoped. They can vary quite a bit in this area, and it seems as if we've been fighting a headwind right off our nose for some time now, slowing our ground speed dramatically. I've changed altitudes several times looking for more favorable winds, but to no avail. We will press on for now, but when we get closer, we will wake everyone and let them know where we stand."

Nodding in reply, Brett began fixating on the speck that was their destination, as if willing it to get closer.

As they approached the islands, Mark noted that the fuel gauges were no longer registering. "Okay, mate," he said to Brett. "It's time to wake the troops."

Turning to wake everyone, Brett shook Dr. Bentley, who was sitting just behind him, and asked, "Doctor, can you wake everyone? We're almost there."

"Why, of course, Mr. Thompson," Dr. Bentley replied.

Once everyone was awake, Mark said, "Okay, everyone, the good news is we've made it to the Falklands. The bad news is I expect the engines to flame out from fuel starvation any moment. If it doesn't work out, I am truly sorry."

Patting him on the shoulder, Dr. Bentley said, "Now, don't you be hard on yourself, old chap. We'd still be freezing our knickers off back on the ice, if not for you. We're all lucky to have gotten this far, and it's not over yet. We have faith in you."

Reaching to Dr. Hunter beside her, Dr. Graves took his hand and squeezed it tightly.

"We're gonna be fine," he said.

"I know. I'm just nervous," she replied.

"What were you gonna tell me back at Williams Field before we departed?" he asked, still contemplating what could have been on her mind.

"Oh, not now, Nathan. Later."

"Okay," he said, squeezing her hand as he looked out the window toward South America, which lay off in the distance to their left.

"I'm afraid there are only a handful of airstrips on the islands, none of which are to the south," Mark said. "I'm going to try to make it to Mount Pleasant. It's a Royal Air Force Base. They will be our best bet in trying to reach the research facility I spoke of," he said, looking back to Dr. Graves. "I dropped the other researchers off there for transportation to the facility."

"But wasn't it the military that bombed us and tried to kill us?" Tasha asked.

"It will be fine. Trust me," Mark replied. "These boys won't do us any harm."

Turning to Brett, Mark said, "Try and reach them on the approach frequency now. If that doesn't work, try the tower; if that doesn't work, just move on down the list on the chart until someone answers."

As the aircraft crossed over dry land for the first time in many hours, the left engine went silent and the propeller slowed.

"Shit," Mark said as he pulled the prop control lever into the feather position, turning the blade into the wind, allowing the engine to reduce its aerodynamic drag from the windmilling effect it was creating.

Seeing that the propeller next to her was no longer moving, Tasha became very nervous and tightened her seatbelt.

"It won't just fall out of the sky," Mason explained as he looked to the right, seeing that the right engine was still running.

"No joy in getting a response," Brett said. "I've tried them all."

Applying rudder pressure into the side with the good engine, Mark straightened the aircraft in order to reduce the drag associated with a side-slipping tendency, caused by the off-center thrust condition of being down to only one engine.

"There she is," Mark said. "There's Mount Pleasant."

No sooner than the words left his lips did the right engine go silent, windmilling in the air.

"Shit!" Mark said as he feathered the prop on the right engine as well. Pitching the aircraft to control his airspeed to his best-glide speed and turning the plane back toward the sea, he said, "I'm gonna make for that sandy strip of beach beside that old white barn with the red roof. It may be a little rocky, but it's the closest thing to a runway that we've got."

Turning to Brett, he dialed a frequency into the radio and said, "Start transmitting a MAYDAY call. Don't stop transmitting until you need to cover your head and brace."

Turning to the passengers behind them, Mark said, "I want everyone to cinch their seatbelts down tightly. When we are near touchdown, put your head down below the seats and cover your head with the your hands. This may be uneventful, but it may not be, either."

Gliding the now silent DHC-6 toward the shoreline, Mark turned to Brett and said, "That's enough, mate. Those buggers aren't going to answer. Prepare yourself."

Looking over his shoulder one final time, he said to those in the back, "Again, folks, I'm terribly sorry. Brace yourselves, and God bless."

As the Twin Otter flew over the shoreline, gliding silently along, Dr. Graves fought through the pain in her knee to bend her leg in order to get into the brace position. Taking one last look out the window, she could see they were just about to touch down. What appeared to be a sandy beach from a distance, was now clearly strewn with large, jagged rocks amidst the sand.

As the main wheels touched down, her heart sank as she felt an impact, shearing the nose gear off, and sending the aircraft into a violent, devastating tumble.

Bashing her head against a hard object, she saw the brilliant morning sun, and then, darkness...

Chapter Thirty-One

"Dr. Graves. Dr. Graves, can you hear me?" a man's voice said as a light shone into her right eye, moving quickly to her left. The pain in her head was severe. It was unlike any headache she had ever felt.

"Dr. Graves, can you hear me?" the voice again said, followed by unintelligible mumbling in the background.

With the blurriness in her eyes starting to clear, she could make out the figure of a man standing over her with a bright light behind him.

Attempting to move her arm to shield herself from the light, the man gently stopped her and said, "Now, now, don't you be moving around too much just yet."

Reaching up and turning off the light above him, he said, "Can you hear me?"

Nodding yes in reply, she heard him say, "Good. Very good."

As the room swirled around her, she saw figures moving about, and heard voices; yet, she couldn't make out who they were or what they were saying.

Leaning in closer, the voice that had spoken directly to her only moments ago, said, "Just lie still. We're going to give you something for the pain."

With the room still spinning, Dr. Graves once again drifted off into darkness.

~ ~ ~ ~

"Dr. Graves. Are you awake?" she heard. Feeling less pain, she opened her eyes to find that her focus was now coming back to her. Seeing a man in his mid-fifties, with peppery gray hair and wearing a physician's coat, she managed to say, "Nathan. Where's Nathan and the others?"

"Dr. Hunter is in the room next door. He's going to be fine, but he's a little banged up, as you are."

"Who are you? Where am I?" she asked.

"I'm Dr. Harrison. I'm a flight surgeon with the RAF here in Mount Pleasant. You are at our RAF medical facility. You've been unconscious for quite some time."

"What? How long?" she asked.

"Almost three weeks, I'm afraid. You suffered quite a serious blow to your head. We were afraid you wouldn't come out of it, but your friend, Dr. Gerald Bentley, spoke very highly of you and said nothing could keep you down."

"Gerald? Where is Gerald?"

"I'm afraid you've missed him," Dr. Harrison explained. "He was able to catch a ride on an RAF transport back to England, or what's left of it, anyway. He wanted to assist with the efforts back there with the new-found information your detailed work provided."

"My work? What?" she asked, still in a daze from her pain medicine.

Seeing a nurse push a wheelchair through the door, Dr. Harrison said, "Well, I've taken up enough of your time. It seems you have a visitor." Turning to walk away, he said, "I'll come back to check on you later."

Looking toward the door, her eyes welled up with tears of joy as she saw Nathan Hunter being wheeled into the room. Reaching out from her bed, she cried and said, "Oh, Nathan! Thank God!"

Embracing her from his chair, he hugged her and then felt her push him back, as she began frantically looking him over.

"I'm going to be fine," he said. "I'm a bit banged up, but it's nothing a few screws, a cast, and staples couldn't fix."

"What about the others? Where are the others?" she asked, desperately wanting to know.

Looking away for a moment, Dr. Hunter wiped a tear from his eye and said, "Mark and Brett... they were in the front, so, they didn't have a chance. Walt Perkins was thrown clear of the aircraft. He was in the ICU for several days, but has been moved to a regular room. He suffered quite a few internal injuries, but is expected to recover. Mason, that lucky bastard, somehow walked away unscathed. Tasha is fine other than some bumps and bruises, and so is Gerald. He has a broken arm, but that's nothing, considering the possible outcomes. You were thrown from the fuselage, just as Walt was when the airplane started to tumble. It seems you hit your head quite hard. Luckily, for those of us who remained trapped inside, there was no fire, since the plane had completely exhausted its fuel."

Taking a moment to contemplate the deaths of both Mark and Brett, she asked, "What did he mean when he referred to the new-found information that Gerald ran off to England with? And what did he mean when he said, 'what's left of England'?"

"The world is in pretty rough shape. The microbes—well, they spread like wildfire once they got to warmer climates just as we'd feared. New Zealand, which was basically ground zero once you got off Antarctica, was completely decimated. It's a no-go zone. It spread from there as they unknowingly transferred patients back to their home countries, spreading it even further. There almost isn't a place on this entire planet that hasn't been touched by it now. The death toll is staggering. I... I just can't imagine what the future will hold, and the battle isn't over yet."

Hearing a knock at the door, Dr. Hunter turned to see someone patiently waiting to enter. Waving him in, Dr. Hunter pushed his wheelchair back from her bed to give the man room. Introducing him, he said, "Linda, this is Dr. Simon Kelly. He's made great advancements with your work."

"Dr. Graves," the man said, taking her hand. "I'm so glad to finally meet you. As Dr. Hunter was saying, your very detailed notes from your studies, taken while hiding away in the Crary Lab and beyond, have had a profound impact on our work here. No matter what we tried, we just couldn't make any headway in trying to figure out how to stop this menace.

"Your notes, though, and the samples you recovered, throughout their various stages of development, well, that's just something we didn't have. Most of the specimens obtainable beyond New Zealand had already morphed into what they are today, erasing the clues we needed to discover their weaknesses and vulnerabilities. Your work has led us to be ever so close to solving the problem of how to eradicate them without killing our entire planet in the process. With your help, once you feel up to it, of course, I know we can fill in the gaps and get on with the business of saving what's left of the world."

Giving her a moment to process it all, he looked her in the eye and asked, "Can we count you in? Will you join our team?"

"Under one condition," she replied.

Taken aback by her statement, Dr. Kelly asked, "And what might that be?"

"The project must be named in honor of Vasily Fedorov. Without him... without him willingly sacrificing himself so that the rest of us could escape, there would be no hope for the future. We owe him everything."

~~~~The End~~~~

A Note from the Author

Unless you skipped to the end, you've just completed Erebus. Erebus had been clawing its way out of my brain for quite some time, even while I was working on other books. It had been so persistent, I had to finally set it free. To be honest, it has become my favorite work to date. I fell in love with Antarctica, MEVO, McMurdo Station, Black Island, and the brave and adventurous men and women who call it their temporary home while working on important research projects that are sure to benefit us all. I owe them all a debt of gratitude for being my inspiration.

I've got several more uncompleted books trying to burst out of my head that will make the shelves in the coming year. In no particular order of release, they consist of a third book in the Society Lost Series, an addition to The New Homefront Series, and another apocalyptic sci-fi thriller based on particle physics. Give me a shout and let me know what you want to see next.

If I have not had the honor of making your acquaintance and if you like my work, please find me on Facebook at http://facebook.com/stvbird
and at my blog/website at http://www.stevencbird.com. You can also follow me on Twitter at http://twitter.com/stevencbird. In addition, my Amazon author page can be found at http://www.amazon.com/Steven-Bird/e/B00LRYYBDU/ where you can see all my available work.

Erebus

I look forward to hearing from each and every one of you, and may God bless you and your loved ones in all of your future endeavors.

Respectfully,

Steven C. Bird

About the Author

Steven Bird was born in 1973, deep in the Appalachian Mountains of Harlan County, Kentucky. Upon graduation from high school, he joined the U. S. Navy where he served eleven years on active duty, obtaining the rank of Chief Petty Officer before transferring to the Navy Reserves. Transferring to the reserves allowed him to pursue a professional flying career while continuing to serve his country. He ultimately retired with just over twenty years of service.

While on active duty, he earned a BS degree in eBusiness, as well as all the professional flight certificates necessary to begin his new career. Once in the reserves, he worked as a flight instructor, charter pilot, airline first officer, airline captain, and is currently the captain of a super-midsized business jet based out of Knoxville, Tennessee.

Steven, along with his wife, son, and two young daughters, currently lives on a farm on the Cumberland Plateau in Tennessee where they raise horses, cattle, sheep, chickens, ducks, turkeys, and bees, as well as grow their own fruits and vegetables.

In addition, they are currently pursuing their dream of building an off-grid, self-sustainable home, as well as developing the land to suit their desire for a true self-sufficient lifestyle.

Over the years, he has been heavily involved in competitive shooting, off-road motorcycle racing, snowboarding, hiking, camping, hunting, fishing, and, of course, writing.

Steven Bird is a self-sufficiency-minded individual with a passion for independence and individual liberty. He puts his passion into his writing where he conveys the things that he

Erebus

feels are important in life, intertwined with action-packed adventure and the struggles of humanity.

More from the Author

Full-Length Novels (Note: All full-length novels are available on Kindle, Paperback, and Audiobook via Audible, Amazon, and iTunes)

The Last Layover: The New Homefront, Volume One
My first work, written casually on a smartphone, and the book that sent my life in a new direction.

The Guardians: The New Homefront, Volume Two

The Blue Ridge Resistance: The New Homefront, Volume Three

The Resolution: The New Homefront, Volume Four

Viking One: A New Homefront Novel

The Shepherd: Society Lost, Volume One

Betrayal: Society Lost, Volume Two

Kindle Worlds Novellas: (Note: Amazon's Kindle Worlds novellas are only available on Kindle, as well as tablets and smartphones with the Amazon Kindle app.)

Civility Lost: A Perseid Collapse Novella

JET: Dangerous Prey

Erebus

Made in the USA
Coppell, TX
26 May 2021